WARRIOR

STERLING FALLS ROGUES
BOOK 2

S. MASSERY

INTRODUCTION

Hello dear reader!

The first book in the series is *Nemesis* and needs to be read before *Warrior*.

Artemis's story deals with some very difficult subject matter, including drug use/abuse, sex trafficking, rape, suicidal thoughts, and self harm.

If you'd like to know a bit more about some side characters and Artemis's history, dive into the short prequel story, Terror (available here: https://BookHip.com/HMPRACQ).

Happy reading!

xoxo,

Sara

1 SAINT

THE TATTOO MACHINE quiets in my hand, and I give my client one last wipe. They stand and go to the mirror, twisting to look at the portrait on their upper arm. It's black-and-gray realism, with gleaming jewels in the frame around the woman.

This piece has been a work in progress for months, and now it's done.

The sense of accomplishment fills me, and I rise from the stool when my client's face breaks out into a huge smile.

"Let me snap some pictures," I say, adjusting my lighting, "and then we'll get it wrapped up. You're already familiar with my aftercare instructions."

"Yep."

The guy is covered in tattoos. He started coming almost a year ago, and we've kind of bounced around his body since then. A mermaid on his thigh, a compass. He works on a fishing boat that comes into port here in Sterling Falls. Sometimes he brings me fish, which has been a fun little barter.

"What are you doing with that?" He points.

I glance over at the sweatshirt slung over the edge of the couch, and my brow furrows.

"Someone left it here yesterday," I say slowly. "I didn't notice it."

My office girl only comes in to confirm schedules and balance the accounts. She would've been the one to spot it, but she's taking some personal time. It's fine by me—I opened this shop by myself and still regularly handle most of the day-to-day shit.

"I..." He turns to face me. "You don't want anything to do with them."

"You've lost me, man."

"The Cyclopes."

My body tenses. It's one of those fight-or-flight reactions, I think, but instead, I freeze. I look again at the sweatshirt, the stitched logo on the breast, and then back to my client.

He's a big guy, but right now his eyes are wide.

"Can you go into a little more detail?" I ask. "I mean..."

"They tried to get a foothold in Emerald Cove and failed," he says. "But it was brutal. They made a strong press, and it was bloody for a while. The police had their hands full, not that the other gangs were willing to cooperate. One of those we'll-deal-with-it things. But my buddy's cousin is familiar with Emerald Cove. Grew up there. He said the Cyclopes were not to be fucked with."

"Why?"

Reese and I had a conversation about them. How he was brought in on a lower level, doing some shit for them as a way to survive. And then Reese came here... We know they're in West Falls already. The roadblocks they set up without police interference, obviously.

"Their main method of intimidation is to take an eye."

He scratches at his wrist. "Just one, not enough to kill you, but it sends a message to everyone else."

Jesus.

"Nobody else wears their shit, man. You had a Cyclops in your shop."

And it's Kade's sweatshirt.

My stomach drops, but I manage to keep a straight face. I go over and snatch up the sweatshirt, shoving it into the bin.

"He's not going to come back," I say. "Thank you for letting me know."

"You see that eye with the snake and you fucking walk the other way, dude." He holds out his hand. "Just trying to… I don't know. Keep you aware? You seem like a straight-up guy."

"I am." I shake his hand.

After he pays for the last session, with a promise to return in a few months, I sit behind the desk and blow out a breath.

It doesn't seem real. Or right.

Kade gave a sweatshirt just like it to Artemis. It had the logo. It made me irrationally angry at the time, seeing her in his clothes, but we thought nothing of it.

The eye, staring at me from the trash, tells me how fucking stupid I am.

If Kade is a Cyclops, that means we're more fucked than I realized.

I call Artemis, but it goes straight to voicemail.

Same with Antonio.

Swearing under my breath, I barely spare time to lock up the shop and sprint to my bike. I hop on and gun it, shooting down the streets toward the hospital.

That place has no cell reception—and it's also the last place I saw Artemis. And Kade...

My heart pounds against my rib cage. I make great time, but instead of a parking space, I just leave the bike on the sidewalk right outside the doors. I drop my helmet onto it and rush inside, taking the stairs instead of the elevator. It's faster.

And when I burst into Reese's room, I find him...

Awake.

Sitting up.

He stares at me. I stare at him.

"When did you—?"

"About an hour ago." He frowns. "No one will tell me anything."

I glance around. Artemis's phone is still on the charger on the other side of the room.

"Was she here?"

"Just a nurse who came in after I woke up." He seems confused. He touches his side and winces. "I don't understand."

"Kade," I seethe. "He had something to do with this, and we've got to find him."

It's irrational. Reese just woke up, he's been in the hospital, but right now my panic—a simmering thing just under my skin and barely restrained for now—is taking charge.

"Kade?" he repeats. "It wasn't Kade who took me, it was Gabriel."

Gabriel. Kade.

Are they both Cyclopes?

I shake my head. "Someone took Artemis, and my guess is Kade. Are you going to help me, or—"

"No need." Kade's voice comes from directly behind me. "I'm here."

I whirl around. "What the fuck is wrong with you? Where is Artemis?"

His expression blanks.

Even Reese, who is arguably seeing Kade for the first time—conscious anyway, and maskless—sits up straighter.

"Laurent," Reese snaps. "Tell us the truth."

Guilt.

Just a hint of it.

"He wanted to keep you unconscious forever," Kade says softly to Reese. "I couldn't let that happen. I had to give him what he wanted."

"Which was...?"

"Artemis. She was the one who he wanted most, and I didn't realize that when we arrived."

Because they arrived in Sterling Falls together.

"Motherfucker," I growl. "Where is she?"

He swipes his hand down his face. "It's too late. Whatever he's going to do to her—"

I'm going to beat him half to death, drag him back from the edge, and then do it again. Over and over again. I'll tattoo him blind. Cut off his fingers—

"Stop." Kade's voice is pained, but it's directed at Reese.

Reese, who is pulling the stickers from his skin, then removing the IV needle. The shrill beeping of the monitor as it loses contact startles all of us, but he doesn't stop. He swings his legs over the edge, putting his feet flat on the floor, and stands.

Wobbles.

Kade is there in a flash, gripping his forearms.

They exchange some wordless conversation, and Kade finally grunts.

"Clothes," Kade says to me.

I scowl.

There's just one problem with that demand. We brought Reese into the hospital in his boxers and a sweatshirt, essentially, after we removed everything to search for signs of trauma. Which means that, besides the boxers they kept him in, he's got a zip-up sweatshirt. That's it.

"Hang on," I bark.

I get creative.

I act a bit like I own the place when I head down the hall and into a utility closet. There are scrubs there, clean and in plastic sleeves. I grab a shirt and pants, then find a bin of slip-on shoes.

When I return, Reese has gone back to sitting. The monitors are silent.

No nurse came running, though, which is even more strange. There wasn't one in the hallway either.

"What did you do?" I ask Kade. Suspicion colors my tone. "Are you going to try to kill me next? Because I won't go down without a fight, that's for damn sure."

Kade rolls his eyes. "Calm down. I'm not going to kill you. I paid the nurses to take the other patients down for some fresh air, so we have a few minutes to ourselves."

Lovely.

I throw the packets of clothes at him and go back to the doorway. He helps Reese change and soon shuffles him up beside us. Reese seems in pain, but his head is held high. I can't see how him coming along on a rescue mission is a good idea.

"Terror," Reese says simply.

Kade narrows his eyes.

"What?" I scowl at him, then Kade.

"Artemis and Gabriel's history goes back to Terror. You

know, the sex trafficking club. If he wanted her, it was probably to hash out some past trauma, or revenge or something."

Kade's getting stiffer by the second.

Why? Because he knows something? Because he and Gabriel are buddies?

This could've been their plan all along. Get close to us, get Artemis' guard down, then attack when we're vulnerable.

An uncomfortable feeling takes root in my chest.

Just how far has Kade gone? Both in his deception and... otherwise.

But part of what Reese is saying doesn't quite make sense, either.

"Why would he need revenge against her?" I ask. "She wasn't running the place."

"No..." Reese continues out the door, his hand on his rib cage. "No, she wasn't. But she still carries a lot of guilt about what happened to him."

There's something he's not saying, but there's no time to piece it together. I dial Antonio's number again and swear when it goes straight to voicemail.

Something isn't right.

"Do you have your car?" I ask Kade.

The stony-faced man nods once. I haven't revealed his involvement with the Cyclopes, but that can wait. If he's helping us now, the accusation could only make him abandon ship.

I'm functioning, and so is he, but Reese...

Reese limps along faster, glaring at us when we're too slow. We take the elevator down to the parking garage, and he finds Kade's vehicle faster than me.

They know each other. I need to keep reminding myself

about that fact, because it means there's a potential alliance there. They could choose each other over me. It sounds like Kade already made his decision regarding Artemis...

A laugh bursts out of me.

They both look at me oddly, but I just shake it off. Reese and I had this conversation. The burning-building question. He said he'd save Kade.

And I picked Artemis.

I will continue to pick Artemis... I just have to make sure she knows it.

We pile in the car, me in the back, Kade at the wheel, and Reese hunched in the front seat. Our drive to Bow & Arrow seems to take hours, even though in reality we arrive in minutes. The club, at this time of day, is not yet active. Even the restaurant isn't open.

But there is someone loitering, and my brows furrow.

"One of the waitresses," Kade says.

We park and hop out, and he approaches her. "Mel, right?"

She nods.

"What's going on?"

"Tem was supposed to meet me to go over the schedule." She shrugs, then fumbles a lighter out of her pocket. A cigarette follows. "I think she's going to fire me."

Not helpful. Minus the fact that she hasn't shown up, and I don't think Tem has ever ducked a meeting with her staff. It's not her way, not when Bow & Arrow means everything to her.

"Did you call Antonio?"

"He didn't answer." She sighs. "I am really getting fired, aren't I? It's because I like to go over to the Hell Hounds' clubhouse sometimes. It's not my fault—"

"Save it," I snap.

We need to get into the building. A tug on the front doors confirm that they're locked, but there's another entrance in the alley. It's where Tem usually parks, and the kitchen staff enter that way. They have direct access to their work stations on the top floor.

Reese heads in that direction, and we follow.

He doesn't stop there, though. There's another door farther down, painted black to match the wall. I can't say I've ever noticed it before, but he seems familiar. He goes and yanks it open, and the squeal of hinges fills the alley.

I check back at the mouth of it, ensuring no one sneaks up on us, then follow him and Kade inside.

I'm not expecting a short set of stairs down, then a long, sloping hallway. It's in much worse condition than anything at Bow & Arrow.

"Where does this go?"

"To Terror," Reese answers.

Again with that name. When Tem said it, it was offhand. Easy, in a way, but more of a brush-over than anything else. Reese says it with a lot more warning in his voice, as if the idea of it makes him sick.

And Apollo said it was a guise for a sex trafficking ring.

One that Artemis was in.

My gut twists. She didn't let us home in on that in the moment, and like an absolute fucking idiot, I let it go. Kade, too. We trade a glance, for once setting aside the fact that we're on opposite sides.

That Kade got Artemis into this position in the first place.

You don't just give the girl to the bad guy.

We reach another metal door, and Reese pauses. He takes a moment, mumbling something that I don't catch, then carefully opens the door. This one is a lot quieter, and we step into yet another hallway.

This has many doors on either side, and the bulbs overhead flicker. The air is stale, and an insidious feeling overtakes me.

We shouldn't be down here.

I glance into one of the open doors, shocked that the room inside resembles a jail cell. Worse, though, because it doesn't even have a bed. Just a dirty, hole-filled pad on the floor. A knocked-over bucket. A single light bulb.

Others are closed, the deadbolt on the outside of each keeping them locked.

Sex trafficking has to keep them somewhere, a little voice in my head whispers.

I'm not the only one horrified. It seems like Kade hasn't seen this place either. We follow Reese down, and I'm still fucking confused at his involvement. Tem was scared of him in the beginning.

"Were you a guard?" I ask.

He shakes his head, then presses a finger to his lips.

Right. Silence.

There are voices farther ahead. We pass what seems like remnants of a doctor's office, although the room's been trashed. There's broken glass everywhere.

Reese looks at Kade. Motions him ahead of us. The voices are louder now, but Kade just scowls and nods.

He takes the lead and rounds the corner.

"Well, well," a voice calls. "What are you doing here, brother?"

I exchange a glance with Reese.

They're fucking *brothers*?

This can't be good.

2 KADE

"WELL, well. What are you doing here, brother?"

Gabriel lounges on the wall across from another hall. A thick black curtain hangs halfway up that one, blocking my view of what's beyond. There's another man with him, a Cyclops who has no problem getting bloody. He's recognizable even with the bandana pulled up over the lower half of his face.

"I came to put an end to this," I say.

I don't bother to refute the *brother* statement.

Gabriel and I are not related—but some days, it feels like we may as well be. Forces outside of our control pushed us together, and while we don't see eye to eye most of the time, there's a familial bond that was created out of devastation.

And desperation.

A wild gleam enters his eyes at my statement, and he straightens slowly. He's unarmed, as far as I can tell. The same cannot be said of the other man, whose gaze bounces back and forth between us with sudden uncertainty.

He's not sure who to follow.

When we were set loose on this city, it was to cause an upheaval. To secure our position in West Falls, then push east. The bounties we were promised...

Well, I suppose I should've paid more attention to what Gabriel wanted. He figured out what I was after and then realized I had Artemis.

Not that I ever had her—but his perception of it was enough for him to move against me.

It was a trade. Artemis for Reese.

But now, that seems unfair. Unfair when I slid the needle into Reese's IV port and watched the drug be injected into his vein. Unfair when his body immediately began to respond, but I couldn't force myself to stay and watch him wake.

The important thing, though, is that he did.

"You don't even want to know what our experiment is?" Gabriel bares his teeth. "It's a little tough love for my nemesis."

"I don't understand."

I am painfully aware that Saint and Reese will be growing impatient at this conversation. That at any moment, they could round the corner.

Gabriel sighs and kicks his foot into the floor. "You're no fun, Kade. I'm not going to kill her. No, no, no. That's not enough suffering."

"And what *is* enough suffering?"

He brightens. "She's not doing so hot in there, brother. She's bleeding out, in pain... but the true agony will be watching the man she looks up to as a father kill himself in front of her."

Fuck.

Antonio. The stern Italian man's features flash in front

of my face, and I take a step forward. The man is loved by more than just Artemis.

Right now, the Cyclopes have a foothold in Sterling Falls, but it's not stable by any means. We've managed to stay under the radar of the Olympians, and I fully believe that's the only reason we've come as far as we have.

One wrong move, and we lose it.

What will happen if Jace King mobilizes before we're ready? If the Hell Hounds strike?

It suddenly occurs to me that Artemis being attacked, not once but twice in West Falls, wasn't an accident.

It was Gabriel.

I lunge forward and grab him by the front of his shirt. I drag him toward me, our chests bumping. He's leaner than I am, and shorter, but his expression is no less vicious. *Or gleeful.*

"What do you think will happen when one of the most beloved men comes up dead? How long do you think it would take them to carve us out of Sterling Falls before we have roots?" I don't have to say more.

His expression shutters, closing down, and he sighs.

"Fine. Go in there and try to save the day. He's probably already dead."

I release him and point. Away from where Saint and Reese stand around the corner, toward what I hope is another exit. Gabriel smirks and jerks his head at the other man, who follows him wordlessly down the hall.

"Come on," I hiss to Saint and Reese. Without waiting for them, I rush up the hall and burst past the curtain—

Just in time to witness Antonio standing over Artemis, driving the knife into his chest.

"No!" I run for the older man, stilling his hand from

pushing the blade any deeper. He folds, and I bring him down to the floor. Artemis lies across from him, blood seeping from wounds in her stomach, and her face is deathly pale.

Too much going on.

He stabbed himself, but I don't think it went too deep. It's in the wrong position, though. Or the right one to inflict as much damage as possible.

"You're not dying," I tell him.

Saint and Reese skid to a halt beside me, and I wordlessly point to Artemis. I don't need to give them orders, they both fall to their knees beside her.

Antonio is running out of time.

And Artemis...

"Fuck." I lift Antonio into my arms. He's stockier than Artemis, but no trouble. I leave Saint to scoop Artemis up, and Reese to follow.

He's not dying today. Neither of them are.

We get upstairs, breaking out into the stairwell that leads to her offices and the restaurant. I shoulder my way outside, not stopping until we reach my car.

"Can you drive?" I ask Reese.

His jaw tics, but he nods firmly. He takes the keys and puts himself behind the wheel. Saint takes the front seat, cradling Artemis in his arms. He's struggling to keep pressure on the wounds. I slide into the back with Antonio, laying him down and folding myself into the space next to his legs.

He isn't losing blood as fast, but he seems to be struggling to breathe. He's panting, even unconscious. He gurgles. The knife could be poking into his heart or lung with every inhale, and I can't do anything about it right now. Taking it out would be a death sentence, bleeding out before we even reach the hospital.

Reese drives like the enemy is riding hot on our heels.

We practically drift into the Emergency Department's ambulance bay. He heralds our arrival with his horn, and doctors rush to greet us. One stretcher for Artemis, another quickly following for Antonio. The three of us hurry after them, but we're stopped at the inner doors by a burly security guard.

I bristle.

Saint grabs my wrist, nodding back to Reese.

Reese, who just escaped from the hospital himself.

He looks a bit bloodless, and he sways on his feet.

Damn it.

"We're going to need another stretcher," I warn, meeting Reese right as his legs give out.

3 ARTEMIS
TEN YEARS AGO

I STAND ON THE STAGE.

My hands don't lift to block the bright lights. My skin stings from my scrubbing. I turn in a small circle, but the gazes latched on my body don't bother me anymore either.

It should, but some part of me has repressed the emotions. In my cell, I scream and cry and beg to be released. But out here, I am nothing.

The voice intoning the bids is incomprehensible, and soon enough I am shuffled out another door. The guard at my back stands straight and tall, using a few fingers along my spine to keep me moving. We go upstairs, into one of the private rooms, and the boy waits for me.

His parents are absent, but the lingering smell of cigarette smoke hints that they're not far.

He's already shirtless, and I can't decide if it was restlessness that made him preemptively strip it off or eagerness. His fingers curl into his palms and release, over and over.

This isn't the first time we've met.

Not the second either.

The guard pricks my skin with that devilish drug. The one that begs me to beg for touch. The need of it crawls along my skin, waiting for any sensation to satiate it. Pain, pleasure, I'm starting to think it doesn't matter.

He leaves, too, and we're alone for the first time.

After all of this, after feeling him fumble his way into me, learning the curves and planes of my body like memorizing a roadmap, I still don't know his name.

"I'm sorry," he whispers.

I shake my head, because I don't know what he's sorry for. Being here? Being shirtless? Choosing me again?

Truly, I don't know if he's ever gone with another girl. I don't know how often he comes—I just know that sometimes I walk into a room and he's waiting, and other times it's scarier, bigger monsters.

The numbness I cling to is being replaced by desire, and I run my hands along my hips.

"What is it today?" I force the words out.

I do not usually talk, not to him or anyone else. There was just that first time, asking whose permission he received to touch me. And the punishment that followed after...

Well, I decided not talking was safer.

There's a camera in the upper corner of the room. There are probably more than that, but it's the obvious one. The one that sometimes draws my attention, no matter what room I'm in. It's all the same anyway.

He hesitates, then steps forward.

I let him because I have to, watching warily as he plucks at the ties of my lingerie. It comes apart easily, the strings unraveling from around my hips and between my legs. They pool around my feet, but I don't step out or away.

His fingers drag along my hip.

I've lost weight. I've lost track of time, too. My skin is

paler than it's ever been, because I cannot remember the last time I've seen the sun.

Even that touch, the soft pads of his fingers, aches.

His body is scrawny, but it's easy to see the changes in just a few weeks. The definition of muscles on his upper arms, even when he's not flexing. A hint of abdominal muscles. He's already lost the baby fat from his face, his square jaw sharp and green eyes examining.

Apologizing?

It's in my imagination.

He just touches my hip, sweeping his fingers back and forth, until goosebumps break out across my stomach.

"Why did you pierce one nipple?" he asks under his breath.

"I didn't." My gaze falls to the brassiere that's more underwire than anything else. The cup is sheer fabric, doing nothing to hide my pebbled nipples and the silver hoop through the one. "It marks us as property, I think."

I don't know why they do it.

Maybe it's to track us? Or just humiliate us?

His warm breath touches my shoulder. I've come to realize that they're using me to teach him how to be a man, and I hate it more every time I'm put into a room with him. It's been different each time, his technique altering.

Sometimes too rough, sometimes too gentle.

Sometimes too fast, others drag on and on until the guard knocks at the door and he pulls away, embarrassed.

"They talked about foreplay," he says slowly. "About making it... intimate."

I meet his eyes. We're nearly the same height, he and I. Over the last few weeks, though, it seems like he's gained a few inches. I hit my growth spurt early, and he's now coming into his. It adds to his lean figure.

Stretch upward, then fill out. That's what I've heard anyway, when my father used to grumble about Apollo's height. Or his skinniness.

Before he went away...

His fingers dip between my legs, touching just where I need, and I bow forward automatically. But then they're moving again, inching down my inner thigh and coming back up on the outside. To my hip, then higher. He undoes my bra clasp, something he fumbled with before and now does with practiced ease.

I can't voice the opinion that he should pretend to struggle more with that the first time he gets with a girl.

Will he know the meaning of consent with her? In the outside world?

"You have to ask," I say roughly.

"For what?"

"Anything." I meet his gaze, but my stance is already widening. The need is bubbling, driven on by a cursed drug. "The girls you'll no doubt seduce. You have to ask them. It's not like here."

He nods once.

He doesn't ask me. Not when his fingers finally return between my legs and his body folds down so he can kiss the swell of my breast. Not when he puts my hand on his cock through his jeans and leaves me to take over that job.

There is no asking here—just taking.

And when he is done, and my knees tremble with the pleasure still rolling through my body, the guard comes and helps me to my feet.

Tears burn the backs of my eyes when the boy leaves, and it's not because of what he did to me. It's because this time didn't hurt, and I don't understand how that makes this place eight thousand times worse.

"You're okay," the guard murmurs.

One I've never seen before.

"Let me get you to the showers. Clean you up, yeah?"

I don't know why he's talking to me like a person, but I find myself nodding and gripping his wrist anyway. I let him guide me away, and I wash the boy from my flaming skin. There's no cure for the drug, and it takes hours to come down. Even the cold water barely touches the fire in my blood.

The guard walks me back, his brows furrowed.

I want to ask him a question, but the words get lodged in my throat. Silence is safer, right? And I can't afford for this to be a cruel act on his part.

"We're not supposed to share names," he says at my door. "But I'm going to anyway. Is that okay?"

Permission.

Asked, and, with a single nod, *granted.*

He gives me a smile, and then his name. "I'm Antonio."

4 REESE

SHE'S NOT WAKING UP.

My private room now has a second bed in it, and Artemis lies unmoving in it. She resembles a corpse, and a pang of worry travels through me again. It seems like every time I close my eyes, I relive our shared past.

With nothing to do in this hospital room—she just returned from surgery, and Saint is elsewhere—I have no distraction from Terror.

My parents told me, the first time we arrived in Sterling Falls, that it was a rite of passage.

It took longer for me to discover that this was something the men in my family had been doing for generations. A way to be wild, yes, but also safe from judgment.

Better to know yourself than figure it out with a girl who could sue. Or worse: end up dead.

Certain proclivities run in the family. Dangerous kinks, one might call them, and without a proper outlet, scandal could fall on the Avery name.

Proper does not mean legal.

They wanted me to learn myself through Artemis. She,

at the time, was just the golden girl my parents bid on for me.

The first time I saw her, I didn't mean to show such interest. Better than the tall blonde, or the petite redhead, she burst onto that stage without fear. Her gaze didn't move across the people—she was too smart for that—but she still stood firm.

Her expression said she would be unrelenting.

I didn't know myself then. I didn't know that learning her body and her mind was a challenge I'd start to crave. Her name, even. She was a mystery I dug into without regard.

After the first time, I sat in a chair in our family theater and watched my interaction with her. My nose still ached from her punch, but it made me smile, too. Watching it back. My father frowned at the screen. He was there, he saw it happen. They left the room to watch what came next from afar.

I didn't take her virginity, but she took mine.

Those months were strange, to say the least.

I went to a boarding school on the other side of town, but my parents came to sign me out every Friday. We took the ferry to Sterling Falls, they would bid on the golden girl, and an hour later I would be inside her in some form or another.

And then I'd return to school. I'd flirt with girls, but I wasn't allowed to touch.

Not until I passed my parents' test.

I learned that the hard way, bringing a girl back to my room after a movie date. My father burst into the room and dragged me out by my ear, and he beat me black and blue in a vacant room down the hall.

No one stopped him.

The girl never spoke to me again, and I...

I focused on the golden girl. I focused on my guilt at having to do such things to her. The weight of expectation threatened to crush me, because I was at odds with everything I knew.

Consent, for one. Parental approval, another. Societal expectation.

I didn't have a girlfriend. As far as anyone knew, I didn't have sex either. There were bands tightening around my chest, the pressure cranked up by the adults in my life.

Do this, don't do that.

The third visit with the golden girl, three weeks in, was supposed to be about foreplay.

That week was my movie date that ended terribly.

On the fourth meeting, I snapped.

Ten years ago

"What do they inject her with?" I ask my father.

While my mother was more supportive in the beginning, she has since stopped traveling with us. She declined at the last visit, wrinkling her nose at the idea of watching me fumble my way around a girl's body.

We sit on the upper deck of the ferry, and cold wind buffs at our faces. My nose is colder than the rest of me, but I keep my hands in my pockets. I still ache from his beating, but I am the proper son. Chastised, I have learned my lesson.

They rule my life, even from afar. I know exactly who is in charge—it's why, when my golden girl's eyes flashed and she asked who had given me permission to touch her, my gaze automatically went to my parents.

They are the authority.

She said last week to ask girls in the outside world, as if it's so far removed from her.

And in a way... I suppose it is.

"Makes them feel lust and desire," my father answers. "Easier to work with a girl desperate to be fucked, especially in that place. It works on the boys, too."

I tense to keep from shuddering.

"This will be your last time," he adds. "You're proving disappointingly plain, and it's not worth our time waiting to see what will come out with comfort, as I suspect that is what's happening."

They sent me a video on bondage, but I could barely get through it. She's already so restrained—mentally—why would I add more? There were videos on knives and blood, hot wax, whips. My stomach turned at all of them.

So maybe I am plain.

"Do something that makes your heart race," he says. "I don't care if they fine me for it."

I nod, swallowing harder.

We arrive in Sterling Falls, take the blacked-out car to Terror, and enter the familiar doorway. Down to the amphitheater, where our seats await. I don't know how much money my father has spilled into this place, but every low ding of an incoming bid from other parties makes me nauseated.

The golden girl steps through, and I nod at my father.

He appraises me, but he doesn't reach for the button.

Someone else bids on her. I stare at him, waiting, but he doesn't push it. He sits back and watches me, a slight smile on his face.

Not a smile—a sneer.

He bids on one at random. I don't look away from him, like this is a test, and when he wins, we're shuffled off to the room.

My nerves buzz, my whole body vibrating with anger.

The girl enters, desperation already crowding me. She pulls at my clothes, the waistband of my jeans, and manages to undo the button fast. She shoves them down and opens her mouth, taking my dick in.

I'm not hard.

My father watches from the corner, his expression severe.

My cock twitches, but it fails to stiffen.

"Do something," my father snarls. "Something you think you'll regret."

I slide my fingers into her hair and tighten my hold. She's fingering herself, too, at my feet. I drag her mouth off of me, practically throwing her back.

She moans and spreads her legs. Her fingers are slick with arousal, and she doesn't stop touching herself. Not even when I stare down at her, disgust curling my lip.

Do something I think I'll regret?

I face my father, then shake my head. I leave the room and storm down the dark hallway. This level, one above where they hold the bids, is lush. Velvets and heavy draped fabric to mute the noises, soundproofed rooms.

I peer into each until I find her, and I shoulder my way in.

The scene that fills my vision is awful. My golden girl is in a similar position as the one I just left, on her knees with a cock in her mouth. But her nose is pressed to his groin, and she makes a choking noise.

Drool runs past her lips.

No.

I know, in the back of my head, that she's not mine.

Not mine to save or keep or protect. But I am inside in a heartbeat, and the older man—my father's age, maybe, in a suit that strikes me as more expensive than my school tuition—sees me only at the last moment.

Pulled from sadistic pleasure, he looks up right as my fist collides with his jaw.

He stumbles back.

She gasps for air.

I haul her up while her chest heaves, and a guard bursts into the room a second later. His hand is on a taser on his belt, the threat clear. I move her behind me, backing into the wall. She grasps at me.

"What the fuck?" the man I hit roars. "Remove this—this boy—"

My father, now behind the guard, clears his throat.

The man pales. "Remy—"

"Nice to see you, Jack," my father says mildly. "Let's trade, yeah? There was a mix-up. Our bidding button was broken." He moves aside, and the other girl's arm is caught in his grasp. He urges her toward Jack, then looks to me.

I take my golden girl's hand and lead her out, my father and the guard following close behind. When we return to the room, someone else awaits us at the doorway.

Someone who feels important.

"Go in," my father orders. "Let me straighten this out."

Okay.

Okay, I can handle that.

My golden girl moves first, slipping past me and taking a seat on one of the plush lounges. I follow in after her, leaving my father and the *important* person out in the hall. As Dad said, he'll straighten it out.

It might result in a donation or something. I'll find out later when he's raging on our way home. He told me to do something that made my heart race—that's this. Driven by *her*.

She's trembling, yes, but she has to know that...

"What's your name?" I ask her. After all this time, I'm desperate to know. I take the seat beside her, but leave a gap between us.

She blinks, her lips parting. Her tongue peeks out, wetting her lips. She's in gold lingerie, and gold dust highlights her cheeks. She rubs at it now, already ruined by the tear tracks.

I've never made her cry, have I?

"Artemis," she whispers.

"Reese Avery." I want to shake her hand, but that's ridiculous after what we've done.

The door opens, and I turn to face my father. He narrows his eyes at the space between us, but I can't tell if he's more disappointed I'm sitting too close or not already inside her.

"You're an embarrassment," he says on a sigh. "Enjoy your last moments with her, son, because you're done."

I already knew we were done.

There's nothing left to try—I don't want to hurt her. I don't want to explore some lost kink. Those genes skipped me.

After a moment, she shifts, then swings her leg over my legs. Her weight settles on my lap, and it puts our faces on an even level. She reaches down and touches my cock.

For fuck's sake, it was out. She strokes it, and it hardens under her sure grip. She doesn't release it until it's standing straight between us, a bead of precum oozing out of the slit. She rises and positions herself above it, lining up.

I hold my breath when she lowers herself. Her pussy lips brush the sides of my cockhead first, and then her warmth envelops it. The pressure, the squeeze, is delicious. She keeps going, taking my length, and finally settles against me.

"Artemis," I test out.

"Reese Avery."

"Nice to meet you."

She scoffs.

I want to apologize. I almost do, especially when she runs her hands up under my shirt and pushes it off. Her gaze drops to the bruises decorating my rib cage, still pretty stark against my white skin. It's a reminder of what I have to do...

She doesn't say a word, but her hips roll. She moves, and I slip my hand between us to touch her clit. I know the way she operates, and bringing on her orgasm is almost easy.

No—it is easy. But it's aided by the drug. Fueled on by it. She doesn't stop after one either. She keeps shuddering and gripping at my cock with her inner muscles, riding it like she's insatiable.

I let her, while my gaze scours her face. I want to commit her to memory, because long after I leave this place, I can't forget her.

I won't.

Too soon, I'm riding the edge.

A knock at the door cements it, and I pin her hips down. I spill inside her, that tingling pleasure rushing from the base of my spine straight through my cock. My balls are tight, and the bite of pain in my ribs and abdomen is worth it.

I lift her off me. Turn away from the door and the

camera to wipe myself clean and put my pants back in place.

She's withdrawing, and my heart thumps extra hard.

I open my mouth, but she waves me off.

"Don't make a promise you can't keep, Reese Avery."

So I don't.

I'm sixteen—I don't know how to find this place, let alone get her out. I have a feeling the price is too high, and my father wouldn't allow it. He mutters about the whores in this place when he thinks I can't hear him.

And now...

When I leave the room, there are more guards waiting. They escort us out, and my father waits until we're in the car to laugh. The worst sort of laughter.

Condescending.

Loathing.

We travel back in silence. He doesn't so much as look at me until we arrive home. Not the boarding school—my childhood house. His hand comes down on the back of my neck, that stoic expression locked in place. The laughter was a break in character—this is the act I was expecting.

It's the same expression he wore when he dragged me out of my room last week, the mutinous anger only cracking a split second before he hit me.

I hate him.

I hate him as he locks me in my room, as I hear him explain to my mother in the hallway what happened. As he paints my infraction as something wrong with me. Something fundamentally broken. He tells her that I might do something truly crazy if I'm allowed anywhere near Sterling Falls.

Once my bruises heal, I'm sent to a new boarding

school. One out of reach of him, yes, but also Sterling Falls. Out of the reach of Artemis.

No matter what I do, though, the guilt-driven nightmares don't abate. Not until the day I graduate. I'm at the top of my class, giving a speech with concealer hiding dark circles under my eyes and drops put in them to cover how bloodshot they are. I stride off that stage and out of the building, and right into the Marine recruiter's office.

They talk about a worthy cause, but I see it as penance.

And weeks later, in cramped barracks on a faraway base, I am finally able to sleep.

5 SAINT

WHILE REESE WATCHES OVER ARTEMIS, I am holding vigil at Antonio's bedside.

He hovered the line between life and death for too long, but six days and two surgeries later, his doctors are optimistic. His wife, who has remained at his side the entire time, finally agreed to go home for a few hours. She deserves a shower and a hot meal.

His kids have come home, too. I know I'm a terrible person, but I can't remember any of their names. They all look alike, even though there are a few years between all of them. One, who I want to guess is named Anna, is asleep in the chair on his other side.

We're waiting for him to wake up and tell us his side of the story.

Another development: Kade has disappeared.

It's not surprising. What Reese and I overheard is essentially that he and Gabriel have been working together.

They're both part of this gang that has moved into West Falls and made our lives hell.

Once Anna—shit, or is it Hannah?—stirs, I tell her I'm

going to step out for some fresh air. Outside, I make a call to Jace King.

He's a pain in my ass. He clocked my angry, self-destructive tendencies early on after the love of my life died, and he essentially ordered me to move in with Artemis. She was asked, but it was with full expectation of her saying yes.

It was a kindness, I think. It was meant to be.

But fuck, living with someone else immediately following her death hurt. I resented Tem to the fullest extent and made her miserable. In my head, we all deserved it. We let Elora die.

It's unfair. I see that now.

Every barb thrown in Tem's direction comes back to needle at me. I haunted her, unaware that she's been haunted by Terror for a decade.

I'm an asshole.

Jace answers my call on the third ring, and I run my hand down my face. When I called Antonio's wife, Vittoria was a mess. When I called Apollo...

Jace and Wolfe had to drag him out of the room she's in with Reese. He wanted her about as far away from him as possible, convinced he was the reason she wouldn't wake up.

Reminding Tem's brother that Reese was literally in the same position didn't help.

"Any update?" Jace asks.

"Not really."

"Yes or no," he says. "Apollo is glaring at me. Is she awake?"

Guilt strikes a chord in my chest. I should've popped into their room—it's right down the hall from Antonio's. Strings were pulled to get them on the same floor. But I went in the opposite direction, unable to bear seeing her unconscious.

"I haven't heard if there's been a change," I settle on. "You are aware of the Cyclopes, right?"

He grunts, which is a poor affirmation.

"What are you doing about them?"

"At the moment? Nothing."

"Why—"

"We can't find them."

I stop and cock my head. "What do you mean, you can't find them?"

My attention goes to the street across the lawn. It must be the lunch hour, with the sun high overhead, because there seems to be an unordinary amount of traffic. The cars rush by. Do they know how many sick people are in this hospital at any given moment? Do they give a shit?

"We went to look for the roadblocks the past few nights, but there's nothing. No patrol either. It's not that I don't believe you—I do. Sincerely. But even Madness seems to be running straight-laced. We went in and asked for Gabriel, and the bartender didn't blink an eye."

Quite the different reaction to when I asked for him...

Although when I replay it, the bartender glanced at Kade first.

Because Kade is connected to the bar, too.

"Find them," I snap. "For fuck's sake, man. I don't think Artemis is going to wake up—"

"Don't say that." Apollo's voice fills the line. "Don't fucking say that about my sister, asshole. She's stronger than anyone I know—"

"I know that," I grit out.

I know it and I don't have much hope either.

"Just keep looking."

"One more thing," Jace adds. "We need to go to Emerald Cove for a few days."

I wait for the punch line.

"It was the favor to Reese," he hurries to add. "And listen, I know he's the last person we should be helping, but I figure some goodwill for Reese Avery might go toward finding Kade. And finding Kade..."

"Would mean finding Gabriel," I finish. Finding Gabriel would put us a step closer to waking up Artemis.

The night the three of us went to Olympus—me, Tem, and Reese—Apollo and I kind of goaded Reese into fighting Kade. It wasn't completely intentional. But then Reese won. As a prize for winning your fight at Olympus, you can ask a favor of the gods.

He asked for their help extracting an *old friend* from Emerald Cove.

I still don't know who they're looking for. I didn't see the paperwork Reese handed to them that night, and we got a little distracted from asking questions.

And even as I consider asking now, I can't get the words out.

It's not my problem.

"Apollo is staying?" I clarify.

"No."

"While Artemis—"

"You're going to call us with any changes," Jace says smoothly. "You're as much her family as we are. Okay, Saint? Can you manage that?"

This is another test, and I fume silently for a long moment. Then I spit out an affirmative and hang up on them. I don't need another test. I'm sick of them.

I backtrack into the hospital and stop into Reese and Artemis's room. Reese is awake.

Artemis is not.

He brightens a little when he sees me, struggling to sit up straighter. I take the chair between their beds, positioning it so I can see both of them. She's by the window. It creates least one layer of protection if no one else is in the room—they'd have to get past Reese, first. Which might not be the best benchmark because of his recent injuries.

Still. Better than nothing.

"How is she?"

"Sweating," he replies. "I don't know why."

I go over and touch her skin, shocked at how clammy it is. "This isn't normal."

"Her vitals..."

"Are low," I finish. "That's low, right?"

He shrugs, then motions to the board. "They've been giving her some medicine every few hours, and I think it's almost time again."

We've been here for six days, and nothing has changed. The blood tests they ran immediately showed normal results, which was the most perplexing part of this whole thing.

How can they not detect the drug that's holding her mind hostage?

They even compared her results to Reese's, with no luck.

I hit the call button beside her hand—in case she miraculously wakes and needs help—and brush her hair off her forehead. A light film of cool sweat has collected there, dampening the strands.

A nurse arrives a few minutes later. She checks Artemis over, frowning, and agrees to give her the meds now instead of waiting. She disappears outside to retrieve it and comes back with two syringes. She snaps on gloves, and I scan the board. It only has one medication listed.

"What are you giving her?" I ask.

"An anti-inflammatory."

"And the second?"

Reese sits up, now watching her, too.

"Just glucose," she murmurs. "It's to make sure her levels stay consistent."

"That would be on her board, wouldn't it?" Reese narrows his eyes. "Maybe you should wait."

The nurse shakes her head and inserts the needle into the IV tube. We watch the amber liquid make its way down and into Artemis.

Something is off, though. My gut twists, and I take a step forward.

I grab her wrist.

She stares up at me in shock, fingers freezing.

"Saint," Reese warns. "What—"

"Tell me honestly," I say in a low voice. "Before I break your fucking wrist."

Her lips part, and then her grip on the syringe tightens. She pushes the plunger down and yanks away from me. She's gone before I can try to hold her back, but my attention is already shifting to Artemis.

The drug enters her system, and her body tenses. Her back arches.

"That's not normal." Reese jumps out of bed, practically falling to her side. He holds the rails erected on either side of her bed, leaning on them, and stares at her face.

The faint furrow between her brows smooths out.

He reaches over for the syringe. There's still a few drops left, which he swipes from the needle. Totally not sanitary—and neither is licking the liquid.

"What the fuck?" I snatch it back and toss it in the sharps container.

He rolls his eyes at me, then frowns. "It's heroin."

I stop.

What?

"They—"

"How many times has that nurse been in here?" I demand. "And how the fuck do you know what it tastes like?"

He flushes, then shakes his head. Guilt flashes in his expression for a moment, then is swiftly overtaken by anger. He turns and leaves me standing there. He limps out of the room. A minute later, he reappears with a nurse.

A different one, luckily.

If I see the original one, I'm going to kill her.

She has something in her hand, and she looks from me to him questioningly. Obviously she's confused. There's been little to no explanation. Artemis was admitted unconscious. It's not like she walked in off the street having an overdose.

"Give it to her," Reese demands. "Or give it to me and I'll do it."

I step away from the bed to give her room, but the urge to flatten myself on top of Artemis and protect her from this shit is hard to ignore. My instinct roars at me that this is my fault.

I should've let Antonio's family watch him—I should've been here to question what they were giving her sooner.

The nurse presses a tube to Tem's nose and pushes a plunger. She steps back, eyeing us like we're about to pounce on her.

"What was that?" I demand.

Reese sighs. "It's Naloxone. It reverses narcotic overdoses."

It's easy to connect the dots—he thinks Tem has been given enough heroin to keep her unconscious? That that is why—

"It didn't show up on the bloodwork," I argue. "And you tasted a drop of it, but are you an expert on opioids?"

He scowls. "Just trust me."

Right.

"As for the bloodwork—I don't know. Maybe it wasn't what they originally gave her." He throws his hands up. "If it works, we'll find out in a minute."

"And if it didn't work, we'll have gotten our hopes up and berated a nurse for no fucking reason."

"Well—"

A low groan from the bed stops our bickering.

Holy shit.

It worked.

6 ARTEMIS

MY BRAIN ACHES AND CRAWLS. I was unconscious for a week—an extraordinary amount of time for me to process. In fact, I'm not processing. I just sit in bed and focus on the ceiling, while people mill around me. Nurses taking my vitals, Saint and Reese hovering.

No Kade.

My thoughts are jumbled, and my mouth doesn't work. I haven't tried to speak, plagued by thoughts of Terror. It felt like I was living there again, stuck in a cycle of vicious torture and long periods of isolation.

Then a rush of heat and pleasure, too quick to grasp before I'm dropped back into darkness.

Saint keeps talking at me.

Reese held my hand for a few minutes, but I didn't squeeze back.

It was real. Him, then. The slow way he tried to creep into my heart, only to leave. And I got in trouble for it. For his insolence. The fear I experienced later wasn't for him—it was because of him.

Because he put me in danger simply by preferring me and breaking Terror's rules.

Eventually, the nurses and doctors leave. Saint mutters something about going down the hall.

Reese has been trying to make eye contact, but I can't look at him. My pupils reacted to the doctor's light, I heard them all say that everything is normal. There's a new bag of fluids hanging next to my shoulder, dripping through the IV stuck in my arm.

To flush out...

Something.

Everything mechanical keeps trudging along. Heart. Lungs. Eyelids.

The things that take effort are out of reach.

Reese sighs. A door closes.

Someone else comes to stand over the bed, his face swimming over mine. "Have to make this quick, Artemis. No time for pleasantries or inquisitions."

He uncaps a syringe. The liquid is cold—colder than the fluids—as it floods into my bloodstream. The rushing euphoria follows.

A hand covers my mouth, blocking my groan.

"Madness," he whispers in my ear.

His breath on my skin should make my skin crawl, but my body has been taken over by other sensations.

"We're all mad, Artemis. When you get out of here, you know where to find me."

I can't.

I can't think about what the fuck he's talking about when I'm floating like this. I lose the sensation of gravity. Every brush of air against my skin is like a thousand fingers coaxing me to pleasure.

I'm lost in it, awake and somewhat aware but totally

blissed out.

Another door opens, the light spilling across my bed, and then it clicks off. Reese doesn't come back over. He returns to his own bed, but I can't tell if he's looking at me. I don't want him to see what I'm feeling.

I remain still and quiet, and his breathing eventually evens out.

I'm left... like this.

TWO DAYS LATER, I am given the green light to go home. The rush receded as the morning dawned, although I hadn't slept. When the nurses came in for their rounds, I was able to focus on them. My brain unscrambled long enough to give them words, pieces of what had happened...

Saint pulls up to the curb. He circles around, offering his hands to me. I take them, my legs still a bit unsteady, and stand up out of the wheelchair. I get into the passenger seat and cross my arms over my chest.

I have bandages on my arm from the IV, many stitches to close up the knife wounds in my stomach and abdomen, and a headache the size of Texas.

I know what I need.

I just don't know how to get it.

Yesterday, the doctors told me I was being drugged, and Saint followed it up that a now-fired nurse was to blame. They gave me something that reverses overdoses, and that's how they woke me up. But the fact that it was a nurse who was giving me something...

How did Gabriel plant so many people around me?

Not just the nurse, but Kade, too.

Reese is already back at my condo. He was discharged

yesterday, and I didn't have the heart to send him away. He had to ditch his apartment because of me…

Or because of Kade?

Because Kade was searching for him.

Is he still? I mean—he set out to do what he wanted. He found Reese.

"Are you okay?" Saint asks.

I make some vague noise. The real answer is no, of course I'm not okay. But how do I tell him that when he's never been fucking honest with me about how he's doing?

And true to fashion, he does not open up and spill his guts to me. He doesn't say that he's not okay, or that he's indifferent, or anything of the sort. He just drives.

My brother, Wolfe, and Jace are in Emerald Cove. That's the only other town in the county, and directly south from Sterling Falls. The easiest way to get there is by ferry. The other way is driving, although it adds almost a half hour onto the journey.

They're there to complete the favor for Reese. The old friend who needs saving.

Hmm.

Maybe them being out of the way is better… Less chance of my brother being hurt by the Cyclopes.

Although isn't it suspicious timing? Them leaving on some errand just as a new gang moves in?

"I have to stop by the sheriff's," Saint says in a low voice. "He wanted my statement, some bullshit about how we found you."

I shrug and slide my phone from my sweatshirt pocket. Someone was kind enough to locate and return it to me, although I haven't been able to go through it before now.

My head is pounding. I don't even unlock the phone,

just pretend to be busy on it while Saint turns toward the center of town.

He parks and glances at me, then rolls down the windows. Like I'm a dog?

"Just leave it running," I say.

He sighs, seeming to want to argue with me, then gives up on it and nods. "Five minutes. Ten, tops."

"Whatever."

He heads inside, his long stride eating up the wide, shallow marble steps. As soon as he's out of sight, I get out and circle around, taking the driver's seat.

My trip won't take me long. I park in front of the bar, pocketing the keys and walking inside like I am meant to be here. Like I'm not currently in danger just by being in West Falls.

Laughable.

I can barely think over my headache, and my skin crawls, too. I'm covered in a clammy sweat, and pretending I was fine for Saint was hard enough.

Pretending I'm well enough to walk into Madness is an entirely different beast.

Squaring my shoulders, I look around at the nearly empty bar and restaurant. I take a seat at the bar, only a twitch of my lips revealing the pain.

The bartender stops in front of me. This guy is new—not the one who got the knife to the back, because I'm fairly certain that guy died. Or at the very least, was physically maimed beyond being able to work here anymore.

"What can I get you?"

I lift my chin. "I'm pretty sure you know who I need to talk to. The last time someone said his name, though, a lot of people got their asses kicked."

He scoffs. "You don't look like you could win against a field mouse."

Well, probably not in this condition. But the comment smarts.

"I'm scrappier than I seem." My head gives another *thud* of pain, right between my eyes, and reminds me why I'm here. "Now, is he here?"

There's a back office. I could just head in that direction, but I figure that's not very polite of me.

He finally sighs and goes to the wall, picking up a phone off the receiver.

Old school.

I can't make out his words, but he disappears around the bar and out of sight a second later.

Gabriel takes his place. He seems fine—physically untouched anyway. No bruising, no circles under his eyes. He isn't addicted to anything except vengeance, I'd bet. His dark hair is growing out a little, and his blue eyes are as clear as ever.

He's beautiful, and as bad as it is, I can see exactly why the people at Terror held on to him so tightly. In that regard, he reminds me of Kade. Similar bone structure in the face, high cheekbones. The only difference, of course, are their frames. Where Gabriel is tall and lean, Kade is a boulder.

I should not think about Kade Laurent anymore.

We stare at each other, and he cracks a smile. His face comes alive with it, an utter transformation, and I dig my nails into my thighs.

"You're looking... alive," he comments.

"Wasn't that the point?"

"No." He leans on the bar, propping his chin up on his hand. "No, stabbing you was kind of a gamble. And Antonio... did Kade get to him in time? He was so disappointed in me."

I narrow my eyes, but I don't mention Saint and Reese. I heard that both were there, although I think I passed out before they arrived.

It wasn't until I woke up in the hospital two days ago that I even learned Antonio survived.

"You had a nurse drugging me, and you don't know if Antonio made it?"

He grins. "Oh! You caught me. Yes, my little birdies are all over the city. They sing the most delicious songs to me..."

From his pocket, he withdraws a syringe. It's capped, the liquid already filled in the chamber. He holds it up, pretending to examine it.

My attention on it sharpens. I can't help it—there's a physical reaction inside me. Like something being yanked just behind my navel.

"What is that?" I ask carefully.

"Heroin," he replies.

Sweat breaks out across my back.

"You knew that, though, tricky Artemis." He holds out his hand, flat on the bar top with his palm up. "Give me your hand."

I don't want to.

But there's a promise of relief if I do.

"Time is running out," he murmurs. "How long do you think the sheriff will keep Saint busy?"

I start, leaning back. How the fuck does he know that?

"Now, now, I just told you." His expression becomes ambivalent. "Little birdies everywhere."

That's not good. I glower at him, but his fingers just wiggle on the bar. Waiting for my hand. The syringe is still in the other. My head is splitting open. Everything is beginning to hurt, pain creeping back in all over me the longer I sit on this stool.

I give him my hand.

His fingers slide down, wrapping around my wrist, and he puts the syringe sideways in his mouth. He uses his now-free hand to shove the sleeve of my sweatshirt up, exposing the gauze tape covering where the IV was inserted.

He runs his thumb over it, then peels up the tape. Just one side. There's a dark-red spot from the previous needle.

When I try to withdraw, he holds fast. "You need this," he says. "I know you don't think so, but I want to help you take away your pain."

"Answer something for me." My voice wobbles, but I push ahead. "Shouldn't you be anti-drugs?"

He bites the cap off. Quicker than anticipated, and with easy practice, he slides it into my skin. He pulls the plunger back a fraction, satisfied when drops of blood enter the chamber with the heroin.

Poised on the edge of giving it to me, he stops.

"What are you waiting for?"

His eyes gleam. "It's your turn."

My muscles lock up, and I force myself to glance around. The shame pressing onto my shoulders is almost too much weight, and the back of my neck burns. It isn't just that, though, or the fact that not a single person is looking at us. It's the headache, the skin-crawling sensation. My stomach is rolling, and every bone in my body aches.

And the heroin will make it stop.

"It'll shut off your brain for a little while, too," Gabriel whispers, leaning closer. He still holds my wrist, a finger pressing down on where the needle meets my skin to keep it in place. "Who needs traumatic thoughts running through that pretty head of yours?"

Not me.

I close my eyes and fight the urge, but it's not enough. My willpower isn't enough.

I reach for the syringe and depress the plunger. As soon as it's injected, Gabriel pulls it out and caps it. He tucks the used needle in his pocket, watching me like a hawk.

It doesn't take long for the effect to hit—although it doesn't immediately drag me under.

No... it's just that I can suddenly *function*. My muscles relax, my headache eases away. The tide of pleasure coasting under my skin is secondary to the relief.

"There you go," he whispers. "You know where to find me when you need more."

I shake my head, already patting down the tape and tugging my sleeve into place.

"I'm not coming back here," I tell him.

His laugh follows me to the door.

7 KADE

GABRIEL and I meet at Bobby's house boat, which is docked up in North Falls near my rented house. I'm already seated inside, and Gabriel hops on board with light, sure steps. I almost miss his entrance, absorbed in my own thoughts.

He enters with no weapon in his hand, no fear of me.

Bobby's house boat, beyond the galley kitchen, is neat and minimalistic. He proclaims he doesn't need much, and I believe him. There's a couch and chair, a radio propped on a table beside a lamp, and framed stock photos on the wall. A ladder leads up to the loft, where he keeps clothes and his bed.

I've taken the chair, leaving the sunken-in couch for Gabriel.

"Where's Bob-o?" Gabriel asks.

"Out."

"Hmm." He pouts. "Are you mad at me?"

"No."

"You're speaking in one-word sentences," he points out. "How else am I supposed to feel?"

I take a deep breath. "You took pleasure fucking with me, then? Taking Reese out from under my nose—"

"You took *her*," he snaps.

He's a rabid dog, calm one moment and foaming at the mouth the next. From Artemis, I learned about his involvement in Terror. And while Gabriel had never mentioned his past—he suddenly showed up in Emerald Cove a few years ago, proving himself in more ways than one—I knew it had to be something bad. What else could twist his brain like it is?

"I didn't take her." I try to remain calm. "You never said who you wanted to find, or what you wanted. I knew of Artemis from rumors, nothing more."

I followed her from Reese, not Gabriel. His clues led me to her club, then her brother's. To the brother and finally, right down the street to Artemis Madden herself.

"How is Reese?" he asks suddenly.

I narrow my eyes. "That's not what we should be discussing."

He scoffs. "It's okay, Kade. I owe him a visit anyway. I'll just ask him myself—"

Rage. I'm up and in his face in an instant. Both hands wrap around his throat, yanking him closer. I squeeze, and something sharp digs into my side.

Hoarsely, he makes a clicking noise.

I glance down at the knife he holds, perfectly poised to drive up under my rib cage. My anger is still boiling, though it doesn't completely cloud my judgment. I throw him back onto the couch and ignore his burst of laughter.

He straightens his shirt, grinning, while I sit.

"So. Artemis, Reese, they're off the table."

His gaze sharpens. "Are we bargaining?"

"No. But I'll fucking kill you if you touch Reese again."

Gabriel waves me off. "Let's talk about your men."

My men. The ones coming in daily from South Falls, slowly replacing the workers there. It's been quiet, since we don't know who has allegiance to those at Olympus. Ships go out, fishing boats go out, factories open.

Diligence, crawling along and doing exactly what is asked of me, the weight of responsibility pushes and shoves at me like the tide.

If I walk through South Falls, almost half of the people are mine.

"Another cargo ship comes in on Monday," I inform him. It's not the cargo that's important—again, it's about the people. The ones who come and stay, while others receive an exorbitant amount of money to get on the boat. Although the cargo matters, too.

Weapons. Drugs.

"And West Falls?"

Gabriel has been filling in the gaps the Titans left. They weren't just holed up in those neighborhoods—the gang leader, Kronos, owned a lot of properties speckled around the western side of Sterling Falls. It's what secured his territory. His lookouts lived there, had friends and family there. When something happened, he was the first one they called.

"It's going." He picks at his fingernail, too nonchalant for my taste. "I want to push east."

I narrow my eyes. "No."

"You don't get to deny me, brother."

"You're too eager," I argue.

This is why we're here, but it feels too soon.

"They're in Emerald Cove." Gabriel looks at me plainly. "They'll be stuck in Emerald Cove for the foreseeable future."

A stone plummets in my stomach. "Why?"

"Because I led them there," he says simply.

He rises and brushes off invisible dust from his jeans.

I follow him out, pausing in the doorway. He hops onto the dock, hands in his pockets, and strolls away.

He hasn't always been like this. In Emerald Cove, he operated with precision, his movements and decisions tactically efficient. But now that we're back in Sterling Falls, it's like a screw has wound itself loose.

He gets into a convertible, sliding sunglasses on his face, and flips me off before he shoots off down the street.

Fucker.

My thoughts turn to Artemis. With her brother out of the picture—at least temporarily—she's going to need more protection. Saint seems like a fine guy, but he doesn't know what Gabriel will throw at them.

Neither do I, for that matter.

But if push comes to shove, I might hold some sway over the Cyclopes. I might save them from being dragged into West Falls and beaten... or worse.

My throat is tight, and I'm still in the same spot when Bobby returns with an armful of groceries. He gives a little start, as I'm still in the shadows, but recovers quickly.

"Hungry?" he asks.

I shake my head and brush past him. "See you around, Bobby."

My options are limited, but I find myself in front of Starlight.

I've never wanted a tattoo before. And yet, Saint is covered in them. They frame his jawline, cover every inch of the rest of him... what I've seen anyway. I climb out of my SUV and try the door.

My biggest surprise is when it opens.

I step inside quickly, half expecting an alarm to go off, but instead there's just the quiet hum of a tattoo machine. It cuts off when the bell overhead swings, announcing my arrival.

From his tattoo station, Saint wheels into view. A black cap sits backward on his head, his white t-shirt loose with the sleeves rolled up. The tattoos on his hands are blocked by black gloves. As soon as he registers it's *me*, he scowls.

Rude.

I frown right back at him, then turn away and resume my examination of the wall of framed drawings. Saint's signature is scrawled in the bottom corner of quite a few.

After a minute, the tattoo machine resumes.

I wait, because I don't really know what else to do. I could round the corner and see who he's tattooing—but I'm not some jealous monster who wants him to tattoo me and only me.

That would be neurotic, and I've done a lot of work to restrain myself in that regard. Possessive, lacks an ability to share, quick to anger... labels a therapist slapped on me when I was thirteen and acting out.

My attention catches on the trash bin. Black fabric hangs out of it, and I pull it out slowly. Nothing was tossed in on top of it, and there's nothing under it either. Which is good, because the sweatshirt belongs to me.

The branding for the Cyclopes was obvious—and right in front of their faces the whole time. I had hoped that Artemis wearing my sweatshirt would keep her safe, or at least let her pass through the roadblocks in West Falls that Gabriel set up. He wanted to test the sheriff's mettle...

And catch a golden girl.

I went about it in a different way, using the sheriff to funnel me information that seemed innocuous. Seeing if he'd break a little rule. Later on, he'll be more likely to break a bigger rule for us.

Artemis being attacked, not once but twice, in West Falls should've been a clear sign that something else was going on. That Gabriel had marked her specifically.

My grip on the fabric tightens, until I'm white-knuckled grasping it. I force myself to breathe out slowly, releasing the tension and loosening my fingers one at a time.

An hour later, I'm reading one of the magazines that featured Saint for the second time, and he's walking the client to the door. The girl sports a brand-new flower on her arm, and she bats her eyelashes at him at the door.

I cough to cover my disbelief, although he shoots me a look.

When she's gone, he flips the lock and faces me.

"What are you doing here?" he demands.

"I want a tattoo."

He rolls his eyes. "Not fucking happening."

"I got Artemis out," I can't help but mention. "She—"

"She's only awake because of Reese and me," Saint snaps. "Get. Out."

I pause. Artemis being awake is new information that I latch on to. Of course she's awake—he wouldn't be here otherwise. He'd still be in the hospital with her, right? Unless he trusts Reese enough...

That rankles.

"Is she okay?"

He stares at me for a long moment, then dips his head. "Yeah, she's recovering. She got home this afternoon."

Home.

The condo that they both live in... and I imagine Reese is holing up there, too. I keep going by the apartment he was renting, expecting to find some trace of him now that he's awake, too. He can't hold things against me forever.

I haven't had a home in a long time—the word is a novelty. There are houses, there are places I rest my head at night, shelters from the oncoming storms. But a home?

"And you left her to come here?" I question.

He looks around his tattoo shop, his jaw muscle jumping. "I have responsibilities. Artemis will be okay lounging for a few hours."

Except I've never known her to sit still. Not that I've known her for very long. If Saint thinks she's going to stay put, I'll take his word for it.

Or not.

Still, I came here for a reason. I gesture to the chair his last client just vacated.

"Tattoo me."

He scoffs.

"I'm serious." I peel off my shirt, feeling the sense of déjà vu, and throw it at his face. "Are you a coward?"

He doesn't answer, but his gaze seems stuck on my chest. I let him look while I take a seat. It's still in the reclined position, so I kick my feet up and cross my ankles.

Finally, he ventures closer and sits on the stool. He wheels over to his counter, taking several minutes to change over the equipment. New needles, ink in little plastic wells, a razor, and a dollop of coconut oil on the side of the tray. He soaks some paper towels and comes closer, gesturing to my body.

I tap my chest.

His eyes narrow, but he cleans the area without comment. Sweeps the razor over the skin, then wipes away the residue.

"Any requests?"

"Something inspired by Atlas."

He pauses. His blue eyes swing back to mine, seeming to analyze me for my sincerity. I keep a straight face while my mind whirs.

Why did I say *that*, of all things?

On my chest?

Picking Atlas when I prepared to go to Olympus wasn't easy. I wanted something that would vaguely represent my struggle, and the Titan called to me in a way that no other did. He helped the gods in their fight against their creator, and in doing so, condemned himself to a lifetime of punishment.

His sentence?

Holding apart the heavens and the earth.

Saint wheels closer.

My abdomen tightens, flexing the kind of muscles I used to envy as a kid. I am fully aware that I'm showing off my body—and right now, all I want is to see if Saint will blush. He pauses, and *yes*, there's the red creeping up his neck and coloring his cheeks.

Hmm.

I don't hide my smug smile when he bites the cap of a marker off with his teeth and leans toward me. I focus on the top of his head. His short, dark hair isn't visible under the black cap. The brim conceals the back of his neck, hiding that blush from this angle. I take in his dark eyelashes, the slope of his nose and slant of his cheekbone.

Did Michelangelo consider his muse for David so critically?

"Do you normally draw your designs freehand?"

I miss his expression, his head tilted as it is, but I imagine it's somewhere between annoyance and anger. His grip on the marker tightens for a moment, then relaxes. I don't look at the design—I don't want to know.

I want to trust him.

Or… maybe I just want to *show* that I trust him.

My mind spins back to Artemis and the fact that she's awake and he's here. I was under the impression that he cared for her, and I don't like being wrong.

"If the design is intricate, I'll use a stencil." His voice rasps. "But I'm confident in my abilities for this."

I hum.

He tosses the marker on his work table and grabs another color, then wheels back to me. He pauses, poised, and continues.

I couldn't tell you what he's drawing.

"How did you get into tattooing?"

He scoffs. "You trying to get information to feed back to your *brother*?"

"Oh, yes, because Gabriel cares so much about that." I roll my eyes. "Didn't I already tell you he's not my actual brother?"

"Then, what?" He sits up abruptly, and his gaze burns into mine. "Where is your loyalty?"

"To—" I cut myself off and laugh. "Never mind."

"Yeah," Saint goads. He shakes his head and points at my chest. "I should've gone with a realistic dick."

I smirk. "Only if it was yours."

His mouth drops open, shock overtaking the anger—but only for a moment. "I have half a mind to throw you out," he says under his breath.

"You won't," I challenge. "You're just scared."

"I am not."

"Then finish what you started."

This is the way to get through to him, I think. Incessant needling.

Saint seems to contemplate it, and he releases a long sigh.

"Good boy," I murmur, his decision clearly made.

My dick twitches, threatening to make itself known... and probably ruin this rapport we've been so nicely building.

But he doesn't notice. Not yet. Instead, he motions again to the drawing. "Take a look and tell me if you want anything changed."

"Do you see anything to change?"

He scowls. Then, when I don't move, stands. He gives me a look, and I do the same. Intentionally in his space. I'm taller than him by a few inches. He has to tip his head back to meet my gaze, and he does it with no small amount of fire.

His body heat rolls off him, and he finally takes a step back. Then another.

I like a flustered Saint Hart, but I keep that opinion to myself.

He bites the cap off again and suddenly is right back in front of me. His hand on my chest sends my pulse skittering, but he just corrects something and then backs off.

"Good?" I ask, my voice rougher than I expect.

"You should see it."

"No."

He sighs.

So much sighing from one man.

I take my seat and close my eyes. Ultimate trust, isn't it?

Or... he should think so.

8 ARTEMIS

"WHERE HAVE YOU BEEN?"

I almost jump.

Almost. The instinct is there, but my muscles don't react. I turn slowly and eye Reese, sitting on the couch with a book in his hand. He wasn't there when I slipped out earlier. When I met Gabriel and took the syringe from his waiting hand.

I didn't immediately succumb. He seemed to wait for me to fall to my knees and plunge it into my vein without any control, and his gaze was calculating when I just pocketed it.

Now, it's burning a hole in my pocket.

The last three times I went to find him, he did everything for me except the final step. I've got it memorized now... not that I *want* to know. I just do.

It's been four days since Saint brought me home from the hospital. Four days of sneaking around both of them—although one is easier to fool than the other.

Mainly because Saint is never here.

Reese, on the other hand, hasn't yet ventured outside.

He sets the book down and frowns. "You shouldn't be leaving without—"

"I don't need a chaperone," I interrupt. "God, you're not my dad. You were abducted, too, don't you recall?"

"And that's why I'm staying here," he replies slowly. "Until—"

"Until what? Until we find Kade or Gabriel or—?" I throw my hands up. "I didn't think you'd be suddenly afraid to live, Reese."

He scoffs. "I'm not. I'm being realistic. What're my chances against literally anyone in my condition?"

Slim.

I break the eye contact, slanting my gaze toward the kitchen. It's never really *dirty*, but the occasional pile of dishes stack up in the sink if I get busy.

Except right now, it's gleaming. The scent of citrus cleaner reaches my nose, and the guilt hits me. While I've been creeping through the shadows, Reese has been here alone. *Cleaning*.

Saint is out, obviously. He's been taking on more clients at the shop, and I think that's more due to him not wanting to be around Reese and me than anything else. He comes home to sleep, armed with groceries or whatever else we need, and that's it.

"Sit with me," Reese says. "We can watch a movie, or..."

"Yeah." I shift my weight.

"You don't have to stand in the entryway like a stranger." The accusation comes gently.

But I still don't like it.

"I'm not." I force my legs to carry me farther in. My hands flutter at my sides, and the urge to cover my pocket climbs. "A movie?"

"Just one," he promises.

A movie in exchange for breathing room.

With a slight nod, I sit on the opposite side of the couch. He has the remote, and I don't even care what he picks. I slump lower and cover myself with one of the blankets on the back of the couch. I stare at the screen, although my brain shuts off at some point.

"That was good."

I blink hard and sit up. The end credits are rolling, and I didn't watch a single minute. I nod my quiet agreement. He only glances at me, then away.

"Goodnight, Reese." I get up and hurry into my bedroom.

Lock myself in before Saint can arrive home.

I take the syringe out and set it on my nightstand. I strip out of my clothes, replacing my shirt and sweatshirt with my sleep shirt, leaving my legs bare. I change the bandages covering the stitched-up stab wounds, smearing an antiseptic across the heated skin.

I can last a while longer yet. It's like a game at this point.

Climbing into bed, I try to close my eyes.

But as soon as I do, they open again.

It's the weirdest thing.

I roll onto my side and watch the clock. It goes from 8:01 to 8:03 before I blink. Then it's 8:10. 9:32. 10:45. 1:13. 4:29.

When it clicks over to six a.m., I throw back the covers and get out of bed.

I stumble. Somehow, overnight, my body must've gone through a meat grinder. Or been run over by a freight train. I catch myself on my nightstand, and my pinkie brushes the syringe.

Ready.

Waiting.

I don't *have* to take it.

In fact, I shouldn't. I rub the crook of my elbow absently, shuffling across the room to gather things for a shower. It'll distract me...

But first, I hide the syringe under my pillow. Just in case.

The shower, if you're wondering, was uneventful. I hold myself mostly out of the water to keep the stitches dry, my body trembling with how I contorted. But my hair is clean, and that feels like a win.

I towel off and dress in the bathroom, mindful that Reese, sleeping on the couch, *might* be awake and *might* catch a glimpse of my ass.

I keep my hair wrapped up in the towel and exit.

And nearly slam into Saint.

He catches my arms, and his familiar scowl appears. "Careful," he chides.

I yank my arms out of his grasp and cross them over my chest. My fingers cover the marks in the crook of my elbow, although they can't fully block the yellowish bruising.

"I am careful," I snap. "Why are you lurking outside the bathroom?"

"To see how you're healing." His gaze drops. First to my breasts, thankfully concealed in a sports bra, and then lower. His attention trips over my arm. "Is that from the IV?"

"I guess." Goosebumps rise along my arms. My heart nearly trips over itself, the lie making me *sweat*. I don't normally lie, but I'm not about to admit the truth, am I? That Gabriel pumped heroin into my body, and now—

"Should you be showering with...?"

"It's fine. I got the all clear." I inch past him. "Now, if you'll excuse me."

"I—"

"We know you're just going to run back to Starlight. Why bother with me?"

His mouth opens and closes. And then, softly, "I saw Kade."

"You saw Kade," I repeat. I pull at the collar of my shirt. "Where? Why?"

"He..." Saint's furrowed brow seems to get *more* furrowed. "He came to the shop."

His tattoo shop. I glare at him, because there's clearly more.

"He wanted a tattoo."

I laugh. It bursts out of me, and I slap my hand over my mouth. Just down the hall, in the open common space, Reese sleeps.

"Elaborate," I finally say.

"He asked for a tattoo."

"And you... refused him?" I finish. "Because he put me in this position? Because he gave me to Gabriel, and you have *some* ounce of loyalty in you?"

His blue eyes hold an apology I cannot comprehend.

No—no, I *can* comprehend it, but I definitely don't accept it. His silent admission isn't going to fly.

"Tell me."

He reaches for me and falls short. "I gave him a tattoo."

There it is.

"A real one," I clarify.

His expression shutters, but he nods.

That hurts worse, actually. That he wouldn't tattoo *me*, but he would give one to Kade? The man who betrayed me...

When will someone pick *me*?

Tears burn the backs of my eyes. I stomp into my room

and grab the syringe from under the pillow. It's back in my pocket, along with the elastic tourniquet and a stupid fucking alcohol swab. I shrug on my leather jacket and lace my boots, tug the towel from my head and finger comb my hair into something acceptable.

When I burst back into the hall, Saint still stands there.

"Where are you going?" He follows me to the door.

I retrieve my gun from the safe, then glance back at him. Where am I going? I honestly want to be anywhere but here. He picked *Kade*. Over me? Over everything that happened?

I blink furiously, willing those tears to get sucked back into my body instead of falling down my cheeks. And I mostly succeed, except an errant one that I dash away with my fingers.

My anger lies with Saint. Poor, sad, heartbroken Saint. But it's Kade's fault, too. He went to Starlight. He asked for a tattoo.

Kade is the problem. We were *fine* until he came into my life, which means the only solution is to get him out. If he leaves Sterling Falls, then... maybe Gabriel will, too.

Maybe everything could go back to normal, and I'll finally get some sleep.

I scrub at my face again, putting my mental mask back into place. My eyes are sandpaper, and the ache that echoes through my body with every move feels like my bones are grinding together.

After a breath, I drop my hands. I smile at Saint, so sweetly, I might as well be proposing.

The difference in my expression has him taking a step back.

"Where am I going?" I repeat his question. "I'm going to burn his fucking house down."

EASIER SAID THAN DONE, but still *totally fucking manageable.*

I toss the empty gas can into the formal dining room. Kade is in the ocean, and I made sure to avoid the kitchen, with its glass wall that faces the water. It would give me away if he bothered to check—and I'm sure he would.

The front door is open, waiting for my hasty exit.

Glancing around, I take in his paltry living. Off the kitchen, his cot is up against a wall and surrounded by his clothes. I was kind enough to avoid splashing the gasoline in that room entirely, for which I feel thanks should be in order.

However, the rest of the house? Fair game.

On the kitchen counter, I spot the folder he tried to get me to take... what was that, weeks ago? The one with Reese's information. The one he used to try and 'hire' me to find his missing friend. I believe some of it... but not his motivation. Not all of it.

I walk in a crouch in and grab it, scurrying back out. The fumes are getting to me. The whole house reeks of the fuel.

I tuck the folder into the waistband of my jeans and hurry to the front door. My nose and mouth are covered by the collar of my shirt.

One last gas can sits waiting for me on the step.

I pour some on the threshold, connecting the puddles in the house to the front steps, then down. All the way to his car, which gets a good douse. He left his windows cracked, and I tip the contents of the gas can in. The liquid pours down the window and soaks the driver's seat.

Down around the tires, over the spot where Nyx died...

I run out of gas, which is fine by me.

It's perfect timing.

I avoid the soaked path and toss it into the house, then return to safety on the road. Every time I get on my bike, now fixed from the crash in West Falls, I'm thankful for helmets and good mechanics.

I flick my lighter on, and the little flame jumps to life. I pull a strip of fabric from my pocket—a sliced piece of the towel I have stashed in the compartment on my bike—and hold it over the flame.

When it catches, I take two steps back and toss it onto the end of the gasoline trail.

Immediately, it alights with an impressive *whoosh*. In a matter of seconds, the fire has climbed up into the SUV. Farther still, it rushes up the steps and into the house.

I tuck the lighter in my pocket and smile.

Methodically, I return to my bike and put on my helmet. I flick the visor down and kick-start it, then wait. My heart rate hasn't settled since I ran into Saint. That's just the adrenaline, though.

So is the spasms in my lower abdomen and the resulting nausea. Another second of watching, making sure the fire catches, and then I'll go to my favorite bakery down the street from Bow & Arrow.

Mmm. Croissants with butter. No, a warm cinnamon roll. Or a breakfast sandwich with bacon on the side—

Nope. I press my hand to my stomach. The pain there spikes, not just the wounds but something deeper, too. My mouth fills with saliva, usually a precursor to vomiting, and I swallow it back down.

White smoke pours out of the open front door. The orange-and-yellow flickering flames beyond it give me an ounce of satisfaction.

Nyx would be glad to see it go, too.

So would Saint, even if Kade and him are suddenly besties.

I put up the kickstand and shift into gear. The bike's vibrations seem more like an earthquake today, and I tighten my grip. The *last* thing I need is to fall off.

The first thing I need is...

Not a cinnamon roll.

My stomach cramps, and sweat breaks out across my body. I hit the throttle until I'm flying, my hair streaming behind me from under my helmet. I get to Bow & Arrow and unlock the back door, hurrying up the stairs to my apartment. It auto-locks behind me, luckily, so I don't need to wait. I just listen for the resulting *slam*, echoing up to me.

I get into my apartment and twist that lock. My hands are shaking. I shed my leather jacket, toss the folder from my waistband onto the counter by the sink, and drop into a chair at the kitchen table. Onto it goes the syringe, the alcohol swab, the elastic. I barely get the elastic on, tightening the knot with my teeth.

The swab comes next. I rip it open and rub it across the crook of my elbow. It's a patchwork of bruises and two prominent needle marks, marked by deeper, purple bruises.

I should find a better place to inject.

No, I shouldn't. I should just stop.

And yet...

Here I go again.

The prick of pain when the needle slides in almost has me groaning. The anticipation climbs, until I need to pause and wipe my sweaty palm on my thigh.

I pull it back a little, waiting for the drops of blood. They swirl and mix with the liquid heroin, and I just stare at how my blood tumbles through it. I want it so bad, but I force myself to count to five.

Then I depress the plunger.

I remove the needle and recap it. I sag back in the chair, my eyes already closing. I don't care that I might be bleeding—the drug rushes through me like high tide, flooding my system, and eradicates my cares. The aches, the nausea, fade as I float.

"Shit," I groan, minutes or hours later.

I don't know.

There's a trail of blood down my arm, a few drops on the table where I rested it. They're dried, which gives away the time loss.

I pick myself up and clean the area. I dispose of the needle—okay, yeah, I just toss it in the trash, sue me—and the rest of the shit. The elastic I stick around my wrist, looped twice. It's innocuous there.

Pull on a cardigan from my closet.

Lock the door.

Go upstairs.

Enter office.

I sit in my chair, running my hands along the smooth, clean surface of my desk.

"What are you doing here?"

Antonio?

It's not.

Mel, the waitress I should've fired when she started handing out my information to the Hell Hounds, stands in the doorway.

"I should ask you the same," I say.

My mouth feels weird. I lick my lips, then lean back in the chair.

"I... it's my turn to do inventory. With Ginger and

Barry." She squints at me. "I saw the light on. But, Tem, we all heard about what happened—"

With Antonio still in the hospital, how has this place been functioning?

"Vittoria."

I flinch.

Mel comes in and sits. "She was in Antonio's office yesterday. She did payroll for us... I thought you knew?"

"Of course," I lie. "I just..."

My desk is clear of paperwork. My laptop is... I don't know. Home? In the apartment downstairs?

Stolen?

"You look like you could use a drink," Mel says.

I narrow my eyes.

"Coffee," she clarifies. "Come on."

A giggle bursts out of me at the misunderstanding. I cover my mouth, but the sound still slips out. It tugs at my muscles—the injured ones—and my stitched skin. I wave off her questioning glance and follow her through to the kitchen.

I sit at one of the outdoor barstools. She fixes me a cup and one for herself, setting cream and sugar down in front of me with a little spoon.

I stir in the sugar slowly, then a dash of cream.

"Want to talk about it?"

I laugh. "So you can tell whoever you're fucking at the Hell Hounds' compound? No, thanks."

She starts. Coffee spills over the edge of her cup.

The faintest hint of smoke is on the air.

"I deserve that," she says. "I'm sorry."

I wave her off. "I don't forgive you for sharing my business. But I've decided not to fire you this time."

Mel blows out a breath.

We drink the coffee in silence, and when both of our cups are empty, I collect them to wash.

What I *should* do is go to the hospital and see how Antonio is doing.

The heroin numbs the pain of being stabbed, and it even eases some of my worry over the closest man to a father I've had.

I snort to myself. If I see them, they'll see *me*. As in, they'll see right through me.

"I'm taking off," I tell Mel. "Have fun with your inventory."

She murmurs a goodbye, and I manage to avoid Barry and Ginger on my way out. I'm not too close with either, which would just make their pity worse.

I don't need pity. Or anything.

I have to return to my apartment to get my bike keys and helmet, then trot downstairs and find my bike exactly where I left it.

Which is good, because I don't take well to thievery.

One thing is out of place, though.

A white envelope taped to the center of the handlebars, blocking the gauges.

There's no one else in the alley. I swing my leg over, straddling the seat, and remove the envelope. It's barely glued shut and cracks open easily under my nail.

Midnight at Madness.
*Unless you want me to burn *your* house down, little goddess?*

A FULL-BODY SHIVER comes over me. Only one person has called me little goddess… and only one would use that threat.

But he's picking Madness?

He knows.

I grit my teeth against that thought. Would Gabriel give me up so fast? Not that he promised this to be our secret, just…

I crumple the envelope and note. At the top of the alley, I toss it in a waste bin. Then continue on toward Olympus. My brother and his friends might still be gone, but that building has long been a safe harbor.

Well, minus the few months it was taken over by the Hell Hounds.

The ride is quick, and I park in the shadow of the behemoth. Instead of going to the cliffs, I head in through a side door. I trigger one of the secret passageways in an alcove and climb the stone steps slowly, my hands on the walls. The tight staircase curves, and I eventually reach the second floor.

Out into the open hallway, down to another alcove. Up again.

The third floor is quiet. I could've gone up the outside, through the window—like old times, when I needed to get a message to Apollo.

Dark times.

The rush inside me has faded to a gentle caress. I step into the room that was once my brother's and sit hard on the bed.

Can't go home because of Reese.

Can't go to Bow & Arrow because of Antonio—or rather, the lack thereof. And also Kade…

Can't go to Starlight because fuck Saint.

The echoing loneliness is removed from me, but it stings all the same.

I care, and at the same time, I don't give a shit.

I'm alone.

Alone-alone.

And it's totally, completely, one hundred percent *fine*.

9 ARTEMIS

AT MIDNIGHT, Kade slides into the seat across from me.

I've been here for two hours, though.

"Artemis," he greets me.

Not Tem, not *little goddess*. He's not quite as singed as I expected. Truth be told, I don't know what I wanted. A loss of eyebrows or arm hair? Soot smeared across his cheekbones?

He looks completely fine. His house, however, is far from it. I cruised by it earlier, noting with a smile that it was brought down to the studs.

His car was toast, too.

"You've switched up our meeting spot," I finally say.

No one blinked an eye when I arrived.

Kade glances around. No doubt he cataloged who was in here the second he stepped through the door, but he's repeating it for show. Men drinking at the bar, a few couples at tables dotted around the place.

No Gabriel. No sign of the bloodshed that took place the last time we were both here.

"What's up, Kade? I got your cryptic message." I toss

the note on the table between us. "Bad enough that you turned me over to Gabriel. Now threats?"

He narrows his eyes. "Don't play dumb. It doesn't suit you."

I lift one shoulder.

I am calm, cool, and unaffected by any of his bullshit.

"You would've thought less of me if I sacrificed Reese to save you."

"Is that what it came down to? His life for mine?"

"He wouldn't have woken up."

I knew that, deep down. Gabriel is crazy, but... I think Kade is just as insane. In a different way, sure, but there's a screw loose in his brain. There's something else he's after, and my distrust of him only climbs the longer he sits across from me.

"What's the real reason you burned my house down?"

"It was a rental." I glower at him. "That's not an admission of guilt, by the way. I'm just saying—it's not your problem."

"I bought it just the other day." He stares at me. "While you were in the hospital."

A sick feeling twists my gut. "Because you're staying in Sterling Falls."

"I had decided on it, yes."

"No."

His brow ticks upward. "What do you mean, no?"

"I mean, you can't stay. It's... you just can't."

He leans forward. He's so massive, he comes halfway over the table and into my space. His brown eyes search my face, but I have no idea what he's looking for. I lean away. My back presses into the booth, holding me from escaping farther.

Not unless I want to rush away.

That temptation is cooled, however, when he returns to a normal position.

"Are you okay, Artemis?"

"Perfectly fine."

"You're flushed."

My skin is hot, my muscles unable to relax. I haven't slept in thirty-six hours. Of course I'm not okay—but the day I admit that is the day I let him hold a knife in my vicinity.

"It's late," I say in a clipped voice. "So you just wanted to ask about your house, that's it."

Not a question.

Where did Saint tattoo him?

Is it visible?

Unwillingly, my gaze drops to his bare forearms. The sleeves of his black dress shirt are rolled to his elbows, and his tanned forearms are corded. The skin there is clear of ink.

"Ah." He undoes the top two buttons and parts the fabric. There, on his right pec, is a bandage. "He told you about this."

I grit my teeth.

"Is that what was behind your act?" His eyes gleam. "Sweet Artemis, are you jealous?"

I choke on my laugh. "In your dreams, Laurent."

I slide out of the booth. My stitches pull, but I ignore the twinge of pain. I catch the bartender's attention and point to Kade. "He's paying my tab."

The bartender's eyes widen when he spots Kade.

They must be real chummy here. It's why he wanted to meet at Madness, with the façade now broken. He's not an enemy in West Falls—he's practically a king.

I thought that meeting with Kade would go better.

Or worse.

Instead, it's left me off-balance.

I mean—of course it's more about Saint than it is Kade. But I thought Kade and I were... on good terms, I guess? It's not like I ever did anything to him.

Minus hide Reese in my condo for a little while.

But that wasn't *bad*, it was just concealment.

This is personal. Giving me up to the fucking madman Gabriel has become, choosing Reese...

Kade chooses Reese.

Saint chooses Kade.

It's all laughable, really, how large the pit in my chest has become. I swipe at my face, making sure there are no tears, but that hollowness has spread to my emotions, too.

I stop on the sidewalk a few feet away from my bike. Someone leans against it, practically blending in with the shadows. In the darkness, it takes me a long moment to recognize Gabriel.

"Care to go for a spin?" he asks.

Without waiting for a reply, he swings his leg over *my* bike.

I stare at him for a long moment. Maybe if I don't move, he'll just get off?

"Better hurry, unless you want Kade to come out and find you in your sorry state."

My exhale leaves me in a rush. I grab my helmet and yank it on. I don't have a second one, and after what he put me and Antonio through, I'm not inclined to give up mine. I climb on and sit well back, gripping the side straps.

His body jerks as he kick-starts the bike. It rumbles to life, and he lets out a shout at the same time that he hits the throttle.

We rocket forward.

I lean into the motion, my knees barely touching his hips. If this were anyone else, I'd hold on to them. Okay, not *anyone* else, but I can think of a few I'd be comfortable enough to wrap my arms around.

We speed off toward South Falls. He seems comfortable enough on a bike, shifting gears with his foot like he's done it a thousand times. Before we reach the industrial district, he turns onto the highway that leads out of Sterling Falls.

I flip my visor up to yell, "Where are we going?"

He glances back with a wide grin. "You'll see!"

I sigh. It only takes a minute of squinting into the wind for me to flick the visor back into place. We ride almost to the very edge of Sterling Falls.

There, just before the town line, is an unmanned toll scanner. It's a small outpost installed by my brother and his friends, meant to collect license plates and bill accordingly. It also tracks who enters, if anyone bothers to use such technology.

He kills the engine and coasts the last hundred yards, sticking his legs out wide until we've slowed enough for him to drop his heels.

He sets down the kickstand and hops off, practically skipping toward the scanner. It by itself isn't anything special... it's the building farther off the road, which houses the generator and computer system, that matters.

I tear my helmet off and set it down, tempted to just slide forward and ride away.

But also...

"What are you doing?" I shout.

He laughs. His sudden kick to the scanner shouldn't surprise me, but I flinch at the *crack* of hard plastic giving way. He slams his heel into it again, his laugh morphing into a wild cackle.

"Try it, Artemis!"

I cross my arms. "You've got to be kidding me."

He pauses, pouting in my direction. "Live a little, would you? You're back from the dead. That's cause for celebration."

I scoff.

"Plus." He drops his foot and faces me. "I heard you burned down Kade's house."

"I didn't."

He tsks. "Liar, liar, pants on..."

A match and book appears in his hands like a magic trick. He strikes the match along the side, and a flame bursts into existence.

"*Fire*," he finishes.

I scowl.

He blows out the match and drops it. "Don't worry, dear Artemis. I approve of the act."

There are a lot of things wrong with this picture. Like how I even trusted him enough to get on the back of the bike, to let him bring me out here...

We're surrounded by trees. A few miles southeast lies the westernmost edge of the harbor, but that's about it as far as civilization goes. Sterling Falls is isolated, well and truly.

It never seemed like a bad thing, though. Not until right now.

"Kade has moved into Madness," Gabriel informs me. "Temporarily, he assures me. Who knows what that means? Real estate in Sterling Falls is taking a plunge... he could get something cheap. But have you seen him? He's so particular."

I follow him toward the building, drifting in his wake as if I'm tethered to him. He kneels at the door and inserts picks. His micromovements are efficient, and soon he has it open.

We enter.

I've never been in here—I'm not sure what I was expecting. But there's a desk, and a handwritten log of people who have been in here, a single monitor. Against the wall are rows of machines. Computer processing whatever. Like straight out of a spy movie. The generator in another corner, protected by a metal cage, hums.

There's a light switch. I reach for it, and the fluorescent tube overhead buzzes and flickers on.

"But..." Gabriel sighs. "Kade being there means our meetings have to stop."

"No," I blurt out. I want to snatch the word back as soon as it's spoken aloud. I should be *thrilled* that I can't get drugs anymore. I mean—besides the syringe currently in my jacket pocket.

He beams. "I knew you liked me."

"I don't," I grit out.

"Boo." He sighs. "I mean, truthfully? Heroin is expensive. I'm afraid I created a freeloader in you, Artemis. What would your father say?"

I don't react.

Can't.

I once told him about my parents in confidence. How my father first sold Apollo to the Hell Hounds to cover his debt, and later me into Terror when he couldn't climb his own way out of the hole.

And now it's being thrown in my face.

"Oh, don't be like that," Gabriel breathes. "It was just a harmless, tiny little question. Honestly. You didn't end up where *we* did—"

That's it.

I knew there was a reason.

"I didn't pay for drugs any more than you have. Well, I didn't pay in cash." He waves me off. "Don't look at me like that. I'm not going to whore you out. The kind of work I'm thinking of goes in a different direction."

Invisible ropes tighten around my throat.

"You're bribing me?"

He gasps. "What? *No.* Bribery is so... *crude.* You're already addicted, aren't you? A baby druggie hiding her sins from those closest to her. You're doing this because you *need* it, not because you want it. What do you call that?"

"Under duress?"

Gabriel snaps his fingers. "You can tell that to the sheriff if he ever catches wind of us."

"There's no *us*," I snap.

"Sure." He nods sagely, then springs forward. Quick as a whip, he has the syringe from my pocket in his possession. I reach for it, but he blocks me. "This godlike feeling is a rush. I giveth, I taketh away."

Those ropes tighten until I can barely breathe. I reach for him, snarling, and he just dances away. My stomach screams when I lunge, and I stumble across the open floor. He dodges, twists. Twirls.

Taps me on the shoulder.

Pointless. In this condition.

Stopping, my shoulder stooping, I take a breath.

Then another, while my brain convinces my body to be rational.

To not do exactly what he wants me to do.

"There." He strokes my hair. "Sit here for a moment."

I sit at the desk. Stare at the monitor, which illuminates under Gabriel's quick shake of the mouse.

A bar for a password pops up. I stare at it, my brow

furrowed, while Gabriel undoes my jacket and maneuvers my arm out.

"Contemplate that, would you?" He hums. "Best guess. You succeed, you get this."

Fuck.

I have no idea what's on this ancient computer. The fans inside it whir. The username is in white font just above the password bar. *AMadden*.

That could be me—but it's not. It's my twin.

My heart aches, but the more pressing distraction is the one at my arm. Gabriel kneels next to the chair, cleaning the spot. The bite of elastic in my biceps makes my fingers go numb the longer he waits.

He presses on a vein, checking it.

And I can't possibly think of a password.

He glides the needle into my vein. Checks that he hit it, then waits.

This is the worst form of edging, because my mind can't operate like this. I type in something that could work, one-handed, then pause. If I get it wrong, it might shut me down.

Gabriel tilts his head.

I hit *enter*.

The bar shakes, clearing, and I frown.

What would Apollo do? It was probably set before his relationship status changed, which means... well, there were significantly more things that meant a lot less to him. Olympus, for example, or me.

Okay. Just...

I roll the chair back and duck down. Gabriel keeps pressure on the needle in my arm, going with me, and I spot the pale-yellow sticky note a second before he does. I pull it loose and slap it down in the light.

Olympus5Madden!

Gabriel scoffs.

I agree. But I type it in and hit *enter* again, and a second later, the desktop appears.

"Good girl," he murmurs.

He hits the plunger at the same time.

My eyelids flutter. This one feels like… *more*. Stronger. The tide that rises, lifting me up and away, doesn't stop when it obliterates my pain. It carries away my brain, too. All my thoughts go, and every little thing touching my skin *sings*.

I swear.

I shift, leaning back, and groan at the way my shirt collar slides across my throat.

He picks me up. It's not sexual in the slightest, but I may as well be having an orgasm. I trap my moan behind my teeth and drag my fingers over my closed eyelids. Across every eyelash, down my cheekbones.

I'm set down, and then I'm moving. The sway of it is like the ocean, all-encompassing, and I happily sink down into it.

10 REESE

I BURST into Starlight and scare the shit out of a girl I've never seen before. I'm not sure if it's my facial hair, which I haven't bothered to handle in the past... since I woke up... or the crazed look in my eye.

Maybe a combination?

At least I'm wearing my own clothes. They're clean, they fit. I won't be mistaken for a homeless person... just one who might've escaped the nearest insane asylum.

Wait, do they still call them that?

Nearest mental institution. The psych ward.

The loony bin.

"Is Saint here?" I demand.

Her chin wobbles, and she points over her shoulder.

I stalk around the desk. Separating his work space from the rest of the room is a half wall, with a curtain currently dragged across it for privacy.

The buzzing noise—his tattoo machine, surely—stops. I yank the curtain back.

Saint sits on a stool, and he's tattooing a man's back. Well, he was up until right this moment. He's wiping a wad of paper towels across it, and his head jerks up at my abrupt entrance.

"Reese." He scowls. "Wait for me out front."

"I think your secretary pissed herself."

He rolls his eyes. "Have you seen yourself?"

I fold my arms over my chest. "No."

He grabs a handheld mirror and tosses it to me. I manage to catch it, raising it to my face.

Ah. Well, apart from the dark-blond scruff, my face has a lovely patchwork of motley bruises that have yet to fade. Black eye, yellowish-green cheekbones. At least the swelling has gone down.

"Right," I allow. "So I'll wait here."

Saint grunts. His attention returns to his client, while I drift toward the far wall. There are sketches pinned or taped to it—not like the framed beauties out front, these seem like works in progress.

There's a realistic arrow. A mask I recognize as one that might belong to Ares—the God of War does not fucking mess around with his bloodshed. A black-and-gray peony.

He's talented.

Obviously he's talented, he's got his face in fucking magazines.

Sometimes the hype just doesn't match the skill, and here, it might be the other way around.

Finally, Saint ushers his client out front to the secretary and we're alone.

"Okay." He snaps off his gloves and tosses them in the trash. "Why did you storm in here? Are you even up for storming?"

I glower at him. "You need to be home more."

"Yeah, right."

"Have you seen Artemis lately?" I step closer. "Like, have you actually looked at her?"

Saint blinks once, then again. It takes him a second to get what I'm implying, and his lips flatten.

"I'll take that as a no." I scoff. "She's falling apart, but she thinks..."

I don't know what she thinks.

She won't talk to me.

"She's not falling apart," Saint argues. "She's just coping. It's a process."

I laugh in his face. *Sorry not sorry, Saint.* "What the fuck do you know about coping? You're a miserable fuck ninety-seven percent of the time."

He doesn't have a response to that.

He goes around the room, cleaning and disinfecting in the wake of his last appointment, and I just... I watch him because I don't know what else to do.

What am I supposed to do?

"She keeps leaving," I say in a low voice. "She barely gets back before you. She locks herself away in her room. We watched a fucking horror movie, and she didn't flinch once—"

"Maybe you're just a pussy," Saint mutters.

"Maybe you're oblivious because you feel guilty for how you treat her."

No, that's not quite right. The hunch of his shoulders tells me I'm almost there, though.

"You feel guilty for liking her," I guess.

He cringes.

We talked about Nyx. The great love he lost. He detailed it one night after Artemis went to bed, drinking whiskey and commiserating about our pasts. Although it started as a game of one-upping the other, I quickly shut up and let him rattle on about her.

All about Nyx—Elora, he called her. Her real name. Their love and her death, played out for me in drunken whispers. When he told Jace King—Hades, I learned—that he wanted to die, Jace came up with a solution. One that involved Nyx's best friend, Artemis.

A year and some change later, Saint Hart is still stuck.

Still grieving, still contemplating dying. But in the abstract...

At least, that's what he tells me.

I thought Saint would feel guilty for living with Artemis. For treating her like garbage for *months*.

But, no.

He treats her that way because he fucking likes her, but he loves a dead girl and can't quite let that one go.

How fucked up is that?

"That doesn't give you the right to treat her like shit," I admonish softly. "Especially after what we've been through."

His nod is disjointed. Up, pause, down.

Then an admission: "I tattooed Kade... and I told her yesterday morning."

Even *I* wince. "You're a fucking asshole."

How long will he choose literally anyone else over her?

Kade picked me.

Saint chose Kade.

Fuck them. I stride out of the shop, irrationally angry. No, no—I'm rationally angry. On behalf of Artemis Madden, I'd like to give the middle finger to Saint Hart and Kade Laurent.

They both fucked up. I did years ago... I learned my lesson.

I won't make the same mistake.

GABRIEL

You promised me a little chitchat.

How did you get my number?

IMAGE]

THE PHOTO IS OF ARTEMIS. Her eyes are closed, and she's on a couch.

Where is she?

You don't recognize that couch?

Fuck, I do. It's *my* old couch—one of the only things I brought into that cramped studio apartment. I paid a guy fifty bucks to help me get it in. It was heavy as fuck, since it had a trundle bed inside it.

How the hell…?

I don't question it. I get in Tem's car—the keys were just sitting there, asking to be used—and drive into South Falls. I park in front of the building and take the stairs, too impatient to wait for an elevator.

The doorknob turns easily under my hand, and I step in.

"Are you armed?" Gabriel asks.

He holds a gun to Tem's head. A small revolver, easily concealable. He's next to her on the couch, one arm thrown around her shoulders to keep her upright. Her head is back, though, her eyes closed.

"What did you do to her?"

Gabriel tsks. He motions for me to spin in a small circle, which I do.

"Lift up your shirt."

I comply. I don't have my gun—I didn't think I would need it to confront Saint. Stupid, really, although it saves me from Gabriel strip searching me.

Which he might, yet.

He whistles. "Nice abdominal muscles, Mr. Avery. Bet the ladies love that."

I glower at him.

He hops up, leaving Artemis in the center of the couch. Without him, her body tips sideways.

"Go on, catch her."

I do. I take his place, but it isn't enough. I haul her onto my lap sideways, angling her head to rest on my shoulder. I brush the hair from her face and check her over.

Gabriel drags a folding chair across the space. Most of the shit I had in here was just stuff I found on the side of the street with *free* signs attached. A circular table that required a bit of TLC to not wobble, two folding chairs, the couch.

Artemis doesn't even stir at the scraping noise.

"What did you do to her?"

Gabriel tsks. He stops close enough to touch, turning the chair around and sitting backward on it. He rests his arms on the back.

"We have to have our chat."

My grip on Artemis tightens.

He clocks it and makes a dismissive noise. "I didn't do the same to her. You were special, Reese. So? Tell me? What do you remember after I drugged you?"

"I..." My voice falters. "I remember not being able to move. You were right, it did burn."

I've done everything in my power to forget about... well, all of it.

His gaze sharpens. "Go on."

"The world went dark."

"I closed your eyes." He nods emphatically.

"There was nothing for so long. The pain faded, sounds faded, but I was still there." My muscles tense, and I force my gaze to drop to Artemis again. Stroke her hair, convince myself we're not in any danger.

A laughable lie.

"And then Kade came," I continue.

"How did it feel to be carried out? Like a baby." Gabriel makes a gesture like his mind is exploding. "And then waking up in the hospital... a rebirth."

"Not quite."

Inside, I was screaming.

And helpless.

"I see your fear," he croons. "I know you don't want to be trapped there again. In your mind. But it was good for you, don't you see? You know what you have to do."

I cock my head. "Do I?"

"Of course!" He smacks his thigh. "Of course you do, Reese. You're going to protect Artemis from all the shit coming down on Sterling Falls... and you're going to realize that you can't."

A chill descends on me. "What does that mean?"

He smiles. "Sometimes, destruction happens from the inside out."

I stand, lifting Tem easily with me. Even though my muscles ache from disuse, and the beating *he* gave me, it's no true strain to carry her. She seems more fragile than she was. The time in the hospital did a number on her... she lost weight, definitely. The dark circles under her eyes only seem more pronounced.

I cradle her to my chest and jerk my chin at the door. "Do me a favor and open that, would you?"

Gabriel leaps to his feet and claps. "Oh, I do like your spirit. You're so different from Kade, you know."

I stiffen.

"Kade is too brooding. He doesn't put up with my shit. They didn't know that they were sending me back to my old playground… I spent a long time crafting my mask outside of Sterling Falls, and returning here, with power at my back, released me from those shackles." Gabriel flings open the door. It slams into the far wall, and he strides out ahead of us. Completely unbothered about having me at his back. "I kind of figured he was in love with you."

"What?" I choke out.

"Kade." He glances back, scowling. "Why else would he risk *her* for you?"

"I saved his life." I shake my head. "It was just…"

He spins around and blocks my way to the elevator. "No."

"No?" I blink. "No, what?"

"You saved his life, so he saves yours. Did that already, rescuing you from *me*. Turning her in was just… extra. I like twisting the knife in people, so I didn't mind." His gaze drops to Artemis's stomach. "I like putting people in impossible positions, because that's where I live."

"It wasn't impossible."

Gabriel steps closer. "That horrible, trapped feeling you had?"

I flinch.

"Ah, see, I knew it. You didn't say it, but it was written all over your pretty face. That terrifying helplessness would've just… continued. Forever. Until one day, maybe when you would've been old and gray and hardly able to recognize yourself in the mirror, the drugs would've released you. And you would've missed decades of your life, and Artemis's, and Kade's."

"Yeah, that doesn't sound like a fun time," I tell him. "Are you crazy?"

He just stares at me.

Right.

I brush past him. He gets out of my way, which is good, and I jab the *down* button with my elbow.

Unfortunately, the lunatic gets into the elevator with me. He hits the button for the lobby, and down we go. He whistles under his breath, his hands in his pockets.

I shift Artemis in my arms.

"I suppose you'd want to know how to wake her up," he says suddenly.

I eye him.

He just shrugs, a slight smile on his face.

"Sure," I relent.

"You can't."

My body goes cold. "Excuse me?"

"She'll wake up on her own." He pats my shoulder. "Just give it some time, yeah?"

"Yeah," I reply, because… what else can I say?

The elevator chimes, and the doors glide open. Gabriel leaves first, exiting the front door and taking a left on the sidewalk. I go right, to my car, and slide Artemis into the backseat. I buckle her in, carefully resting her head on the seat, and hurry to get us out of here.

Do I take her back to the condo?

Or…

Fuck.

I don't know. Bow & Arrow?

The last I heard, Antonio was still in the hospital. I'm not the one they call with news, though, and Artemis hadn't mentioned anything else.

My phone vibrates. At a red light, I scan my screen.

KADE

We need to talk.

Fuck off

I toss my phone on the seat. While stuck in Tem's apartment, I ordered a new one. New number. But I suppose since he and Saint are chummy, that's how he got my number.

And through Kade, Gabriel. Of course, I should've suspected. It didn't even occur to me, though, because I guess I just presumed Gabriel to know everything.

Funny how everything twists around and around until something breaks.

Namely—me. My sanity.

Artemis groans.

"Where do I take you, golden girl?" I twist around, checking she's okay.

She blinks slowly, focusing on her hand curled in front of her face.

"Olympus," she mumbles.

Her eyes close again.

Fuck.

At least I know how to get to Olympus. I leave South Falls, heading up a windy road that follows the water—barely visible through the trees—and will eventually bring me to Olympus. Or, if I kept going, into North Falls and Bow & Arrow.

Resisting the urge to take her far, far away from Sterling Falls, I keep driving north.

I pass a driveway, and a motorcycle pulls out behind me. I don't think anything of it until another one does, then another. Suddenly, there are at least a dozen on the road, the purr of each engine blending into a symphony.

One puts on a burst of speed and comes up beside me.

I glance over, tempted to flip the rider off, and recognize the man who found me in my apartment.

Malikai.

A Hell Hound.

He falls back, and two more shoot forward. They ride ahead of me. More surround me. As a unit, they slow, and I'm forced to hit the brakes or run over the two bikes in front.

"For fuck's sake." I check Artemis. Her mouth is open, her breathing deep. "Hope you're having a nice nap. I might get shot."

Nothing.

I'm not sure how to explain to them... any of it.

I kill the engine and hop out.

Malikai does the same, hanging his helmet on the handle of his bike and ruffling his hair.

"To what do I owe this pleasure?" I ask.

"You're driving Artemis's car."

I dip my chin.

"She's here, boss," someone calls out. "She doesn't look so hot."

Great.

In a flash, Malikai has a gun drawn from his hip and pointed at me. "You harm her, Avery?"

I slowly raise my hands. "No. In fact, I only just got her back."

"From?"

How the fuck do I answer that?

Movement out of the corner of my eye draws my attention. They've got the backseat door open and are hauling her out.

"Careful," I bark. "She was stabbed—"

"Hold," Malikai calls.

They freeze.

"Stabbed?"

I ignore him and shove toward Artemis. I take over where one has her shoulders, then shift her weight and bring my other arm under her knees. Because Malikai won't rest, presumably, until he knows she's safe, I carry her over and set her ass down on the hood of the car. Her body is like a rag doll, lolling forward.

He grips her chin, angling her face up. Pulls at her eyelid. Takes her pulse.

"She woke up briefly and told me to go to Olympus," I explain.

I'm not one to get nervous... I mean, it's not like I've done anything wrong, right? I just have an unconscious girl in the backseat of her own car, we can't wake her up, and it's looking more and more like I'm in the wrong.

I straighten my shoulders.

The rip of a motorcycle engine comes from a far way off.

Malikai glances over his shoulder, and someone shakes their head.

The noise grows, until it's a low roar coming toward us. Around a bend, sloping down a hill, comes not one, or four, but probably twenty bikes.

"Who the fuck?" the Hell Hounds leader questions.

I shrug.

He releases Artemis, and I pick her back up. I put her gently in the backseat, closing her in, and pause with my fingers on the handle of my door.

The closer they get, the worse the sinking feeling in my stomach gets.

I recognize the front man.

Kade Laurent.

"I don't suppose you need backup?"

Malikai shakes his head. "Nah."

"Great, then I'll let you handle this." I get in the car and reverse it, leaving his guys to scramble to get their bikes out of the way. I speed in reverse until I get to the Hell Hounds' driveway and spin the tail end into it. The car bumps to a halt, gravel dust kicking up around us.

One last glance down the way gives me a clear shot at Kade.

He's off his bike, squaring up with the Hell Hounds.

That sinking feeling only grows.

I yank the wheel and hit the gas, and my back tires kick up rocks, spinning uselessly for a second until they grab traction. We take off back the way we came.

Kade bringing a group into East Falls? Practically begging for a confrontation from the Hell Hounds?

He probably didn't imagine the scene he'd come across... but then again, neither did I.

All I know is, this city is fucked.

And I'm taking Artemis out of it.

11 GABRIEL

MADNESS.

Descend into madness.

I follow the steps down, down, down. Into the subway tunnels long forgotten by this city. A year ago, they were used against them. Like some scene out of an action movie, dear Artemis and her twin brother entered the bowels of the city and very nearly perished.

Explosions seem so peaceful.

I get to the electrical room that once stored generators for those nasty little subway cars. The metal door swings open easily, the hinges kept in tip-top shape.

The generators stored here were removed by the city—funny, that, since the *city* doesn't seem to give a shit about anything else—and repurposed after the gang war spilled over to the water plant at the edge of the reservoir up in West Falls.

It took out running water for almost three days to half its citizens.

But does anyone care about that? *No.* Not hardly.

With the room free and clear of all except dust, I felt

obligated to take it over. Give the dust a new home, carry in my equipment, and set up a secret shop.

It's dark and creepy down here, and it reminds me every second that I could easily be swallowed by tons of rock and dirt. I could get trapped in this room, suffocate and die. I could be buried and crushed, then die. I could starve, go wild with hunger or thirst, and die.

Die, die, die.

The laptop in the corner is hard-wired into the power source, a delicate ethernet cable run down through some venting and attached to Madness. A concealment, I think, if anyone were to come looking.

The laptop is also connected, by a nifty invention, to the toll building at the edge of Sterling Falls. Bit of a fun turn of events, Artemis discovering that password.

Who would've thought to look *under* the desk?

Not me!

But she did, proving her worth.

Would you believe me if I said giving her the drugs makes me sick?

But also... Sort of happy, too.

Heroin is a nasty business. As long as it has her in its grip, she's off the chessboard. She'd do anything, even betray her brother. She didn't think about it like that, but that's what it is.

Twisting up her insides, making her do things she'd normally never cave on... the *old* Artemis was so righteous. She was confident in her morality. She would've been a crusader for honesty and ethics.

Ethics. Gah. They're so boring.

But now I have access to the scanner. I replaced the plastic I broke—my rage might be vapor, but it ignites at the slightest spark—and now I have a record of all the vehicles entering and exiting Sterling Falls.

And the income to boot.

With a few keystrokes, I up the tolls a fraction. I divert the payments into a new account, one that will fund Kade and all his toys.

An alert pops up, and I pause. I duck forward, clicking the notification, and my blood goes cold.

There's not much that can do that nowadays, but...

My pretty little nemesis has flown the coop. Who said she could leave Sterling Falls?

That just won't do.

Closing the laptop with a slam, I move to the far side. The metal wire shelving that houses my fun supplies. Plastic explosives, wire, random bits and bobs to use as detonators or filling to cause damage. I don't do that so much, preferring the sheer brilliance of fire to lead the way.

It's peace, as I said earlier. A single spark, a timer running out—okay, sure, that part might not be relaxing—and then it's just *over*. It burns too hot for anyone to consider running, especially if they're up close and personal.

I set to work crafting the perfect bomb to draw my dear Artemis back to Sterling Falls. She left? She's not allowed to leave. It's an unwritten rule, and maybe even unspoken. But that doesn't mean shit.

She's never left before, has she?

An entire life spent within the confines of this city.

What happens if she likes the outside better?

She won't. The outside world is different. There's order there... and order, in the wake of chaos, feels unstable.

She'll return here, and she'll breathe easier when she does. Even as she returns to find everything in ruin.

Bomb made, wires carefully in place and waiting final attachment, I run my fingers along the edge of it, humming under my breath. There's someone creeping closer, out of the shadows, and I only hum louder. I add some words, my shoulders already lowering back into a nonchalant place.

People come to spy.

People come to stare.

They don't understand me. They don't understand what I've been through, where I've been. They don't *get* to judge me for something that was forced upon me.

One person doesn't judge, and he doesn't even really stare. He watches from the shadows as I close up the bomb in a box.

Ha—*bomb in a box.*

I should stick it in the mail. Perhaps I'll ship it to the sheriff, just to watch his arrogant face when he realizes he fucked up. But no—the sheriff is off-limits. He does Kade's bidding, drawn by the allure of deep fucking pockets.

If I ever give *that* much of a shit about money, I'll deserve a bullet to the brain. I'd take it happily, too. If Kade didn't buy Madness, well, formerly Descend, if he didn't pay for the renovations and fund it entirely for me to then take over... I don't know.

I wouldn't have a place to sleep at night, surely. Or I'd be sharing his house.

A giggle bursts past my lips.

He doesn't have a house anymore. Artemis burned it down, down, down.

Box taped shut, I write *Nemesis* on it. I put the box back, carefully patting it goodbye.

"Who's that one for?"

I'd almost forgotten Kade came to see me. I face him, cocking my head. "An empty building far, far away."

He rolls his eyes. "Right."

"How's Malikai?"

He pauses. "How—"

"Do I know you took your men and rode down the main road of East Falls like you owned it, thereupon stumbling drunkenly into the leader of the Hell Hounds and eleven of his men?" I wave my hand. "It doesn't matter. I want to know how you think it went."

Oh, I wish I had been there.

I nearly clapped with glee when I was informed. Hadn't I just said to Kade that I wanted to push into East Falls? Perhaps not quite so dramatically... no, wait, *absolutely dramatically*. Kade Laurent took a page out of my book!

Except, it didn't end quite the way it should've.

Malikai Barlow is not one who bows. Naturally. Men like him are practically born with iron spines. If only I could've seen Kade's expression when the Hell Hounds' leader met him eye to eye without flinching...

"Tell me," I demand.

Kade sighs. He leans on the doorframe, crossed arms, crossed ankles. "One of ours got stabbed."

I cackle. Fuck those guys Kade rides with—they're loyal Cyclopes, sure, but they're narrow-minded to the point of detriment. Sometimes I think Kade is right there along with them, and it's *sad*. He used to have a mind and goals, but now that Reese is nice and safe... what's a guy to do? Lose his brains and flush our hard work down the toilet?

"It's not a laughing matter," he hisses.

I pick up the box I just taped, crossing out *Nemesis* and writing *Barlow* on it instead. I shove it none to delicately into his arms.

"Solve the problem, then, brother." I smile. "Let me know when you want it to go *boom*."

He holds it like a baby, cradling the thing carefully. Which is good, because it's always wise to have caution around explosives. It's not armed, though. Not until I pop the tape off—which I do while he holds it—and slide the last plug into the black box.

It blinks to life.

"Shit," Kade mumbles.

"All it takes is a phone call." I brighten. "And only I know the number."

I usher him to the door. "Go forth and deliver."

"We need to talk about—"

"About your massive fuck up?" Every fiber in my being goes still and focused. "I told you *I* wanted to go east. I didn't want to wave a giant red flag and declare our intentions."

He glares at me. "I didn't."

"You went for a fucking joyride. Get the fuck out of here."

When he leaves, the hard armor in my expression melts away. Alone, I can return to being *me*. Which... doesn't leave much to be desired, sure. To be normal is to be an oddity.

No one is fucking normal, least of all me.

I trail Kade back the way he came, taking care to step lightly and stick to the shadows. He takes the stairs back into Madness, and I continue on. The hallway ends in the subway tunnels. The actual ones. They go almost everywhere, and it's my own personal playground.

No one's brave enough to venture under the streets.

Anyway.

I stroll along the tracks, always considering running my fingers along that infamous third rail. It could still be *hot*, as they say, or... well, since the generators are gone, it could just be my imagination creating the buzz of electricity in the air.

My eyes are well adjusted to the dark, and the route is memorized. I traverse it easily.

Half a mile away, I come upon a man handcuffed to one of the normal rails. There are ties on either side, ensuring he can't slide like an inchworm down to one of the abandoned platforms.

He comes awake when I bring more sound into my movements. Skittering my toe across a loose collection of pebbles, landing harder with every step. Thud, thud, thud.

I locate the flashlight I left behind and flick it on. It illuminates the man ahead.

He squirms and lifts himself into a sitting position.

There's an awful lot of blood on him.

Might be due to the missing eye and all.

"Hello, Jeff." I squat beside him, poking his shoulder.

Poor fella flinches back like I stabbed him.

Might've done that, too.

A few stabs never killed anyone.

Much.

"Jeff," I admonish. The beam of light lands on his face. "Where are your manners?"

"H-Hypnos," he stutters. "Please let me go. I won't tell anyone—"

I scoff. "Sorry, Jeff, you sing like a parrot. It's a proven fact now. Maybe if you kept your mouth shut *sooner*... Alas. Much too late. And I still have details to extract from you."

"Please." His Adam's apple bobs. He squints, trying to see me. Maybe. Or maybe he's just trying to conceal that he still has one working eyeball. "I've told you—"

"A fair amount about your favorite Olympians," I

concede. "But now we're going to talk about Malikai Barlow."

He stills. "I don't—"

My scoff silences him.

I have an excellent scoff. Sighs of disdain. Huffs of exasperation. Many a men have fallen still after such an exclamation.

I'm getting off track.

"Focus, Jeff."

"My name isn't—"

"*Malikai Barlow*," I interrupt.

He sighs, and it's not nearly as powerful as mine. I creep closer and grasp his shoulder. The light is still on his face. His pupils—sorry, fuck, *pupil*—is a tiny pinprick.

Hmm.

"Tell the truth. Cross your heart, hope to die... stick a needle in your eye." I tilt my head.

Do I have a needle on me?

"No." He scrambles back, seeming to forget that he's handcuffed. His shoulders bulge, his arms reaching the end of their limit. His chest rises and falls sharply. "No, um, Malik. He rarely goes by his full name. He, ah, he's the leader..."

"Of the Hell Hounds." I release his shoulder. "Do you have anything *new* or *interesting* to tell me?"

He considers that.

"For your freedom, Jeff," I whisper. "Don't you want to see sunlight again?"

"I do," he agrees. "I just... I don't know what you want."

"Let's start with a little history lesson." I rock back on my heels. "And maybe some pain management. Would that loosen your lips?"

His eye widens. The other one flaps, the eyelid shredded. At least it's stopped bleeding... terrible thing, eye wounds. All head wounds just bleed and bleed and *bleed.* This one is evident by the dried blood down his face, staining the front of his shirt.

He's lucky he didn't die.

I pull a vial and syringe from my pocket. I make a show of uncapping it, tipping the glass bottle upside down, inserting the needle in through the cap. Drawing a few millimeters of morphine.

He sways toward me now.

Fucking junkie.

"Talk," I demand.

"A h-history lesson." He wets his lips. "Okay. Um. The Hell Hounds used to be led by Cerberus James. Malik was his number two, but Wolfe James—Ares, you know—was his son. So everyone assumed Wolfe would take over. But then he said he didn't want it, and neither did Jace or Apollo.

"Wolfe appoints Malik, and it's part of the whole city clean-up thing in the wake of the end of the war. So I don't know, I guess Malik is kind of—"

"When did Apollo and Jace go into the Hell Hounds?" I thumb the plunger, letting a drop or two of morphine ease out. Our chats about the Olympians didn't cover their early years.

"In their early teens," he tells me, his voice fucking *eager* now that I have what he wants within reach. The metal handcuffs clink and scrape as he readjusts. "Malik was like an older brother to them, like a guiding force, you know?"

"No. Keep going."

"He, uh, took them under his wing. Artemis, too."

I perk. "Artemis?"

"Apollo's twin," he says needlessly.

As if I could forget who *Artemis* is. Was. Will be.

"She hung around the Hell Hounds a lot, when they were sixteen or seventeen..." He swallows sharply, his Adam's apple dipping.

Kind of want to cut it out, just to see if he could still talk.

"So Malik has a soft spot for her, too?" I consider that.

"He must."

I thought I knew the players on the board.

Apollo, Jace King, Wolfe James.

Sheriff Nathan Bradshaw.

Antonio Greco.

Reese Avery.

Kade, grudgingly, is added to my mental list.

And Malikai Barlow was never really *on* it, he was just there. Something to conquer, lumped in with the rest of the Hell Hounds. One bike slut is just the same as all the rest.

But now...

I rise.

His gaze goes to the syringe. "Please..."

The gleaming point catches on the beam of light, and I suddenly smile.

It looks like I have my needle, after all.

12 ARTEMIS

REESE WAITS for me in a small galley kitchen. He has a mug in his hand, and the scent of coffee reaches me from the doorway. I step in, dragging the sleeves of my sweater down over my fingers, and cross my arms.

My mouth is dry, my head vaguely hurts, but I cannot recall getting here.

He reaches behind him and shakes a bottle of painkillers. It draws me deeper into the kitchen. The walls are cream, the tile backsplash between the butcher block counters and cream, upper cabinets seaglass green.

In short: it isn't familiar.

"Where are we?" I accept the bottle, then the glass of water he sets between us.

"Emerald Cove."

I choke. Sputtering, I cough up the pills I had been in the process of swallowing. The wet, dissolving tablets land in my palm, and the bitter taste coats my tongue.

Try that again, I guess.

He waits for me to swallow, then polish off the glass of water, before continuing.

"I didn't know where else to go. I'm more familiar with Emerald Cove, although I was sort of hoping your brother and his friends could meet up with us..." His eyes narrow. "What do you remember?"

What *do* I remember?

The first thing to jump into my mind is sitting at a booth in Madness, waiting for Kade. But Kade didn't...

I left him sitting there, and Gabriel awaited me.

"Gabriel," I answer. "He..."

Reese pulls out his phone and flashes the screen at me. An image of me, unconscious and on a couch. Laid out, my hands folded over my stomach.

I could be sleeping, but I know I'm not.

And now I'm here.

I swallow sharply around the sudden lump in my throat. My eyes burn.

What is this reaction?

I blink and try everything to keep my expression blank, but it doesn't work. It takes me too long to pinpoint why my body is doing this.

"You came for me?" My voice squeaks.

He tosses his phone on the counter and takes my hands. His brows furrow. "Of course I did."

"I..." I pull back ever so slightly. "Where's the bathroom?"

"Down the hall on the left."

I nod and scurry back the way I came. I pass the bedroom I woke up in, find the bathroom, and lock myself in.

What the fuck is wrong with me?

Panic claws at my throat.

Saint's ire I can handle.

Kade's betrayal, sure.

But *Reese*? Reese coming to my rescue?

I pat myself down. Gabriel drugged me—I remember that much now. Sitting at the computer in that little building on the edge of town. The sting of the needle entering my arm...

My heart skips just thinking about it.

And then my fingers brush my pocket, and my heart full-on stops.

I know what it is before I pull the slender syringe out of my pocket. It has the amber liquid already in it, the needle capped and ready to go.

Without thinking, I shove my sleeve up. I flick the cap off with my thumb and slide the needle into my skin. Draw it back to confirm I hit a vein, *pause*. The bite of it is delicious, and anticipation claws at me.

Then there's no more waiting. I remove the used syringe out and recap it before I forget. My hands shake, and I stuff it in my pocket. I tip my head back, my eyes closing, and wait for the rush.

There's nothing quite like it. It's being in the center of a symphony. It's a thousand mouths on my heated skin. It's the freefall leaping off a cliff.

It hits me hard, and I grip the counter.

Oh *God*.

My knees buckle.

After a long moment, I take a breath. My first breath in what feels like a decade. I exit the bathroom and go straight for the kitchen, where I find Reese. He seems lost in thought, but that changes when I don't stop in the doorway.

"I'm so glad you came for me," I breathe.

I kiss him.

Dazzling electricity bursts across my lips, the teeth of his touch burying in my mouth. I cup the back of his neck, and it only takes a moment for him to respond. Eagerly. He kisses me back, his hands at my waist.

More.

I push at his shirt, sliding it up. We separate just long enough to get it off. His skin is so soft. Never mind the healing bruises. He's like silk. I tear my lips from his and drag them down his jaw, his throat. I nip and suck, my hands roving down farther.

"Tem—" His voice hitches.

I unbutton his jeans and shove them down.

"Artemis—"

"Shh," I whisper, going to my knees.

His dick quickly rises to meet me. I avoid looking Reese in the eye, taking in a familiar cock. Familiar. Familiar. *Familiar.*

Yes. Right.

Terror held me hostage, but now I can't seem to grasp at the trauma. It's just... away. I curl my fingers around him, jerking him off slowly. Until my mouth is watering and precum beads at his slit.

I want to taste him.

I do.

He fills my mouth, and he makes a noise above me. I fall upon him, until he hits the back of my throat. I barely gag. My cheeks hollow, sucking him until his hips jerk forward.

Deeper, harder.

I want him to fuck more than just my face, but the taste of him is addictive. I keep going until his fingers twist in my hair and he pulls me off of him.

His expression is dark.

"You sure?"

I nod.

He stands me up and tears my shirt and sweatshirt off. I

unbutton my jeans, careful to not dislodge my hidden contraband, and stand in just a sheer bra and panties.

His gaze locks on my nipples, visible through the bra.

I reach up and unclasp it, letting it fall.

He reaches for my right breast, his fingertips grazing the ring. "You kept it?"

"And got a matching one." I tip my head back. The way my hair moves sends a tingling sensation through my scalp and down my back.

"Fuck," he breathes. He hoists me up on the counter, knocking aside the empty water glass. He touches at the edge of one of my wounds, the stitches tight, the skin pink as it heals.

But that's all the attention he pays *that.*

His head lowers, and he licks at my nipple. My back arches. The new feeling is overwhelming, so much so that my vision goes white. I hang on to the edge of the counter, so tight my nails might as well be cracking. Not that it matters—I'd happily trade that for his mouth on my breast.

He sucks the piercing into his mouth, tugging at it, and I groan.

Fuck.

While his mouth is busy, he tugs my panties down. I squirm, making the job easier for him, and the fabric falls away. My legs spread, and I urge him closer.

He obliges.

He releases my nipple and palms his length, pumping quickly once, then again, before positioning himself.

"You want this?" he confirms.

"Please fuck me," I whisper. "Right now."

He slides inside me.

I let out a shaky exhale. My muscles immediately tremble. I've never felt sex like this. Every sensation is compounded. I could orgasm just from him being there, the fullness of him stretching me open…

And then he moves, and it gets better.

The friction alone brings a gasp to my lips.

He catches my jaw and draws my face to his, our lips reconnecting. He swallows my sounds. My breasts rub against his chest.

There's no way to possibly be closer unless I cut him open and slide under his skin. But he's already inside me, so what's the point?

Connection.

I'm going to burst.

I'm on cloud nine.

I'm going to come.

His fingers on my clit bring me close to the edge, but he backs off too fast.

Then again.

"Reese," I groan, and it comes out a bit chiding. Even though the ride is well worth it…

He smiles. "I just wanted to hear you say my name."

Fuck. Fuck me.

I don't realize it's a chant until his thrusts get harder, spearing into me with vigor. I grip his shoulders and hang on, because this is the Reese show.

"You feel so good," he says, kissing me again. Slower, deeper.

It's so at odds with the way his dick slides in, it's hard to focus on both at the same time.

He's at my clit again. Working me just right, until I'm on the edge.

Shivering pleasure rolls over me, and he's right there with me. Gasping, moaning. It takes a long time for the orgasm to slip away, and Reese's gaze shutters when we separate.

Our bodies are misted with sweat. The cum between my legs—ah, so that's why he's making that face—slowly seeps out.

I peer down, then back up at him.

I should care about that, right?

But… it's right.

The rush has left me wanting more. More touches, more Reese, more sex. More heroin, as fucked up as that is.

Heroin will lead me back to Gabriel… something that cannot happen again.

Reese runs his hands down my arms, and he pauses at my elbow.

I yank back, but he holds tight.

"Those damn nurses," he murmurs after a moment. "I thought you had an IV? Is it normal to bruise this much?"

My mouth opens and closes.

His gaze comes up and crashes into mine. "Tem?"

"I don't know," I finally say. "I've never had an IV before."

He examines the area again, the lines between his brows deepening.

He doesn't believe me.

I twist my arm out of his grasp and loop it around his neck. "I think you've been holding out on me."

"How so?"

"That was better than…"

"Than in a sex club under duress?" He rolls his eyes. "I sure hope so."

He helps me down, then picks up my clothes.

The fallen panties and bra. Shirt.

Jeans.

I reach for it too fast, practically ripping the fabric away from him. I cradle the denim to my chest and shrug.

"Feeling self-conscious," I lie.

Even though I really don't.

I don't care that I'm naked. He's looking at me strangely, though. At any moment, he's going to figure it out. The panic that creeps through me is distant. I'm aware of it, but it doesn't change my expression or my heart rate.

It just flutters in my stomach.

My gaze drops down to Reese's dick, and I tilt my head. There was something he always liked...

Overcome, *again*, I go back to my knees. For the second time.

"Artemis," Reese protests.

Don't care.

In an instant, I've reverted back to the fifteen-year-old who had to do anything to survive. I lift his dick and open my mouth. I take my time licking his balls, until his cock no longer hangs limp but stands up straight out.

"Stand up, golden girl."

A shiver races down my spine.

I release him and stand.

He grabs me and spins me around, kicking my legs wide. I gasp when he presses in close, and he thrusts inside me without an issue. His cum and my arousal make it easy. He grunts. His chest connects with my back, and his arms wrap around my torso. He somehow avoids the stab wounds, but the pressure barely aches.

The way he's bear hugging me is stabilizing.

His teeth score my shoulder, and I cry out. I can't go anywhere. He takes his fill, and only once he comes does he touch my clit. He rubs me to another orgasm, one that nearly takes out my vision again. The room goes silent, just the pulse in my clit under his fingers, and then everything tunes back in.

Our panting breath, my thundering heart. The tick of a clock.

Distance. As soon as he's pulled out, I step away. I don't look back at him, just pick up my clothes and hurry back to the bathroom.

13 SAINT

COMING to see Antonio was a mistake.

The older man has been moved from the hospital to a rehabilitation center. When I arrive, a nurse directs me to the physical therapy room.

It's about the size of a high school gymnasium, broken down into different sections. Some people are using weights, others are doing guided stretches. Along the far wall, on one of the exercise machines, sits Antonio. A trainer is right there beside him, helping form or coaching him through it...

And getting cursed out in Italian, by the sound of it.

I catch Antonio's eye and wave.

He scowls at me.

The trainer tells him to go again, and Antonio slowly pushes his arms forward. Like a vertical bench press. He has two grips in his hands, each with a length of cord that feeds back into the machine. Where one might put a pin in the weights, at the center of it, a two-pound bar rises.

"Good!" the trainer says. "Two more."

Sweat dots Antonio's brow. He continues his Italian tirade under his breath, but the trainer seems to not mind.

The trainer, in a royal-blue polo and slacks, introduces himself to me. "Jared Brown. Physical therapist."

Right, therapist. Not trainer.

"Saint," I greet him. "How's he doing?"

"Good."

"You have experience?"

He lifts his pant leg, revealing a metal ankle. It disappears under the hem. "Real-world experience plus training. Antonio asked me the same thing."

"Right." I nod once, forcing myself not to focus on my embarrassment.

"That he's talking through the exercise, even swearing, is a good sign," he adds.

Antonio finishes his set, and Jared takes the handles back. He helps Antonio stand, and the older man glares at me.

"What are you doing here?" he asks.

I raise my hands in surrender. "I came to check on you."

"Bah." He scowls. "You spent too much time at my bedside."

"I don't see it that way." I shove my hands into my pockets, or else they'll be balled into fists in no time. "Artemis—"

"Artemis," he interrupts. "Yes. Exactly. *Artemis*."

"No. She would've—"

"I have a family," he snaps. "Who does she have?"

She has her brother... who is currently out of town.

She had Nyx... who died.

"Reese was with her," I argue. "She was sleeping. Unconscious. The nurse—"

"Jace told me," Antonio interrupts. He eyes me. "You

haven't talked to Jace King, have you? Been skipping his calls to hide in your tattoo shop?"

I lift my chin. The words hit home, but he doesn't have to know it.

Doesn't stop him from seeing right through me anyway.

He sighs. "Stop hiding."

Right.

"Do you need anything done at Bow & Arrow?"

He shakes his head. He walks slowly, his physical therapist right beside him. I follow along on his other side, tempted to reach out and grab him. But why would I, when it's clearly unwanted?

"Vittoria is handling the bills." He glances over. "How's Tem?"

"She's..."

"You don't even know, do you?"

"She's fine." It's a bald-faced lie.

He's right—I don't know. All I have is Reese telling me to be home more, to *see* her, and Tem avoiding me. Or starting fights. She's been acting flighty, but why wouldn't she? I could see how I devastated her by informing her about Kade's tattoo.

She left. I presume she's staying at Bow & Arrow to avoid me, and Reese hasn't been around either. Which is fine. I could use some alone time...

Lies.

At least I haven't been back to Elora's house in West Falls.

That's something, right?

And that reminds me—

"I think she burned down Kade's house."

Antonio pauses, then bursts out laughing. Immediately,

he presses his hand to his chest and doubles over. He gasps and takes a long moment to straighten again.

"You *think*? I would, too. I hope the fucker was inside it."

I wince.

He waves me off. "Your heart is too kind sometimes, Saint. And sometimes, it's far too cruel to the wrong people."

Maybe so.

My conscience is clear, though, now that I've at least confirmed that Antonio is awake and kicking.

While I'm walking to the car, my phone buzzes.

KADE

Where are you?

Leaving rehab place.

??

Antonio.

Come to Starlight.

My tattoo shop? I gulp. The sudden anxiety that takes flight in my chest is foreign. I don't get *anxious*. And I do not come when called.

Bite me.

If you're into that...

I shake my head and delete his texts. I *was* going to head to Starlight, funny enough. Now, I'm going to avoid it. I grab a sandwich from the local deli, then make my way to North Falls. I'd like to see that Bow & Arrow is being looked after first-hand. Vittoria might say she's got things under control, but she can't be in five places at once.

Except it's not open when I get there, and I don't have a stupid key to get into the club.

Turning on my heel, I pause long enough at the car to empty my pockets, kick off my shoes, and tear off my shirt. I'm left in jeans and boxers. I rub my hand over the hourglass branded on my chest. Of all the things that happened last year, that was one of the worst.

The inked skin under the angry, raised brand is blurred, some sections gone entirely where scar tissue took over. The important thing is that it didn't obliterate the tattoo I dedicated to Nyx—a galaxy over my heart.

My skin prickles. The weather is slowly shifting, summer sliding headfirst toward winter. The water will catch up later, but for now... it should be manageable. Nice, even.

I cross the street, then the boardwalk, and finally put my feet in the sand. The waves at this section are gentler, better for swimming, while farther down tends to favor the surfers. It's strange how different the ocean sounds at different points.

It's angry at Olympus, beating the cliffside.

It's soothing at Jace's house, and also at the jump spot halfway between here and Olympus.

And here, it's calm.

Calm is good.

I walk into the ocean, and it's weirdly reminiscent of the day Elora died.

The same water, which is nearly warmer than the air, greets me with little splashes against my thighs. It comforted me and held me close when I wanted to pitch myself in and let it take my last breath.

And when they dragged me out...

I wade in up to my waist, then dive under an oncoming wave. I swim out past the break and pause. Considering.

Only a mile or so down is the remnants of Kade's house.

I swim in that direction, my thoughts on my breath, my stroke, the waves that push me toward shore and back out. A rocking lull.

I approach the house sooner than I expect, and I angle toward the beach. It isn't until unusual splashing draws my attention, and I jerk my head up a second too late.

Someone collides with me.

Our limbs tangle, and I'm dragged under a wave. I kick, forcing some distance between us, and come up just as Kade's head pops above the water.

"What the fuck?" I snap.

He laughs. "Why are you cursing at me? You're in front of my house."

He treads water easily. We can't touch here... I guess I drifted out a little farther than I thought. It's a good thing sharks aren't known to lurk around Sterling Falls' water, or else I'd be hightailing it to land at the realization.

"Saint."

"What?" I stare at him.

The water plasters his dark hair to his head. It's slicked back, a quick head-toss when he first came up achieving that. I run my hand through my hair. I trimmed it last night, maybe too much. It barely moves under my fingers.

He catches my wrist and drags me closer. "You seem unsettled."

I scowl. "I am."

"Did you come to gawk?" He shifts us, so I have a better view of the house. "I was in the ocean when it happened. I was so focused, I didn't..."

"You shouldn't be swimming with a fresh tattoo," I blurt out.

My gaze lands on the art on his chest. It's loud and proud, a black-and-gray masterpiece of Heaven and Earth. And a pillar between them.

"You're right," he says evenly. "Come on."

He still has my wrist, and I don't resist him pulling me back.

It rings in déjà vu, although a very different kind. He tows me effortlessly through the water, until he's striding. And then my toes brush sand, and I stagger along behind him.

He doesn't stop until we're right at the edge of the house.

The remnant of it anyway. It stinks of smoke, the still-standing metal pillars coated in soot. The rest is ash. Even the glass walls, the giant, impressive glass walls, have melted.

That's some fire.

"Artemis," Kade says with a frown.

I glance at him. Then away. I don't know what's wrong with me. The breeze is cold, but I fight off a shiver. The *last* thing I need is to show any sort of weakness. Instead, I slick the water from my torso with my palms, shedding the droplets. I shake out my hair.

Kade, in swim trunks alone, goes to a surviving chair. He grabs a towel and wipes his face off, then tosses it to me. I dry briskly. My jeans are a hopeless matter, but as soon as my upper body is try, I give it back.

He smirks, carefully blotting his chest, then firmly swiping it down his abdomen.

"You didn't want to see me," he said. "I suppose I should be offended by that."

Ugh.

"Maybe ask next time instead of making it an order." I wrinkle my nose. "Why are you swimming here anyway? Shouldn't you be in West Falls?"

"This is a natural intersection of West and North."

It sounds like he's agreeing with me?

"Where do you and Artemis stand?" I ask suddenly, facing him.

"That's what you want to talk about?"

"Yes."

He frowns. "I'd say Artemis and I aren't standing anywhere near each other right now."

"Because...?" I just need him to admit it. And then I need to make sense of why me giving him a tattoo led her to burn down his house. I'm eighty-seven percent certain it went in that order anyway. She went on the defensive after I told her, which means...

I need to get my head out of my ass when it comes to her.

And Kade can't come between that.

"Because Reese Avery saved my life," Kade says on a sigh. "And when it came down to it, I owed him the same. So I did that."

"I don't think Reese is your biggest fan," I point out. "Didn't he come to Sterling Falls to stop the Cyclopes?"

He inclines his chin. "He... yeah."

"So you are going to clash at some point." I move around the house's footprint, toward the road. I'll thumb a ride back to the beach or walk—it doesn't really matter. The rubble blocks my view of the road and driveway.

Kade follows me.

"Presumably, yes, but I'd like to avoid that." He sighs. "It's not my choice."

"What isn't?"

"How this is playing out."

I face him. Like this, I can't help but flash back to our fight. I didn't know him at the time, of course. Just the faceless *Atlas*, who remained silent during the briefing before the fights, who warmed up quietly in the corner on his own, who kicked my ass…

At some point in the future, I want a rematch.

No, need one. If only to prove that I can hold my own.

Kade examines me. "There are more moving pieces than meet the eye, Saint."

Reese, Kade, Artemis. Jace and his friends. The sheriff? The Hell Hounds?

"So don't let it play out the way it's going," I say.

He shakes his head and brushes past me. He follows the sandy path around what's left of the house, and I trail after him. His burnt-to-a-crisp SUV is gone, replaced with a shiny new one.

"Some things are more easily replaced than others." He opens the trunk, which faces the house, and unzips a bag. From it, he pulls out a pair of shorts.

Without warning, he drops his wet ones.

My gaze goes straight to his dick. I don't know if the piercing is a magnet or the cock… It twitches to life, and I whirl around. I stand with my back rigid, until his low chuckle reaches my ears.

"It likes you," he says. "Nothing to worry about, Saint. I won't fuck you unless you ask for it."

What the hell?

I spin back around, and he's *still* naked. I ignore his lower half and stab a finger in his direction. "In your dreams."

"Yeah. I've been cataloging your comebacks. I think

they're just suppressed desires. Biting..." His gaze heats. "Fucking."

"No." It's actually laughable.

"Okay." He shrugs. "Want a ride back?"

I stare at him. "I'm not getting in a vehicle with you."

He waits. "You'll chafe."

"Maybe I'll swim back."

He scoffs. But the humor only lasts a second, and it morphs into something more serious. "Get in the car, Saint."

"No."

He raises an eyebrow.

I stare him down.

"Get. In. The. Car." The corner of his lip ticks upward for the briefest moment. "Or I'll force you into it."

He seems serious. And a threat of being manhandled is worse than giving in, so...

I do it. I circle to the passenger side and reach for the door handle, and it flashes under my fingertips.

Locked.

"What the fuck?"

He's followed me, a towel in his hands. "Strip and sit on that."

I hold his gaze and do it.

And I feel a bit rebellious, actually, letting my soaked jeans and boxers fall around my ankles. His gaze flicks down, then back up. His expression is amused, and I am wholly unsettled. I grab the towel, wrapping it around my waist. When we get back to my car, I'll...

I don't have anything extra.

Whatever. It doesn't matter.

A pair of briefs hits me in the face. I catch them and glare at Kade. Humiliation coats my skin like another layer, and my face burns.

He smirks. But instead of staring, he leaves me be. He circles around and gets in the driver's seat, and I slowly loosen the towel enough to pull them on. I keep the towel, positioning it over my lap as I sit.

I need to hide my suddenly erect dick.

Why is it malfunctioning?

He doesn't so much as glance over. He asks where I parked, his smile widening when I tell him Bow & Arrow. By the time we get there, the sun has dipped below the water, and the line for the restaurant disappears around the corner. He finds a parking spot halfway down the block and shuts off the engine.

Kade whistles. "We going in?"

"To...?"

"Talk to Artemis? That's why you came here, right? And maybe you couldn't get in or reach her so you..." He hikes his thumb toward the water. "Decided to go for a four-mile swim."

Shit. Was it four miles?

I thought it was shorter.

He chuckles. "I wouldn't mind using you to talk to her anyway."

"To do what?" I eye him. "She's..."

I can't say fragile.

I can't do that to her, not when she's helped hide my self-destruction from Jace.

"She might not want to see you," I finish.

"Obviously." Kade reaches over and unclicks my seat belt. "I think I have pants that will fit you."

He does. My freak boner has luckily subsided. I throw the towel at his face and quickly pull the sweatpants into place. He offers a shirt, but I decline. My car is just around the block, and I retrieve the rest of my clothes. Shoes and socks, shirt, sweatshirt. Wallet, keys, phone.

I have a missed call from Reese, but I ignore it. I'll call him later, when I'm on my way back to the condo.

Kade and I skip the line. The bouncer, Barry, waves at me. He holds his hand out to Kade, though, and the big man beside me glares down at Barry.

"He's with me," I tell Barry. "Is Tem here?"

He narrows his eyes. "I'm not at liberty to say."

"Okay. Are you going to let us in?"

"Any funny business, and the report goes straight to the top," he warns.

"Understood." I clap him on the shoulder. "Thanks, man."

He unclips the red velvet rope barring the entrance, and we enter through the heavy metal doors. We go to our right, straight up a set of stairs with a glass railing on the left. It gives an impressive view of the dance floor below—which is better when the club is open—and the different levels with glass walls, both even with us and higher.

We get to the restaurant, which is buzzing. A hostess blinks at me, seeming to take a second to recognize my face. Her expression closes.

"Sorry, Antonio isn't here," she says. "And neither is Artemis."

"I'm hoping we can cut through to get to her apartment," I explain.

Kade watches passively.

The hostess seems to debate, then finally nods. She leads us in through the kitchen, which is a flurry of activity. Down a hall with closed doors that hide Tem's and Antonio's offices, then into a stairwell.

"You know the way from here?"

"Yeah, thanks." I trot down the stairs and land at Tem's apartment door. I've been here a few times, usually coming to seek her out and drag her back to the condo on Jace's orders. Never because I wanted to be in the space...

Kade, however, seems perfectly comfortable kneeling and picking the lock when no one answers our knocking.

It swings inward, and he glances up at me.

Jesus, why is a *glance* erotic?

Why am I thinking about the word erotic and *Kade Laurent* in the same sentence?

I shake it off. He goes in first, flicking lights on.

Weird that she's in the dark...

"Tem?" I call.

I never call her Tem.

I am seriously so off my game, it's not funny.

"Artemis?"

Nothing.

Kade moves to her bedroom—I don't want to know how he knows where it is, but I suppose it *is* a small apartment—and peeks in. "She's not here."

"What?"

I check for myself.

Bed is made. Clothes are on hangers, not spread across her floor.

What the fuck?

"Why do you look like you've just seen a ghost?" he demands.

"Because..." I cross to the refrigerator. There's nothing in it besides a few condiments. Nothing in the trash except an old plastic wrapper. "I thought she was staying here."

"When?"

"Last night." I lick my lips. "And the night before."

How the *fuck* did I lose Artemis?
And this isn't even the first time.

14 ARTEMIS

I'VE DECIDED TO QUIT.

Heroin, that is.

Obviously.

And I say that not because Reese just burst into the bathroom with the empty syringe in his hand, holding it up like the single piece of evidence will condemn me.

Maybe it will.

Also, the lock on the bathroom door?

Shitty as fuck.

"What is this?" he demands.

I finish clipping my bra closed and slowly slide my arms into my shirt. Over my head. I fluff out my hair, then cast a glance in the mirror.

I look fine. Normal, really.

"I don't know," I say. "Where'd you find it?"

"Where your jeans were on the floor."

"Well, it's not mine." I stare him down. "Is that what you think of me?"

He gapes. "I'm not thinking anything *of* you, Tem. I

want to know what the fuck you've been injecting yourself with."

"I haven't."

"Bullshit," he hisses. "I saw the track marks. The bruising."

I sigh and shake my head.

What else can I do? *Admit it?* No, thanks. I've already decided to quit, so I don't need to confess my sins to Reese and leave it up to him.

"Whose house is this?" I ask. "I was just in the hospital, Reese... Of course I have marks on my arms. How many times did they try to get an IV in my vein?"

"And a nurse was giving you an illegal substance," he whispers. "Under our watch."

"I'm not on drugs," I snap. "Jesus, Reese. I have more self-control than that."

Maybe.

He drops the syringe on the counter and puts both hands on his head. He goes into the hallway and paces back and forth. I don't know why he's so freaked out, there's no confirmation of anything.

I'm not on drugs. I told him that.

It's the worst lie in the history of lies, but still.

It's actually kind of nice, not giving a shit about his freak-out. I lean my hip on the counter and watch him.

"Reese." I finally push off and step in front of him. I grab his wrists. "I'm okay. Maybe Gabriel planted it to sabotage me."

"Yes." He latches on to that. "Oh God, when will his manipulations end?"

He sways and presses his forehead to mine.

"It's okay," I soothe. I release his wrists and rub his arms. "We figured him out."

"Yeah." He kisses my cheek.

"Now... we should really get back to Sterling Falls."

He straightens. "You want to go back?"

I huff. "My whole life is there."

"Okay..." He seems to debate. "Do you want to see your brother while you're here?"

Do I?

He, Jace, and Wolfe might see through me. I pretend to think about it, counting to ten in my head, and finally frown.

"They're fulfilling your favor, aren't they?" I tap his chest. "Saving someone?"

Reese nods. "If they're successful, yeah."

"Then we shouldn't distract them. The sooner they finish, the sooner they'll be home."

So... we do just that. We leave Emerald Cove.

I sit in the passenger seat of my car and watch the unfamiliar city flash past my window, and I have the oddest experience of wanting to jump out. To explore it more, to just *see* it.

But I don't, and soon we're on the two-lane highway that leads back to Sterling Falls.

We leave my brother behind, and I easily bat away the guilt that creeps up. He doesn't need me like I need Sterling Falls. He's so wrapped up in his family, it doesn't even matter.

Right?

At some point, I doze off. I come to when Reese touches my shoulder, and I bolt upright.

"We're back at your condo," he tells me. "I figured you'd rather walk than have me carry you up..."

I nod. Really, though, I'd rather be anywhere but here. When I climb out, I pause and stare at my bike.

The last time I was on it… Gabriel and I were going to the toll house. He was driving. So how did he get it back here? And why?

An uncomfortable feeling crawls over me, but I don't show it. God knows Reese would see and misinterpret it. But if Gabriel did something to my bike… I just know it'll be a while before I get back on it.

I beat Reese to the elevator, although I wait for him to arrive with my car keys. He scans the fob that will allow us to hit the button up to my floor, and ride in silence.

"Is the sex making things awkward?" I ask.

He winces.

It's either that or the drugs, but I'm sure as fuck not bringing that up again.

On the bright side—I reconnect with my phone, which had been forgotten in my room when I left to burn down Kade's house. I scroll through the few messages, which mainly consist of my Bow & Arrow managers checking in with updates, and pause on one from Barry.

The bouncer rarely texts. But he's alerted me to the fact that Saint and Kade are in my club, and then the hostess at the rooftop restaurant letting me know they went down to my apartment.

I grit my teeth and kick my door closed.

They're in *my* club? Did they break into my apartment, or were they just hoping to sneak up on me?

I change into a short, tight gold dress, strap on gladiator-style gold sandals that have a little heel, and unzip my makeup bag.

Fifteen minutes later, I'm ready.

Reese starts when I emerge, his eyes rounding. "Where are you going?"

"To see the look on Saint's face when I kick him and Kade out of my club."

He scrambles after me.

Which is probably good, because I still shouldn't drive. I dangle the keys from my finger in the elevator, and he takes them with a shake of his head.

We arrive in record time, and he glides the car into my reserved parking space at Bow & Arrow.

"Where to?" he asks.

"My apartment first." I hop out, leaving him to follow once again.

We go upstairs, and I try the handle of my door. It swings inward. I curse, stepping in fast to catch them by surprise.

But it's empty.

Seems they checked it, came up with nothing, and left.

For... the club?

It's open now. The faint notes of electric dance music reaches the hallway.

I text Sam, the nightclub manager. She replies with their location in under a minute. I flash it to Reese, and he sighs.

VIP lounge.

Naturally.

That's where I found Reese. Well, Reese found me. It's where Kade went, too. Not every time—occasionally he slums it with the rest of the patrons. When he's sneaking in and trying to get my attention...

The VIP lounge they've chosen is on one of the upper levels. It has its own private bar, U-shaped booths in black velvet and leather, and a wall of glass that looks down on the dance floor.

We find Saint and Kade at the bar.

My shoulders hike automatically, and I stop.

"I don't think I can do this," I whisper to Reese.

He nods and brushes past me. He steps up between them, one hand on each of their shoulders, and leans in. I don't know what he says to them, but they don't seem particularly surprised to see him.

What the fuck do I do?

Kade is with the Cyclopes pushing into Sterling Falls. I don't believe they're just filling in the gaps that the Titans left behind... but I don't know for certain. I don't know who's in charge. Is it Kade? Is it Gabriel? Some combination of the two?

Is either man responsible for the dead informant pinned to my club?

It had to be Gabriel... he was sending a message.

Then what hand has Kade played in my torment?

And for Saint to just...

"Artemis." The devil—Saint Hart—swims in front of my face. "Are you okay?"

His voice comes from a long way off.

"He wants to make things right."

He's talking about Kade.

I blink hard, and the bubble around me pops. "Then why'd he send you to champion him?"

He steps back. Careful, cautious, angry Saint. Am I just supposed to forgive everyone? Pretend the last few weeks didn't happen?

I didn't wake up.

Kade and Gabriel—

I turn away. Not just that. I don't stop. I keep going, until I fully admit to myself that I'm running away.

ONE PLACE they won't look for me: Jace's old hideout on the water.

I curl up on the cot, which reminds me a little too much of the one Kade had set up in his lonely, evil, empty house. I hope Nyx agrees that the place deserved to be burnt to a crisp. I hope she got a bit of satisfaction out of it, too.

My sleep is restless, to the point where I'm not sure if I actually fell asleep or simply tricked myself into believing it because of how still I lay. When the sun creeps up, lightening the sky through the far window, I give up on pretending.

Jace kept the place stocked well enough.

My phone, plugged into an outlet just out of my reach, lights up with an incoming message. I groan and reach for it.

I scan the message, and my heart sinks.

Another body.

I call my brother.

"Hey," he answers on the second ring. "You're up early."

"Early bird gets the worm," I reply. "I don't suppose the sheriff called Jace before he texted me?"

Pause.

"No," Apollo replies. "What's up?"

"Another body. Can you send me some details on your missing informant?"

He swears. "Where was it found?"

I press my lips together.

"Olympus?" he guesses.

"Yeah," I finally murmur. I tug on my boots, keeping the phone trapped between my ear and shoulder while I lace them. "I'm headed there now."

"You should stay far away."

"It's Olympus." I wait, and when he doesn't reply, I huff. "You can't say it's your territory alone to protect."

You're not even here.

"I..." There's a sliding sound.

Suddenly, a new voice fills my ear. "Tem."

"Wolfe."

"How's my, uh, second-favorite girl doing?"

"Perfectly fine, thanks."

He chuckles. "Try again, but make it more believable."

"I'm actually doing great. Is that why you interrupted my conversation with my brother? To ask me how I'm doing?"

"Apollo thinks he knows how you're doing," he admits. "So he won't ask too much. But I don't think you show us everything."

Of course I don't.

"I'm on my way to examine a dead body left at Olympus."

"Well, fuck. We're coming home."

"Did you find Reese's friend?"

Reese didn't go into detail... and neither have they. I don't know who they're looking for or how much of an extraction this person needs. All I know is that Reese gave them an envelope with the information in it.

"We're working on it," Wolfe hedges.

"Who is it?"

He sighs. "I shouldn't tell you."

That's bullshit.

"Wolfe. Seriously? What am I going to do...?"

"You might be tempted to abandon Sterling Falls and come to Emerald Cove yourself."

Because...

It's someone I know.

Someone Reese knows, too?

No one immediately jumps out—but there must be a connection. Maybe to Terror? To our teen years? Who would we both have come into contact with, and of that small pool, who left Sterling Falls?

It's a mystery I fear I'll be turning over for a while.

"Okay," I finally relent. "When will you be back?"

"In an hour."

I scoff. "No. Stay, do your job. I'll handle this."

"And are you handling everything else? Saint, Reese..."

Kade.

I finish getting dressed and yank open the somewhat flimsy door to the hideout. It's no more than a shack adjacent to the marina. I trudge up the gravel path to the vine-covered gate, which I drag open only enough to slip through. Then it goes back into place.

"Tem."

I wince. "I'm fine. I said that. Why don't you believe me, Wolfe? Do you not want me to be okay?"

"It's not that."

"You just don't think I'm capable." I snort. "I'm stronger than you think."

It's why I'm quitting heroin. It's been twenty-four hours... give or take... since I've even thought about it.

Okay, that's not quite true. I've thought about it a lot. But I haven't even considered texting Gabriel to get more.

I just need to keep myself preoccupied with other shit.

Like...

Boom.

I nearly fall into the gate.

"What the fuck?"

"I have no idea. I'll call you back." I hang up and shove my phone in my pocket. The good thing about fleeing Bow

& Arrow without any of the guys is that I was able to get my car back. My car, which has my spare firearm in a lockbox in the trunk. I rush to it, my gaze sweeping the streets.

Smoke rises in the air in the east.

Shit.

I grab the gun and holster, attaching it to my pants at my hip, and jump into the driver's seat. My bike would be so much better in a situation like this, but the car will have to do.

I fly toward Olympus, but the closer I get, the more I realize the smoke isn't coming from that far north.

South of Olympus is the Hell Hounds' compound and Apollo's house...

Obviously, we have priorities. I drive down the dirt driveway to Apollo's house, only to find it perfectly intact. I spin the wheel in their large drive and head back out.

Hell Hounds' compound next.

The smoke is rising thick and fast from just beyond the trees, and I press my car faster. I'm glad for the bells and whistles that allow it to attack the road, speeding down the lane.

The front portion of the clubhouse is *gone*. Bikes are scattered, blown back from where they were surely parked in an orderly fashion along the porch.

The roof of the porch—what's left of it—hangs down in the center. The support posts closest to the middle are broken.

It was a localized blast, I guess?

From *what?*

Malik bursts around the corner. There's ash and soot smeared across his face.

This club has bad vibes.

Bad luck.

I cover my mouth so I don't laugh.

It was only a year and a half ago that someone else blew it up. That one, however, had a much more devastating impact. It resulted in the whole place being demolished and rebuilt.

Kind of like how Kade will have to rebuild his house...

I don't think I'd mind that. If it was a new house, then I could stomach it.

Not that I want to stomach anything to do with him, I'm just saying. I *could*. And maybe Saint could, too.

"Artemis!"

I flinch.

Malik flings open my door and ducks down to stare at me. "What are you doing here?"

"I heard—saw—"

He grunts and reaches past me. Kills my engine, unclips my seat belt. Tows me out. All in swift movements. He looks me up and down, and if I didn't know better, I'd say he was tempted to pat me down, too.

I had jeans in my car, buried under some towels—and the gold dress from last night is tucked into it. It can pass as a shirt, so that's what we're going with. Because I tend to cliff jump spontaneously, I've learned to keep an assortment of clothes with me. Stashed under my seat on my bike, in the trunk, et cetera.

Not that it really matters.

He pushes me against the car, his expression sharpening. "Where were you that you saw it?"

I open and close my mouth.

I once had a crush on Malik. It's faded now, but I can't help the tug of worry in my gut.

"Someone tried to kill you," I say weakly.

He rolls his eyes. "Really? You think?"

"I—"

"I was being sarcastic."

Right.

"The last I saw you, you were unconscious in the backseat of this car." He slams his hand on the roof. "How did that happen?"

My breathing hitches. "Um..."

"Artemis," he warns.

"Was the car parked?" My tone is hopeful.

"No." He crosses his arms. "Reese was driving. Right past us, here."

I swallow. Reese didn't mention that. At my confusion, Malik sighs.

"He said he was trying to help you, and then Laurent and some of his guys rode up on us. Reese took you and split before they reached us."

My eyes widen. "They... what?"

"Cyclopes in East Falls." He shakes his head. "I thought Kronos had a pair of balls, but these guys..."

I scrunch my nose. I shouldn't think about Kade's balls. And *definitely* not the former Titans leader's wrinkly old set.

Gross.

So, so gross.

"What happened with Kade?"

He shrugs. "They wanted to prove their mettle."

My stomach knots. "And...?"

"And one walked away with a blade in his stomach."

I grimace. "Is this payback?"

"No, Artemis." He stares down at me. "The knife to the gut was the punishment for trespassing. This was... something else entirely."

Great.

Someone calls an all-clear, and the Hell Hounds come out of the woodwork. They're armed to the teeth, their leather cuts gleaming in the sunlight. They busy themself yanking away the savable pieces of roof and porch. Someone sprays a still-smoking wall with a fire extinguisher.

Malik and I venture closer to the blast zone. The dirt and gravel, in a ring starting at the heavy metal door that now lies flat inside the club, is charred. There are nails and bits of metal everywhere.

"It was a package." He dips his chin toward one of the guys sitting on the far end of the porch. He's being taken care of by another guy. "He didn't notice it, and opening the door jostled it. He was partially behind the door, which saved his life."

"Damn."

He sighs. "I thought we'd hold on to peace a while longer."

"Because you want peace, or because Wolfe does?"

His palm rests on the butt of his gun, strapped at his hip. Realizing he's armed isn't shocking—I'd be more shocked if it was absent. I grew up around the Hell Hounds, and ninety-nine percent of them carry.

"I wanted it. I wanted to stop my guys from dying in the streets. But... I think this will be worse."

"How so?" My skin prickles at his words.

I just need him to say something that I can refute. Like that this gang is bigger, meaner, or stronger... he doesn't know that. He couldn't possibly.

"They want it more," he says quietly. "There's a desperation underlining their actions."

Shit.

I don't think I can argue with that.

15 KADE

I STORM into Gabriel's creepy room under Madness. To no one's surprise, he isn't there. He's like a ghost sometimes, only appearing when you least want to see him.

He *bombed* the Hell Hounds.

I knew... I mean, he gave me the box, but I didn't do anything with it. I didn't write Malikai's name on the box—he did. I didn't mail it. I carried it up and left it, forgotten, at the base of the stairs that hides Gabriel's underground world from above.

But now, he's gone and blown up their front porch—a nice little welcome gift, he'd probably say. But the madness that will fall upon us...

I don't feel ready.

I'm not convinced this was the way to go about things—I didn't want it to come to violent terms. I didn't want to coat Sterling Falls' streets in blood after they just recovered from one war.

"Gabriel!" I spin around, but the room is most certainly empty. The boxes that lined one shelf are gone, too.

Ice coats my skin.

He put the bomb in a box.

But there were more boxes...

How many more bombs are there?

Where would he send them?

I check my phone, but there's barely any service down here. I do have a missed call from Artemis, of all people, though.

That gives me pause.

Why is she calling me?

Leaving Gabriel's cave behind, I head up into the heart of Madness. I'm about to push through the door when I freeze.

Gabriel's behind the bar, and Artemis is talking to him.

Why?

I lift my phone and call her.

She scowls at Gabriel, then checks her phone. She slides off the stool, and her hips sway as she exits the building.

"Hello?" Her voice is breathy.

Not hard, like I was expecting.

"Where are you?"

"I *was* with Malik."

I narrow my eyes at Gabriel. He hasn't noticed me through the glass. Or maybe he did spot me, and now he's playing dumb. Neither of them were here when I stormed through not five minutes ago. He's not clearing any sort of glass from where she was sitting...

"And?" I reply.

"You don't strike me as the bomb type," she admits. "But your interaction with the Hell Hounds outside their club left a bad taste in their mouth."

"Mouths now filled with ash," I supply.

Internally, I curse myself *and* Gabriel.

He set me up, then took advantage of my foolishness. This is going to come down on me, not him. After all, it's my prints on the box—if anything remains—and my bitter confrontation the other day that can be traced back.

"Meet me," I say suddenly. "Name the place."

When she doesn't reply, I clear my throat.

"Please," I add.

She sighs. "Okay. The reservoir waterfall."

I pause.

"Yeah," she adds. "I know about you and the sheriff."

My phone beeps, signifying that she hung up on me.

I think I deserve that.

ARTEMIS LEANS on the trunk of her car, which is backed carefully into a spot that gives her a view of both the road and the waterfall.

Same place I met the sheriff when he delivered Reese's mother's phone records—which proved useful only in that I was able to narrow down two burners. One that, at the time, was working but wasn't used frequently enough or long enough to be tracked. And the other was dead.

It confirmed what I already knew: Reese Avery still talks to his mama.

I park my new car and climb out, stopping a good distance away. This is the first time I've seen her since... *since*. She's thinner. Her hair is in a bun on top of her head, and her gold shirt is skin tight. It's tucked into a pair of high-waisted jeans.

She's too pretty. It's devastating, a bit.

"What do I have to do for you to leave Saint alone?" she asks.

I narrow my eyes.

"I mean, you've already fucked me over," she continues. "And Reese, too. So is Saint next? Is that why you keep inserting yourself..."

"There are much worse places I could be *inserting* myself." I smirk. "We could find out."

She doesn't react. Not physically anyway, and she's just far enough away mentally that I can't get a read on her frame of mind.

"I wanted to explain myself." I rub the back of my neck. "I..."

"I don't really care." She raises one shoulder. "I came to see about Saint. Not for you to make excuses."

My brows lift. "Excuses."

"Yes, Kade, excuses."

She crosses and uncrosses her arms, then straightens. She goes to the railing, leaning her forearms on it and staring out at the waterfall. It's an impressive sight. A force of nature.

Artemis, I mean, not the falls.

"It's not an excuse." I approach before she can run away. I won't corner her or trap her, but damn it—she needs to listen. "It's a reason. I owed Reese, and he was never going to fucking wake up. I knew Gabriel wouldn't kill you."

She laughs. "You know that, do you? What he did was so much worse than that."

I stare at her.

I hadn't considered that.

"Artemis..."

"No. Fuck off, Kade. Go on your killing spree, pin bodies to my club and Olympus, fight with the Hell Hounds. I'm so far done with all of this shit."

I don't know how to respond to that.

She faces me and reaches out. I don't move. I don't want to scare her away, but the thought of her touch has my heart thumping harder.

She yanks the collar of my shirt down, revealing the tattoo Saint gave me. The heavens and Earth separated by a marble pillar...

It's very much inspired by Atlas.

Just what I asked for.

She sighs and releases it.

"I didn't give him a choice," I tell her.

"You always have a choice."

There's the hurt. It shines in her eyes, and the air leaves my lungs in a rush.

I hurt her, and Saint still...

She touches the ball of her shoulder, as if remembering something, and her expression closes. All of it leaves her, until she's just staring at the rushing water.

"You and him should talk," I say.

"Talk or argue."

I nudge her. "You're a good debater. Surely you're not afraid of getting into it with Saint?"

"He just makes things bigger than they are. And I'm tired."

I nod like I understand. I'm not in her shoes, though. I can't understand shit from over here.

I hold out my hand. "I don't want to be your enemy, Artemis."

She glances down at it, then up at my face. "You're with Gabriel. And he..."

Her eyes fill with tears. They spill over, and I reach for her. Like she reached for me. But she doesn't swat me away or move back.

She lets me catch her tears with my fingers.

"Don't cry."

There's something in me that demands I protect her in all the ways I couldn't. Against my better judgment, I pull her into my chest and wrap my arms around her.

It takes a long moment, but she carefully hugs me back.

I breathe in her floral scent. Dip my head to let my nose brush her hair. Inhale.

I don't want to exhale.

"I'm sorry," I tell her. "It won't happen again."

She sniffs. "I don't believe you."

That stings. But I can't make her trust me... it's got to be earned.

And I want that.

"I'll prove it to you."

She slowly extricates herself.

"Gabriel is the problem." Her words are more for herself than me. She looks me up and down, seeming to decide something, and slowly nods. "I'll see you around, Kade."

"Yes, you will."

I watch her go.

Then I head to Bobby's boat, parked back at the marina, because I'm starving. And there's nothing left to do today except mourn how much I fucked things up.

16 SAINT

THE MOMENT I FIND TEM, I settle.

Everything with Kade left me off-kilter. It should be natural that I seek out some form of comfort. Except... why is it her?

Why am I standing in the doorway of her room, watching her fold laundry, instead of immediately retreating to the safe haven of my room?

When did she have time to do laundry, is the better question?

"Why are you staring at me?" Tem's voice is stiff.

I cringe. "I'm not."

"Yes, you are." She drops the shirt onto her bed and plants her hands on her hips. "I have a sixth sense about that kind of thing."

"Staring?"

"You." She meets my gaze.

Oh.

"I didn't realize how tattooing Kade would hurt you," I say.

I either say it now or I hold on to it forever.

She winces. Continues folding. Busy work to steady the slightest tremor in her fingers.

"So for that, I'm sorry. If I knew... I should've known, that's not an excuse. I just..."

"You just can't help yourself," Tem says quietly. She laughs. "Of course you can't. You torture me, Saint. All the fucking time, you just *kill* me. And now you're going to come in here and tell me that was the one time you forgot Kade was a sore spot?"

I rear back. "No."

"Yes," she argues. She's given up on folding and comes closer, her expression more mad than I've seen her. "Yes, Saint. You know exactly how to drive the knife in deeper."

Apt analogy. My focus drops to her stomach. She's wearing a cropped top, and the stitches of the lower stab wound are visible. They're healing surprisingly well, which means she's taking care of them the way she should. She's not scratching at them, or jumping into the ocean, or...

"Even the tattoo," she mutters. "Not his—*mine*."

"Your—"

"My lack of a tattoo!" She throws her hands up.

Strands of hair are escaping the bun on top of her head. Her black leggings match the cropped shirt, and both make her tanned skin seem even more golden. There's not a speck of makeup on her face. Just a few necklaces, a ring on her index finger...

Her lack of a tattoo.

She's talking about when I tattooed her with no ink?

"I thought you didn't care about that." I eye her. "You didn't want me to—"

"No?" She huffs. "You're so thick."

"I am not."

"You are," she goads.

She comes closer, pressing her palm to my chest. "You're so stupid, Saint. You don't see what's right in front of you."

"What's that?"

Her expression closes.

I know the answer, though. Belatedly. It's *her*. She's right in front of me.

Before she can retreat, I grab her neck and tow her back to me.

I bend, leaning over her. Our lips are close enough that barely a movement from either of us will let them touch.

"I see you," I whisper.

She shakes her head. "You see what you want to see."

"I want to see your pussy," I counter.

My dick is already at attention. Whatever freak incident earlier was clearly a result of not getting myself off enough. But with everything happening, there hasn't really been time...

"Strip," I order.

Her gaze darkens, her pupils dilating. She hooks her thumbs in her leggings and drags them down.

I take care of her shirt as soon as she's kicked the leggings away, lifting it and exposing her breasts.

No bra.

Should've figured.

"Saint," she breathes.

"Yeah?"

"I..." She shakes her head. "Never mind."

My brows furrow.

Her hands go to the button of my jeans, but I still them. I kneel in front of her and drag the last strip of fabric hiding her cunt from me. She shudders, and I guide her backward. She sits hard on the bed, and I spread her legs. Lean in.

"Don't tease me," she says, "I don't think I could bear it."

I take my jeans off. She scoots backward, knocking the clean, folded clothes to the floor. I crawl over her, palming my length. I should pause and get a condom, but the way she's looking at me...

Fuck.

Sliding inside her is the most normal, natural thing in the world.

Why would I ever want to be somewhere else?

She groans. I use micromovements, trying to bury myself deeper. She's wet and tight—almost too tight. It takes a few long moments of stroking, of rubbing her clit, for her to relax enough to take all of me.

"Pretty girl," I tell her. "No teasing. Just orgasms."

She nods at me.

I deliver on my promise. She comes while I'm seated inside her, and the waves of euphoria that clamp her muscles down around me is a true test of my willpower. The need to move is almost overwhelming.

"I slept with Reese," she confesses.

I pause, swallowing the questions that bubble up. Like *when* and *why*?

I could guess the why.

I could also probably hazard a guess at the when.

"Saint."

I pull out and flip her over. On her hands and knees. I spread her legs and drive back into her harder. Just because she slept with someone else doesn't mean I won't fulfill my promise. It's almost too late to back out anyway. No teasing —just orgasms. Mine. Hers.

She drops her face to the bed, and the slope of her

spine, her waist, down to her curved, wide hips, nearly makes me blow my load right then.

I slide my palm down her back, keeping her bent low.

"Say something," she begs.

Can't.

A little busy.

I fuck her until her headboard slams against the wall with every thrust. I fuck her through another orgasm, and reach around and tweak her nipples, tugging on the piercings until she squeaks out a protest.

Part of me wants to see her face.

Another part wants to question how the sex with Reese was.

Another... the more selfish option... is to make her forget all about him by obliterating her mind with climaxes.

I pull out of her, flipping her over, and use my mouth. My cock is so hard it aches, but I'm not about to ruin it by coming early. I can wait. I do wait.

She comes on my tongue.

She comes with my fingers buried in her pussy and my mouth latched on her breast.

She comes, she comes, she comes.

Until she lifts onto her elbows, and her muscles tremble and shake so much, she falls back to the mattress. Only then do I climb over her and thrust back into her warmth. I bury my face in her neck, inhale her scent, and pump my hips. The friction is just barely there. Her cunt is drooling with arousal and her cum.

My balls tighten, and I groan. I bite her neck, and a flash of Kade's threat to bite me flashes in my mind.

Shit.

I spill inside her, my cock throbbing and pulsing.

"I didn't mean to do that." I almost pull out of her, but she grabs on to me.

Wraps around me.

"Just stay here." Her voice is more vulnerable than I've ever heard. "Stay."

I exhale. Long and slow. "Okay, wildcat. I've got you."

We shift onto our sides, and I keep her close. It's the oddest feeling, staying inside her while my dick softens. It doesn't lose all of its hardness—in fact, its half-mast shape lets me remain in her even longer.

I hook a hand around her knee, drawing it up to my hip. Her arms are tucked like little wings between our bodies, but I don't mind that. I drape my other arm around her waist.

Hold her tight, keep her here.

Pretend this is enough to set us right.

And finally, finally sleep.

17 ARTEMIS

NADINE BRADSHAW SEEMS nothing like her asshole brother. And yet, they're cut from the same cloth. Same outlook on a lot of things—with different approaches. Different morals, but often things come to the same conclusion.

We sit in her office early on a Tuesday morning.

It's been a few days since the bomb at the Hell Hounds' compound and the body was found at Olympus. Longer still since the sheriff executed a search warrant on Bow & Arrow.

Nadine holds a seat on the city council. While that doesn't exactly give her oversight of the sheriff—I suspect that would be a conflict of interest—both are elected positions. Both, in theory, answer to the people.

"I just want answers," I say plainly.

Antonio has been in the rehab place for over a week. I haven't seen him, but Vittoria has sent daily progress reports. Soon, he'll be cleared to go home. And after that, he'll return to work.

Probably.

Maybe he'll retire.

The answers I need are in reference to the warrant. It shouldn't have been signed in the first place, but I need to know which judge okayed it.

And why?

"I'm sorry," Nadine says. "I can get you a copy of the warrant. Nathan should've given it to you already, but it has all the details."

"It won't say what they found." I cross my legs and reach for one of the two coffee cups I brought with me. She hasn't touched hers, but I'm not going to take that personally. "A body was found *outside* my club, and a judge signs a warrant for my computers? Really?"

She winces.

There *is* something there.

"It's not Bow & Arrow—" She presses her lips together. Guilt flashes across her expression.

It's not Bow & Arrow... which means this has to do with Terror?

Does someone want to see if I'm still running Terror?

As if I'd do it through my club's books.

Although... a lot of cash comes through the bar, especially in the summer. Tourists *love* cash. They don't want evidence of how much they spent on liquor or champagne on their credit cards. If there was ever a need to clean money, Bow & Arrow would be a great company to run it through.

"Fine," I say in her silence. "I'll take a copy of the warrant, then, please."

She nods and gets up.

She leaves the office.

I hop up and circle to her chair. Her computer is still unlocked.

To be clear—I don't suspect *her* of anything. But I do think the sheriff is wrapped up with Kade, which means Gabriel has access to him, too. And depending on how deep their wallets are...

I hate that Nathan Bradshaw isn't loyal. He's always followed the money, and for a while, he was fine. He was doing well, actually. Until Kade came along.

Fucking Kade Laurent.

Fucking Cyclopes.

I go to her recently sent emails and take a picture of the list. Then her inbox, just for the hell of it. And her deleted ones. Most people hide shit in their deleted folder, and it's obtainable because they don't wipe that browser.

Other than her slender laptop, her desk is clear.

Her heels click on the tile in the hall, and I race back around the desk. I drop into my seat and cross my legs again just as she reenters.

"Here's a copy," she says, extending a folder to me. "Is there anything else I can help you with?"

"You don't know anything about your brother's investigation at Olympus, do you?"

She gives me a *look*. "You know I can't say."

"Family dinner discussions? Anything?"

"I'm sorry, Artemis."

I sigh. "Okay. Thanks." I tuck the folder under my arm and head out, taking my coffee with me. In the hall, I flip open the pages and scan the warrant. It granted the sheriff's office access to Bow & Arrow's hard drives, including but not limited to: point-of-sale systems, accounting systems, office computers and phone lines, and identification scanners.

Weird.

I keep skimming, all the way to the bottom line, signed by a judge.

Justice Marcus Graves.

My heart sinks.

Graves... as in, Wesley Graves? As in—the fallen leader of the Titans, who went by the name Kronos.

Things just got a bit murkier.

There might not be a connection. It *could* be coincidence...

But there are a whole lot of reasons a potential relative of the man who drove Sterling Falls to war might want to see the whole city burn.

I'VE COME to two conclusions: Gabriel is going *down*, and heroin is no fucking joke. It's been a week since I caved, and I'm feeling it. Everything hurts. Seriously, everything. My *hair* hurts. How does that even happen?

The guys—Reese, Saint, Kade—have so far left me alone. Saint is probably still freaked out from me needing him to hold me. Reese is watching me with hawk eyes, still not one hundred percent sold on my lie. And Kade... well, Kade can fuck off.

I'm lying in the bathtub, fully clothed, when the fucker enters.

The water has gone cold. Actually, I'm not sure it was ever warm. My teeth chatter. They hurt, too, for the record.

"What are you doing?" Kade asks.

I glare up at him. "What do you mean, what am I doing? What does it look like I'm doing?"

I'm fighting the urge to slip under the water and drown

myself. That might be more pleasant than the shitstorm wreaking havoc on my body.

He squats beside the tub and dips his fingers in the water. Instantly, his mild concern deepens. "This is ice-cold."

"It's lukewarm."

"You're shivering," he points out.

I shrug.

Let's backtrack to Gabriel, and how the son of a bitch is going down. I've been contemplating this for a while, but with no true leads, no idea of his motivations, I'm stuck.

There's one avenue I could explore, but I hesitate to venture down it. It would probably result in him going absolutely bananas, and I'm not sure I'd survive that. Although it sure is tempting...

No, no. That will remain on the back burner until I'm even more desperate. If such a place exists.

He has to go down in some other way. Like... well, maybe not murder. Imprisonment?

Shit, I can't do that to him. It would be what he deserves, but it's kind of like putting someone back in the trauma that made them this way.

Well, not *kind of like*. It *is*.

Imprisonment is out. Killing him is out. Public embarrassment?

I'm losing it.

I focus back in on Kade. "How goes the destruction of Sterling Falls?"

He grimaces, which I have to assume means it's not going well.

Or it's going too well?

He reaches into the tub. Water sloshes everywhere and soaks his sleeves in the process, but he doesn't even flinch.

He grabs at my knees, wraps one arm behind my back, and hauls me up.

It's actually impressive. I'm solid. A lot of muscle, a bit of fat. Some depression... You know, the usual.

"How come you haven't seen Antonio?" he asks.

I blink up at him. I hadn't realized my eyes were shut, and it takes effort to force them wider. He perches me on the counter and strips me. If his movements were anything less than methodical, I'd fight.

I promise. Really. I'd fight to have a big, strong asshole try to get me naked.

But he's not doing it to be sexual, he's being *nice*. Arguably the worse of the two.

Once I'm out of the wet clothes—he tosses them back in the tub, where they make satisfying splashes—he bundles me in a towel. One around my body, another slung over his shoulder. He opens drawers until he finds a wide-toothed comb and carefully runs it through my hair.

My painful, aching hair.

But the teeth against my scalp doesn't feel too terrible, and my eyes flutter again.

"Where'd you learn to do this?" I ask when he blots my hair with the extra towel. "This care-for-a-girl stuff."

He meets my gaze. "A sister."

"Right." I hum. "The medical bills sister."

The wall behind his eyes? The one I hadn't realized was missing? Yeah, that slams back into place.

I catch his wrist. "I didn't mean to say it like that. You said she was sick?"

"She had a long hospital stay," he says on a sigh. "Yeah. It doesn't matter."

"Well, it mattered if you were brushing her hair. That's an act of service. Love and stuff." I raise my eyebrows. "It's okay to admit you love and care for your sister."

Or… love*d* and care*d* for his sister.

I don't actually know if she's alive—and I don't want to know. To learn that someone close to him died some terrible way would be too tragic for me to handle.

Doesn't that sound bad?

It would be too tragic for *me*?

Someone needs to slap me before it's too late.

"Where are your parents?"

"Throw me back in the water, why don't you," I mumble.

He wraps that second towel around my hair and rubs my arms through the other towel.

"Why are you even here?"

"To ask you probing, painful questions about your family. Obviously." A hint of a smile appears, then vanishes. Worry takes over, but he never looks away.

I sigh. "Right, well, Dad's an asshole and Mom's a pushover. That's about all you need to know."

"Uh-huh."

"What? You don't think a girl just *ends up* in a sex trafficking ring, do you?"

He stops.

Yeah, he didn't think of *that* one.

"I wasn't kidnapped in the middle of the night. I wasn't snatched out of the house where I lived with two loving, peaceful parents. My father put me in the car on my fifteenth birthday and drove me to meet a man who ran Terror. That man put me in the back of a truck with others, and off we went. With an exchange of money, of course." My gaze stays on Kade. "After all, someone had to pay off his gambling debts."

Kade's mouth opens and closes.

I've actually stumped him?

"You hadn't said any of that," he finally mutters. "I mean, we talked about Terror, but..."

"It's embarrassing." I glare at him. "You think I'm proud of what happened to me? So many more girls—and boys—came out of that place with physical scars along with the emotional trauma. My scars are just mental."

He winces. He looks like he's about to say something, then clearly thinks better of it. I kind of wish he would say what he thinks, though. Cracking open his brain and digging into his thoughts might be the only way I inch closer to forgiving him.

It doesn't happen, though. His movements stay methodical. He unplugs the drain in the tub, finishes rubbing down my limbs with a towel. He leaves me on the counter and comes back with clothes.

A t-shirt, leggings, his sweatshirt.

I spot the Cyclopes logo stitched on the breast, and my anger flares all over again. He put me in his sweatshirt so nonchalantly—and for what?

"Why make me wear that?"

"I was hoping it would keep you safe," he admits in a low voice. "But it didn't."

I sigh.

No, it definitely did not. It didn't stop the target on my back. It didn't signal that I was *protected*. Clothing doesn't work like that in Sterling Falls.

My conversation with Nadine returns, and suspicion prickles at my skin. She said there was outside influence. The sheriff alluded to the same, hinting that it wasn't his decision to search my club. To take all the computers, our hard drives...

"Did you push the sheriff to search Bow & Arrow?" I ask.

He meets my gaze. "What? No."

Yeah, right.

"You guys planted a body—"

"I had nothing to do with that," he growls. "I'm not a fucking murderer."

Okaaaay, Mr. Crabby Pants.

He gives me his back while I put on the new clothes, and I clear my throat when I'm done. I leave the sweatshirt sitting where he placed it, because if there's one thing I cannot handle, it's more fucking Cyclopes.

He only frowns a little when I lift a forgotten one from the hook on the back of the door. Once it's on, he opens the bathroom door again. This time with the intention of us exiting.

When I entered the bathroom, I was aching. Kicking off my shoes was painful, so I lowered myself into the hot water fully clothed. No one was home to stop me, anyway. I was allowed to wallow in my misery.

I guess I did that a bit too well.

There's something in his expression now that seems... regretful. But is it for something he's actively doing? Or his past decisions?

I eye him.

His hand lands on the small of my back, ending my hesitation. He guides me out and turns me away from my bedroom. I move faster into the main living space, just so his touch will stop.

Reese and Saint both wait for us.

Oh, fuck.

The reality of the situation crashes down on me, and I bite back a grimace.

Is this an intervention?

18 ARTEMIS

"I DON'T HAVE time for this." I spring forward, away from Kade's hand, and make a beeline for the door.

Saint follows me into the hall, and I laugh to myself at the stupidity of it all. Kade being in my condo. Saint tattooing him. Reese being—*I don't know*. Fucking Reese. Good or bad, he's unexpectedly kind.

"Honestly, Saint," I call over my shoulder. "I don't think I can do any more betrayal from you."

I can't. I thought he would stand with me in this. Didn't he see me in the hospital? Didn't he help rescue me from Gabriel's fucked-up game?

"Tem."

"Don't call me that." I hit the button for the elevator. Jab my finger onto it again when it doesn't immediately light up, then again a few more times. "Why'd you even follow me out here?"

He sighs.

"Don't *sigh* at me," I snap.

"You burned down Kade's house." He stops beside me. "You're acting erratically."

"Maybe I'm just traumatized." I glare at him. It's true, though. Maybe I *am* traumatized. By betrayal and lies and backstabbing. It's a lot for a girl to go through on her own. I'm totally on my own, aren't I? Saint and Reese and Kade are only just visitors in my life. My brother is out of town. Antonio... I can't go to him.

I'm alone. I'd be more alone if Saint stopped chasing me.

The elevator chimes, and I step in before the doors have fully opened. Saint follows. His hands are in his pockets, his expression stricken.

Ha.

"Why did you follow me?"

The doors slide closed.

"Because I care."

"You have a funny way of showing it," I mutter.

He shakes his head. "You just don't want to see that I'm trying to keep everything together. All the time."

"Oh?" I face him. "What are you trying to keep together? Me? You?"

"Yes," he hisses. "Yes, Artemis, *you*. And the tattoo shop. And my own fucking traitorous brain."

"Because of Kade," I surmise.

He reels back. "Excuse me?"

"You're dealing with your own form of betrayal from him—"

"No." He comes closer. "No, damn it. My brain is telling me to stay true to Elora. I loved her. I can only ever love her. And this fucking attraction to you is overwhelming and *endless*. Do you think I want to want you? Do you think craving you is *easy*?"

My jaw drops, but no words come out.

"It's not," he whispers. His hand slides around my neck,

to my nape. His nails dig into my skin, and he drags me toward him. "It's the worst torture I've endured."

His lips slam into mine.

I gasp into his mouth, my brain still caught between *craving* and *torture.* It fast forwards to our parting lips, the chase of his tongue in my mouth. It's furious and sweet at the same time.

I press up on my toes, clutching at his shirt. All I can hear is the rushing of my blood in my ears. The headache, the bone-deep ache, it all becomes secondary to this kiss.

He's kissing me.

I'm kissing him back.

Knowing he feels just as guilty as me soothes some of the knots in my stomach. My fingers hook into the waistband of his jeans, and I yank him closer. He groans into my mouth. I almost draw back, but his fingers tense against my nape. Keeping me with him.

This is happening?

We've fucked. Fucking, in retrospect, had practically no intimacy.

And this is the complete opposite. It's just a *kiss*, and I may as well be standing in front of him with my soul cupped in my hands.

Letting him examine it.

The elevator doors slide open, but I can't stop.

He doesn't either. I angle my head and suck his tongue into my mouth. My heart pounds. He tastes like watermelon.

The doors close.

He chuckles into my mouth. We're swept upward, and I finally push back against his chest just as it stops at a new floor.

We separate, me stuck to my wall and Saint stepping

back to press his spine to the other. His eyes are wide, his cheeks flushed. I'm sure I look no better, but the couple that enters don't seem to notice. They hit the button for the lobby.

I carefully run my fingers through my hair. It's still quite damp, and every tug through it spikes pain along my scalp.

You know what would fix it?

A drug that I'm not going to think about.

The elevator chimes. Saint and I follow the couple out into the lobby, but I pause. I don't actually have a plan for where to go or what to do. If I was alone...

"Come on," Saint murmurs.

We walk in silence. My joints hurt, but I push it aside for the peace between us. It's too rare, and I find myself hesitant to open my mouth.

What if I ruin it?

I could easily say something snappy, and he would retort with a patronizing comment. It would dissolve into an argument, and the peace would vanish like it was never here in the first place.

By our third turn, I know where we're going.

Starlight.

My chest tightens, but I don't say anything until we're standing in front of the tattoo shop. He unlocks the door and ushers me in, and I glare at him.

"Don't look at me like that." He flicks on the lights and gestures to his tattoo chair.

"Another trick?"

"I'm righting a wrong."

A lump forms in my throat. He goes to the counter and starts prepping a tray of supplies while I fidget.

"Take your shirt off," he says without turning around.

A chill sweeps down my spine.

I'm not wearing a bra. Something Kade seemed to have forgotten when he gathered clothes for me... or maybe he just didn't want to dig around my top drawer?

How kind of him.

The last time Saint saw me shirtless, he couldn't take his gaze off my nipples.

So...

Fuck it. I lock the front door, then yank the privacy curtain. Saint glances over his shoulder just as I'm pulling off my shirt and sweatshirt in one go, and predictably, his gaze drops to my chest.

My nipples pebble in the cool air.

"Artemis," he groans. "What are you doing?"

"You told me to take my shirt off," I say as innocently as I can.

He tilts his head. "Do you trust me?"

"Is that a requirement?"

"No." He takes a seat. "I was going to do your shoulder, but... I'll do wherever you want."

I consider that. My sweatshirt and shirt are in my arms, covering my stomach—and more importantly, my arms. God forbid Saint notice the bruised veins in the crooks of my elbows.

Nothing would kill this mood quite like that.

Where do I want a tattoo?

Wordlessly, I tap my collarbone.

He nods and points to a spot in front of him.

Damn. My knees shake on my way over. I'm feeling a bit vulnerable like this. Who wouldn't? I hug my clothes tighter, tempted to cover my breasts, but they've got Saint enraptured.

When I come to a halt within arm's reach, he inches

forward even further. He presses on a spot on my collarbone, then sweeps his finger outward.

Goosebumps rise on my skin.

"Stay still." He grabs a marker and returns. He flicks the cap off and braces his other hand on my shoulder. Right before he makes contact, though, he pauses. When he looks up, his face is only inches from mine. His eyes, this close, are too blue. Wide with earnest. "I'm not going to blindfold you, but I'd like you to not see until I'm done drawing."

I swallow, then slowly nod.

He nods back. His head dips, his concentration focused on my skin.

His canvas.

The marker's tip scratches against my skin. I sway, and he places my hand on his hip. Another stabilizing point. It keeps me upright, which is all he probably needs. The marker, after a few minutes, hurts like a tattoo.

I keep my gaze fixed on where the wall meets the ceiling in front of me.

He hums under his breath. At one point, he switches to a finer-tipped pen. I still don't peek. I concentrate on the burning scratches, my body aching. The pain has traveled from my scalp down my spine, settling in my hips. I fight the urge to shift my weight.

Finally, he caps the pen and takes a step back.

"You can look," he says in a low voice. He directs me to a mirror hung on the wall. "Tell me if you hate it."

I shoot him a look. I've *seen* his work. Through countless hours sitting on the white couch in the front of his shop, taking *my* work here just because I was terrified he would slip out and kill himself when I wasn't watching.

The way he acted right after Nyx died was a scary time.

He held it together for everyone else, but I saw through it. I hurt right along with him, but that solidarity wasn't enough.

I don't know if he even felt it.

I was more of a planted watchdog than a friend.

But that need to make sure he stayed safe slowly faded when he didn't act out. It was impossible to tell if he was just pretending or if he really didn't mean it when he told Jace he wanted to die.

Or when he ran into the ocean and had to be dragged out.

Too many examples for comfort spring to mind. He went through a phase of running himself ragged, which he said was just to be exhaust his body enough to sleep.

But he didn't stop tattooing. If anything, he took more clients. He wanted to be here all the time—and I get that. It's the best sort of distraction for his brain *and* his body.

All that is to say, he only grew better. Magazines came to interview him. Famous people, even NHL players, traveled to Sterling Falls to see him. His work was worth it. *Is* worth it.

He did that all with a broken heart.

I step up to the mirror, analyzing myself first. Hair: curling and a bit frizzy. Dark circles under my eyes. The wounds I suffered at the hands of Gabriel—the stabbing and subsequent heroin-induced coma—made me lose too much weight.

I feel similar to how I felt emerging from Terror. Hollow.

But my gaze finally drops to my collarbone, and my breath sticks in my chest.

Through the layers of marker, from a light blue to a darker purple, I make out the scales of justice exploding with wildflowers. It's about the size of my palm, and some of the flowers extend down toward my breast, and others up to the ball of my shoulder.

My eyes burn.

I blink rapidly, but I can't really make sense of it.

"What does it mean?"

He steps up behind me. "I think you'll figure it out... if you want it. Should I change anything?"

"I want it exactly as it is," I say immediately.

"Okay."

I turn away from the mirror and take a seat. I hold the sweatshirt over my breasts, but after a long moment, slowly lower them.

He groans through his teeth. "You want to make this difficult?"

"You could've picked something easier," I answer. "My thigh."

"Seeing your thigh would not have been any easier."

I smirk.

He takes a seat and rolls the stool closer. He adjusts my chair to a better angle, tilting it back so I'm reclined.

With one gloved finger, he traces the hoop in my nipple.

I almost fly out of the chair.

It's his turn to smirk, but it fades fast. "Tell me about Terror."

Oh.

My mouth dries. "Why?"

He lifts a shoulder. "Because I should understand, and I don't."

"No one *should* understand."

"Gabriel does." He's not even facing at me anymore. Black ink in the little wells, a few different needle sizes.

My palms sweat.

"Gabriel does," I agree. "He had a different experience, but... yeah."

"So?" he questions. "Please, Tem."

Oh, there he goes, using the name only friends call me. I wouldn't say we're that—but he did admit to craving me, didn't he?

The tattoo machine in his hand comes alive with a sudden buzz, and he picks up ink from the well. He scoots closer. "Ready?"

"Yeah." My voice is hoarse.

He touches my skin with his left hand, steadying me, and I try to relax for the first prick of the needle.

It hurts more and less than I thought it would.

I know that makes no sense, but...

It's all I can focus on. And it's by choice, so it makes it better.

After the first line, the first taste of this kind of pain... maybe I have an addictive personality. Maybe Gabriel knew, and now Saint will, too. Because I'm not sure how one tattoo will be enough.

The only way to keep myself sane is through punishment. And that's why I start talking.

19 ARTEMIS

Ten years ago

AFTER REESE, I was transferred.

They call this one a brothel, because there's less pomp and circumstance.

A lot of the women here are drugged. The men who roam the halls always have stuff on them, using it to tempt the women into submission—or threaten the sober ones.

Sometimes I crave the unknown substance. It makes them malleable, like dolls. They don't seem to care what the men do to them.

If we're not in a private room with a client, we're out in the open on the first floor of the house. There's not much to do except wallow in self-pity. Doing anything else would draw the attention of the guards.

In quiet moments, my mind strays to the guard who gave me his name. Antonio. There was sadness in his eyes when he locked my cell, a certain sort of helplessness that I hadn't seen before. *I* was helpless. *I* was trapped. But... his expression made me think maybe he was trapped in his role, too.

And also Reese. The way he touched me to make my body shake and quiver—and not out of fear. I think about his eyes when the world gets too hard, and try as I might, I can't figure out if he's a good guy or bad.

If he bought me and raped me without complaint, or if he was forced into it, too.

The men who come into this place pay at the door for an hour, they select which one they want, and then... well, beyond that, I don't think there are any rules. Just don't kill us, right? But I'm sporting a black eye from an aggressive guy who came in the other day.

He tried to suffocate me, and instinct kicked in.

I fought back. I'm not ashamed to admit that.

But once he was *compensated for his trouble*, the guards locked me away from the other girls. They threatened to drug me into an oblivion and offer that guy another pass at me.

Fear rolled down my back.

I babbled promises. To behave and whatever else might save me.

Now, the night ticks toward dawn, and I am the only one awake. I lie on a pallet in the open room, surrounded by other women, but I don't think I've slept in weeks. Not the kind of sleep I need. I doze. Any little noise jars me from rest.

That's exactly what happens tonight.

There's a scraping noise, and then a louder click. Someone murmurs—a guard, perhaps, stationed outside. They don't have to be in here with us because of the cameras always on us. They torment me almost more than the men, because there is no such thing as privacy here.

At least at Terror, I had my own room. A door that locked, albeit from the outside.

I sit up slowly, clutching at the thin blanket covering my legs.

There's a muffled *thump*, and then a piercing shout.

Male.

Angry.

Pop-pop-pop.

More girls are waking up around me, and I shush them. I can't see anything. The moon is gone, shifted away from the window, leaving nothing for me to go on. My eyes haven't adjusted—it's impossible in this kind of pitch-black.

Pop-pop-pop.

A woman screams. "Those are gunshots!"

That riles everyone. I leap to my feet and back up, pressing my spine to the wall. The brush of hands across my chest, stomach, as they stumble and feel their way to safety, makes me all the more rigid.

There's another volley of shots, this time louder, higher-pitched. There's no softness to it.

Different gun.

I cannot move.

After a long moment, it goes silent. Everyone, everything. My breath even seems loud and ragged. I hold it in for a count of five, then slowly exhale.

The door blows inward. Light from the outer room, where the guards stay and payment is made, that was previously blocked, now floods in.

I glance to the side, checking the women. They're bunched up together, clutching at each other's arms, expressions twisted with fear.

I won't die like that. I think I decided that a long time ago.

Cowering will give me nothing.

It won't save me.

A man steps into the doorway, silhouetted by the bright light. It sears, but I can't look away. Can't stop blinking, trying to get my eyes to tell me what I'm seeing is a lie.

"Artemis?" a rough voice calls out.

Another door opens, and a man staggers into the room. He raises his weapon, a rifle that has prodded me in the back many times. Before the muzzle lifts high enough, a shot comes from the front entrance.

He drops like a stone.

"Artemis," he calls again, and the voice finally registers.

A voice I didn't think I would ever hear again.

"She's here," one of the women whispers.

An overhead light flickers on, and my heart cracks open.

My twin brother, Apollo, enters the room with his gun at his side. There's a spray of blood across his face and chest. Only when he spots me, as if I have a spotlight on me, do I move from the wall.

How long has it been since I've seen him?

He was sold to a gang.

I was sold to Terror.

But I've lost track of time.

My staggered steps become a sprint toward him. He catches me easily, his arm banding around my back and his other hand cupping my head. He holds me steady for a minute, then slowly releases me.

"We need to go," he says. "Are there other women?"

I glance back and catalog them.

When I look back, he's removed his shirt. His gun stowed in the waistband of his jeans, he takes a second to wrangle my arms through, then my head.

The loose fabric falls around my body, hitting mid-thigh.

I don't have it in me to blush. I've been in a state of undress since I arrived at Terror.

"Come on," he says softly. "Hold it together, Tem."

I swallow and lift my chin.

I've never had to *hold it together* before. When Mom told me Apollo was gone, I cried until I couldn't breathe. This whole experience has made me numb, but that's not keeping my composure.

That's shock.

That's trauma.

He curls his arm around my shoulders. "Tell them."

My throat has closed.

I'm no saint. I'm certainly not the warrior he thinks I am.

It doesn't stop him from saying, "The guards are gone, ladies. Let me get you out of here."

They unpeel from the wall, from each other, and creep toward us. Some grab blankets, wrapping them around the shoulders of the others. The ones who escaped the drugs guide out the incoherent ones.

We exit into the front room. I'd imagined what it looked like. I was shuffled in through the back when I first arrived, never seeing the client entrance. There are couches, a desk.

But now there are dead guards. At least five of them, one fallen across the desk, another on the couch. Blood pools under their bodies. A laptop lies smashed on the floor.

"You're okay," Apollo assures me.

He's my brother.

My twin.

I trust him to know me when I cannot... but I don't think there's any way I am *okay*.

And I don't think I ever will be again.

20 SAINT

THE TATTOO IS DONE.

We took some breaks, of course. I couldn't make her sit still in the chair for six hours straight. We ordered dinner, stretched our legs...

Meanwhile, I've been fighting a freaking hard-on since I turned around and her breasts were staring at me. It didn't diminish much when she told me about Terror. Specifically, about Reese and then, later, Apollo's rescue.

I can't figure out if I hate Reese or if I want to give the poor guy a hug. From watching Wolfe operate with his father, I know that some things cannot be helped. Like controlling parents putting their kids in impossible situations.

It speaks to Tem's panic attacks, however. Seeing him after all those years must've been a shock. And having him appear in Bow & Arrow? The very building that used to hold Terror.

Now, I wipe over the tattoo a final time and release her to look at it.

Her legs shake, and she glances at me with a frown.

I frown back. "What's wrong?"

"Nothing."

Right... why don't I believe that? The downturn of her lips remains in place until she sees the final tattoo, and then a wide smile overtakes it. She leans in, her finger hovering over one of the delicate flowers at the top of the scales.

She asked why *this*.

It's because she is the balance.

"Tem."

She turns back.

I apply the second skin—a film that will protect it in its initial healing stage, then touch my fingertips to her shoulders. I back her against the chair, and she sits on the edge. Her lips part. I drop onto the stool and inch closer.

My cock is rock-hard now. It strains against my pants, but I manage to ignore it in favor of the girl in front of me. She told me a story—a truth—I'm never going to forget.

Time to show my appreciation.

I move slowly, pulling down her leggings. She rises a bit and helps me get it down, and once the fabric is around her ankles, I lean in. Hands on her knees, pressing her wider. Her pussy is wet and flushed, and I can't help but lick my lips.

"You don't have to do that," she whispers above me.

Have to. I don't—I want to taste her so bad it hurts. My anticipation has been building and building, and I cannot resist any longer.

This isn't totally about me anyway. I just put her through pain, and now she should get pleasure.

She sat so beautifully for me.

I kiss the inside of her thigh, by her knee, then drag my lips higher. She shivers and grips the chair on either side of her. I keep moving, licking at her soft skin, kissing. Nipping.

I switch to the other leg and continue the climb, until I reach the crease of her leg.

I inhale her scent, then lick at her outer lips. I suck one into my mouth, testing how sensitive she is to me. I want to bring my hand up, to slide my finger inside her, but they're glued to her knees. I spread her open wider and settle in, my hot breath hitting her core.

A pause.

I look up, and she nods hurriedly at me.

My tongue touches her slit. I flatten it as I go up toward her clit, giving her a bit of pressure. Then down. I open my mouth wider, thrusting my tongue inside her.

Her muscles squeeze at me, and her back arches. A tremor runs down her body.

Good.

All the bad things I've called her, the demeaning words said in anger, come crawling back over me. *Filthy whore* and *slut* as I pounded into her. *I hate you* and *you disgust me.*

She's not any of those things. I'm seeing the reverse of it, the angel on her shoulder, the way she tastes like my favorite dessert. The caring girl behind the mask.

I wrap my lips around her clit. My tongue flicks at it, and I alternate the light pressure and sucking hard, until her fingers slide through my short hair.

It's moments like these that I want to grow it out. Give her something to grip and pull.

"It's too much," she says. "I want you inside me."

I chuckle. We haven't even crossed *enough* yet—too much is a far way away.

But I oblige her needing something in her. I slide my hand away from her knee and push two fingers into her. I eat her pussy and finger-fuck her, my mouth too full to offer apologies for how I treated her for the last year.

This is just the start of that apology.

She comes on my fingers. My muscles strain to keep her legs open. She clenches on my fingers, her cunt pulsing, and I lick at the arousal that seeps from her.

Dirty girl.

Gorgeous girl.

The front door rattles hard enough to ring the bell.

I pause, looking over my shoulder. The privacy curtain hides us—*her*—but there's no denying that I'm here. The lights are blazing.

"Saint," Tem whispers over my head. "Ignore it."

I can do that.

I kiss her clit and rise to my feet. I kick away the stool and undo my belt buckle, shoving my jeans down my hips. My cock is red and swollen. Precum has been steadily making a wet spot on my boxers like a teenager.

"You're the sweetest torture," I tell her.

She takes a moment to kick her leggings and shoes off, then scoots farther back on the chair. It's reclined, so she lies along it and spreads her legs again. There's room for me to kneel between her legs on the chair, or...

I shake my head and duck down, hitting a release. The part her legs rest on folds down. She jumps, grabbing on to the armrests, and barely stops herself from slipping off.

It would be a normal chair now, if the back wasn't leaned back at such an angle.

No matter. I straighten and grip her knees. My hands skate to her ankles, guiding them around my waist.

Her eyes light. Her gaze drops to my tattooed dick, then back up to my face. She sucks her lower lip between her teeth.

"I can't decide if I want to repay you for that, or—"

"No," I interrupt. "Tem. No."

She goes quiet.

What could she possibly be thinking?

She was used for sex. Over and over. *Sold* for it. And yet, she's overcome that with Reese. She seems to have forgiven the one boy who was there on the other side.

If only Gabriel...

Stop it.

Thinking of that monster only makes my thoughts shift to Kade, and the inexplicable *thump* of anxiety behind my ribs.

I fist my cock and stroke it, although it's unnecessary.

What is necessary is a condom, but I don't have one.

Selfish, stupid... a combination of the two.

She still covers herself with her sweatshirt, her left arm banded across her stomach.

"You hiding from me, wildcat?" I lean into her body. Sweet, welcoming, warm. I take my time inching closer to her mouth, until she comes to me.

The kiss is deeper that way. It shows me she wants me just as much as I want her. I mean, I figured from how she kissed me in the elevator and the look in her eyes right after.

One hand on my dick, lining myself up with her entrance. The other pulls the sweatshirt away and tosses it to the floor. Her breasts will be my next focus, but first—

I thrust inside her, and she gasps into my mouth.

The perfect noise.

I rock my hips forward, inching deeper. She's tight, and I concentrate on her lips instead of her pussy so I don't burst immediately. After a long moment, I bottom out in her.

Heaven.

Staying there, I drag my lips from her mouth and down her throat. I cover her mouth with my hand, the fingers that were inside her slipping past her teeth. She makes a surprised noise, but I don't stop until I've got her nipple in my mouth.

My fingers move in tandem with my dick. I keep her jaw open. Her tongue curls around the pads of my fingers.

She shudders.

My hand leaves her mouth and goes to her clit. Flicking it, pinching it. She arches, forcing her breasts into my face, and I gladly take more in my mouth. Her pink areola. Her nipple ring sits on my tongue.

Her body trembles with each thrust. I move faster, stroke her harder. We're racing toward a cliff, and I want to feel her milk my cock as I come.

A thought I keep to myself, though, as I work both of us up.

It takes every bit of control to slow a fraction, easting the tightness in my balls. I want to come *now*, but she's only just rising.

Until she's there, and I let go of my inhibitions.

She comes with a cry, her nails digging into the back of my neck, and I follow.

It's every bit as good as I imagined.

I rise off of her chest. Her breast that I was mauling—leaving the other untouched, by contrast—is red and puffy. Her nipple stands at attention.

My hips move, and I shake my head at the sensation.

"What's wrong?" she asks.

I focus on her face. "I just don't want to pull out just yet."

"Ah." She makes a clucking noise. She crosses her ankles behind me. "Guess you should stay there, then."

I nod. But...

Well.

I pick her up, keeping us connected, and take her seat.

Her knees land on either side of my hips, seated on my lap, and I smile up at her. I *smile.* Something must truly be wrong with me.

"Better," I say.

She hums.

My gaze locks on the scales of justice. Balance. But also... more than that.

She *is* the justice in this town. The moral compass her brother has always followed, unknowingly or not.

I can only hope she'll guide Kade's Cyclopes the same way.

21 KADE

NATHAN BRADSHAW MEETS me at the reservoir after his shift. The roll of his cruiser's tires on the dirt lot reaches my ears at six o'clock on the dot.

We're not at the falls, where we had previously met. This time, I picked the location. I arrived early, scouted ahead. Artemis spying on my meeting with him—and to learn of it later—was *embarrassing*. I should've kept my eyes open for that kind of thing. Should've known that she would be suspicious of the sheriff.

He's pushing too hard.

I think he has a habit of leading with his greed, not his brain. Not a desirable trait in a stand-up sheriff, but acceptable for what I need of him.

I stand with my hands in my pockets on the rocky shore. The gun in its holster at my hip shouldn't surprise the sheriff, but I can practically feel his intake of breath when he spots it. I don't look back, but I picture his hand landing on his weapon. Not necessarily to draw it, just out of habit.

Because he doesn't trust me, and I don't trust him.

Keeping my back to him is either an act of stupidity or power.

The reservoir, which supplies water to Sterling Falls, stretches out ahead of us. It's a protected body of water. No boats. No fishing. No swimming.

"You called?" the sheriff drawls.

I smirk to myself but drop it when I face him. "Tell me about the body at Olympus."

He wears his uniform, the dark-green helmet-hat hiding his red-brown hair. Sure enough, his hand is balanced on his holstered weapon. He seems at ease on the rocks, however. So he's either a great liar or he doesn't think I'm a threat.

"Why should I do that?" he replies.

I scoff. "We have a quid pro quo relationship, Bradshaw."

"Oh? And what do I get out of this?"

"You get a warning."

He raises an eyebrow. "Not sure I buy that, Laurent."

I sigh. Getting him to turn over Reese's mother's phone records was easy. I should've expected him to pump the brakes once things got too real. Too much like the war zone Sterling Falls once was.

I wish I had been around to see it. It would help me understand Artemis and Saint a little more. They're both gun-shy about the Cyclopes.

Who wouldn't be?

"The Hell Hounds' compound bomb was a warning, too," I say. "But the wrong kind. They didn't listen to me at first. We had to send a stronger message. Do you understand what I'm saying?"

For a second, he doesn't know what to do. His mouth opens and closes, his face reddening.

"Tell me about the body at Olympus," I say again.

He takes a breath. "One of their informants. Jace King reported him missing a few weeks prior..."

I motion for him to continue.

"The coroner's report came back. He overdosed on heroin, and that combined with severe trauma to the face and neck..." He looks away. "One eye was completely removed. The other was... disfigured."

"Disfigured how?"

"The heroin was injected into it." He shakes his head. "Turned my stomach just looking at him. Otherwise, he was completely identifiable. Wolfe James gave us his name on a video call. There were no other toxins in his blood... but there were signs that he was held hostage in the time between his disappearance and his body being found."

Gabriel is going off the rails.

I nod once. The sheriff contemplates me for a moment, seeming to wait for my promised warning.

"One more thing," I say.

He stiffens.

"Did you find anything incriminating at Bow & Arrow?"

"Tem's club?" He pauses. "The computers were sent to an independent company for analysis. I don't have anything else."

Someone pushed him for that... and here I thought I was the only one applying pressure.

"Thanks, Sheriff." I check my watch. "You'll be just in time if you hurry."

Alarm sweeps over his features. "Hurry where?"

"To the docks." I smile. "The last deep-sea fishing boat should be docking as we speak."

"So?"

"So… you should meet the newest Sterling Falls residents, don't you agree?"

He swears under his breath.

Deep-sea fishing boats stay out for a month at a time, sometimes more. They have a relatively robust crew, since there are so many duties to keep a boat like that in running order in the middle of nowhere.

But that's just the ruse.

In reality, the boats have been diverting to Emerald Cove, and the crews replaced with my guys. Every ship coming into port, for months. Out with the old, in with the new.

Except this is the last of them.

They're *my* men. They listen to me, they trust me. Only with trepidation do they follow Gabriel's orders, because they know me to be rational. Sane.

Even in this insanity we're about to begin.

I follow him to the parking lot. His pace quickens, and he bypasses my bike—a new acquirement—and hastily climbs into his cruiser. He guns the engine and spins the wheel, sending gravel skittering toward me, and races back down the way he came.

My phone is already in my hand.

I make a phone call. One I've been itching to make since the sheriff showed his proclivity for bribes, for *weakness*. This town has elected him again, knowing everything that happened could've been stopped from the beginning if he did his job.

"He's on his way," I say when my call is picked up. "Take it."

I stash my phone in a zipped pocket and climb on the bike. It used to be owned by a Hell Hound, but… well, he won't be riding. He'll probably barely miss the bike.

At the end of the road, I follow the sheriff's path south. But I take a left and zip through the empty streets of West Falls.

The citizens understand.

There must be lingering trauma here for them, too.

I want to tell them that the takeover will be peaceful. That once we're established, restrictions and roadblocks will ease. They'll barely notice our presence.

But it's a lie even I can't stomach.

There's no easing into this, no soft approach in the middle of the night. We've been doing that for months—this is the time for fast action, for violence. It's the surge of power that scares people, but it's the quiet after that which is the most dangerous.

I fly through the center of Sterling Falls and coast to a stop outside the large marble building that houses both the city council and the sheriff's department. There are still people working at this hour. A whole building full of them, I'd reckon, who all follow the sheriff's lead. Plus extras, like the city council.

My nose wrinkles.

The sheriff is a problem. He's always been a problem. Corrupt, vile. Some, like Artemis, might argue that he has a heart.

I know differently.

He follows money. Always has, always will. He would stab his sister in the back if it meant saving his own skin. We're going to find out very, very soon if my opinion of him is correct.

I look across toward where three of my men sit on bikes, and I gesture for them to continue. They each rev their engines, and the answering call echoes around the building. From all sides, the motorcycles flood in. My masked men—

not like Olympus, where they cover their eyes and leave the rest blank, they have bandanas tied around the lower portion of their faces—stream off the bikes and into city hall.

In a matter of moments, screams and the sound of breaking glass are carried out on the wind. Flames flicker in the first-floor windows, and suit-wearing men and women sprint outside.

More of my men wait for them, corral them.

Soon, black smoke billows from the windows. It represents the deterioration of the office, of Sterling Falls' government. We're going to burn everything rotten to the ground, and they'll be lucky if we deem Sterling Falls worthy enough to start over.

Or maybe we'll just revel in the ash.

22 ARTEMIS

I EXAMINE the tattoo in the mirror. Saint went out front to draw the blinds down across the wide windows, not wanting to strictly rely on the privacy curtain I pulled. I'm still bare-chested, *satiated.*

Sex with him, this time, was totally different from the quick-and-dirty fucks of the past. Not that I can complain about them—putting aside the guilt that crawled over us afterward, they were hot.

It was also a baring of my soul. Telling him about Terror... I'll admit, I skipped some of the more brash moments. I went with the feelings of helplessness and vulnerability. I didn't want to discuss the clinical aspect. The way the doctor spread me open to check my hymen when I first arrived, then gave me a tranquilizer to relax.

Docile was the name of their game.

He wouldn't want to know about the men who bought me. The way their rough fingers gripped at my skin. A million ways to bruise me, but it seems like my soul took most of the battering.

"Tem."

I glance toward Saint.

"I..." He looks down. "I'm sorry for how I treated you this past year."

My heart thumps extra-hard. "You don't have to apologize."

"I was cruel." He meets my gaze, his expression pained. "How do I recover from that? I... It wasn't just what I said when we had sex. It was every other little action. And you were hurting—"

"No more than you."

He comes closer. "Men took what they wanted from your body. How is that any different than what *I* took from you?"

I slide my hands up the front of his chest. "Because I goaded you into it. If I didn't want you to fuck me, Saint, I would've said no. And I believe with all my being that you would respect that."

He nods, but the haunted expression doesn't go away.

"I want both," I whisper. "I want to take your misery and pain and twist it into pleasure. But I like this version of it, too. I like the softness after."

"A combination," he agrees.

He pulls me toward the white couch, sitting and drawing me onto his lap. I straddle him and rest my arms on his shoulders. This way, we're nearly eye to eye. He's still a bit taller than me, though.

"Is that wickedness you crave a piece of you from Terror?" he asks. "Did they... condition you to like pain?"

I shake my head.

His hands roam slowly, first across my hips and back, then higher. Up my sides, across my ribs. He palms my breasts and skates his thumb across my nipple.

"They pierced one when I arrived," I tell him. "It hurt so fucking bad."

"Why?"

"A sign of their ownership, I think. Like tagging a cow's ear to mark it as part of the herd."

His brows furrow. "That's awful."

"I know." I scoot back and unbutton his pants. I'm not sure why he put them back on. But his dick is already stiffening again, and I stroke the inked, soft skin to full hardness. "Tell me about this."

He laughs quietly. "It was a punishment."

"For what?" I meet his gaze.

I love his eyes. Dark blue, like the ocean in a storm, they can be so impossibly expressive. It's how I knew he was in pain. And somehow, he can sharpen them to cut like a knife. He can also, I think, see straight through me.

"After Elora died, I wanted to feel something. Anything."

He keeps touching my breasts, just soft little movements, and I fight the urge to shift my hips. What he's saying is important, I think.

"You didn't see me accidentally walk into the bathroom when you were showering," he continues.

There's a tub—which I contemplated drowning myself in—and a glass-walled shower.

"The glass was fogged over, but I saw you. Your silhouette. Your ass, your breasts... although if I had seen the piercings, I don't think I would've been able to stop myself. I was hard in a fucking second, and I hated myself for it. At her funeral, I promised myself that I'd never fall in love again."

I blink hard.

"Do you remember what's on her plaque at the mausoleum?"

Yes, of course I do. I used to visit it. I haven't in a few months, though. The urn isn't there, so *she* isn't there. I think her parents took her...

Why Saint allowed that, I'll never know.

"The darkness only makes you shine brighter," I recite.

It fit her, both as Elora, a glorious star, and Nyx, the primordial deity. Goddess of the night. She picked that name with care, I know. From her first fight at Olympus, then set on the path by my brother and his friends. With Saint.

They were intertwined, always.

"What made you think of that?" I cup his nape. "And what does that have to do with the tattoo on your dick?"

He leans forward, brushing his lips against mine. I accept the kiss, but I don't let him deepen it. It's a rare day for Saint to talk, and I find myself greedy for his words.

"It was you," he murmurs. "You in the shower. You were singing."

I scoff. "I don't sing."

"You were, though. That song about walking on sunshine. And it hit me—*you* are that sunshine. You're warm and alive and sometimes you fucking glow with it, Tem. How could the stars ever compete with the sun?"

Oh God.

Tears spill down my cheeks, but he beats me to wiping them away.

"There's no darkness that could blow out your flame."

I wish that were true. But I allow a shaky smile to curve my lips, nonetheless.

"I couldn't cope with that realization. The fact that I already was attracted to you, that you were around me all the fucking time. The scent of lavender haunts me. It's your shampoo, isn't it? I once tried it, just to feel a little less lonely."

My heart breaks all over again. "Oh, Saint."

"I might be cruel," he continues. "I might be a bastard. I might pick fights, or drink too much, but I didn't want to take something from you in that moment. I didn't want to ruin the memory of Elora for you—for either of us. So I went to Starlight and let myself remember your silhouette in the shower, and the sound of your voice in my ear, get me hard. And keep me hard through the pain of tattooing myself.

"I knew the next time I thought of you, I could slip that agony in with it, and hopefully, eventually, I'd stop." He threads his fingers through my hair. "It didn't work like that, though."

This confession feels fragile.

I don't want to move to scare him off, but my heart beats out of control, and my breathing comes in shallow gasps.

All this time, he's been fighting grief and attraction.

"I..."

"It's okay." He strokes himself, his hand twisting at the top and smearing precum down his length. "I blocked out your pain for so long."

He's still blocking it out.

I haven't tried to hide my arms. It didn't occur to me once his mouth landed on my pussy. I threw caution to the wind, and now it feels precarious. It's almost too late to go back? I will him to look at my arms, to see that the track marks are not from the hospital.

It's more.

It's worse.

When he doesn't, I rise and let him find my slit. I slide

back down slowly, taking him inside me, and groan. He feels good.

Right.

I ride him, while his fingers work at my clit, and I hold his shoulders. I tip my head back, my hair so long it nearly brushes the crack of my ass.

"Are we really doing this?" I ask him.

"Do you mean having sex?" There's a bit of humor in his tone. "Or allowing ourselves to be happy?"

"That second one."

He chuckles. "Yeah, wildcat, we're doing this."

Okay. I accept it.

He thrusts his hips up, hitting deeper than before, and I groan. He pulls my face toward his, kissing me hard. Tongue and teeth and lips. Heart and soul.

Finally.

23 REESE

I STEP into Antonio's office at Bow & Arrow. The man sits behind his desk, glasses perched on his nose. His attention is fixed on a stack of papers in front of him, one held up so he doesn't have to lean forward.

His gaze cuts to me, but his expression doesn't change.

The man has a poker face, that's for sure.

"Mind if I sit?" I point to the chair across from him.

He inclines his chin, which I take for a yes. I pull it out and drop into it, kicking my legs out and crossing my ankles.

He goes back to reading. His skin is paler than I'd seen previously, although I don't have a ton of experience with the man. The hair on his head is more silver than brown, his goatee the same. Everything is trim and proper about him, except that his button-up shirt seems a size too big, and he occasionally presses his palm to his side.

He stabbed himself to save Artemis.

If that isn't love, I don't know what is.

After a long few moments of silence, he sets the paper down.

"So," he says, "I presume you have a reason for visiting."

I sigh.

Artemis ran out of the house like her ass was on fire. Saint chased her. When they didn't come back, Kade tried to make conversation.

Then he got a text, and he made some excuse to leave in a hurry.

And now... well, I wasn't going to sit home alone.

"Have you seen her?"

His expression is blank, blank, blank.

I wave my hand toward her office door, which is closed up tight. No light emanates from underneath it. She hasn't been here, that's for sure. But when she isn't at home, I kind of assumed she was with Antonio.

Now, I'm doubting that.

"You tried to save her." I will his façade to crack. Just a little. "Luckily, it didn't cost you your life. But... it could've. And she lost consciousness thinking you killed yourself. She *thought*—and now she's avoiding you?"

"Did you come here to press on my wounds, boy?"

"Yeah, maybe I did." I lean forward. "What you did was foolish."

"I'd do it again," he swears. "She's my family. As surely as I'd sacrifice myself to save my wife or children, I would do anything to protect Artemis."

"I believe you," I say. "But... she's not doing well."

"I gathered as much. I came here hoping she would show up." He tilts his computer screen toward me, revealing the rows of camera feeds. "Barry is keeping an eye out for her at the front door. The servers know to alert me if she appears in the club."

"Why would she bypass you to go into the club?"

He lifts one shoulder, then winces. "I'm not at a hundred percent. Getting out the door this evening was a fight with my wife. She's currently down the hall, supervising the restaurant closing for the night."

"Smart of her to keep you in one spot."

He cracks a smile. "That's my Vittoria. Smart as a whip."

I stand. "I'll leave you to... this."

"Off to search for Artemis?"

"Something like that."

Not really, though. Once I leave Antonio, I descend to the ground floor, then continue down to the giant metal doors of Terror. There was an elevator entrance once upon a time for the clients, although even searching Bow & Arrow didn't locate it. It makes me think Artemis had it bricked over in her rebuild.

The hinges squeal when I yank the door open, and I hurry to close it behind me. In the complete darkness, panic constricts me.

I'm okay, I tell myself.

I use my phone's flashlight to navigate down the hall. Everything about this place sucks. It's creepy and old, the air stale and sour. The farther in I walk, the more guilt presses in on me. It's almost as old as this place. My guilt is suffocating and hot, pressing down on my shoulders.

At one door, I stop.

It resembles a doctor's office but beyond disrepair. A reclining examination chair is on its side, broken glass littered across the tile. I step into the room and crouch in front of one of the bottle labels. It's legible after I swipe the dust and dirt off, and wince at the tiny print.

Ketamine.

I take myself out of my experience and put myself in Tem's shoes. Being brought here, maybe even dragged through the same doors I just came down.

Drugged.

This place was no stranger to needles. To using whatever methods they could in order to elicit the desired response. Whether that was enthusiasm or complacency or lust... maybe some combination of the three.

I straighten and go to the chair. There are straps on the arms. One big band hanging loose from the middle of the chair, half disintegrated or eaten by rats. There's another cuff on one of the stirrups that remains attached. The other lies across the room.

Horrible.

My gut turns, and I shine the light around again. Some of the glass comes from the broken medicine cabinets, but the cloudy shards seem to be remnants of fluorescent tube lighting. There would've been no hiding here, under glaringly bright lights.

But it wasn't just Artemis who was here.

Gabriel existed in this space, too.

Terror formed him.

Do any records exist?

I leave the sham of a doctor's office behind. The amphitheater is just down the hall, but I don't care to revisit the pools of blood Artemis and Antonio left behind on the stage. I went there the last time. I found the bomb left by... Gabriel?

We assumed it was him. But with Kade in the mix of Cyclopes, and them knowing each other... anything is possible. They tried to blow up the Hell Hounds. They've been killing informants. Well, two informants who were loyal to Tem's brother and his friends.

Jace King.

Wolfe James.

Apollo Madden.

They're not in Sterling Falls. It was my task—my *favor* —that sent them to Emerald Cove. It seems, in hindsight, like a manipulation. But it was in earnest. There's someone there I met, who I care about, who is *trapped.*

Standing in Terror, I seem to be filling my well of empathy for caged individuals.

Gabriel, Artemis...

I go to one of the cells and step inside. Imagine the door shut. The thin, horizontal window at the top of the far wall has been boarded over, but perhaps it wasn't always that way... Besides the window, there's a single bulb in the middle of the ceiling.

My stomach turns.

Why am I down here?

This is stupid.

And yet, I can't stop. I continue past the amphitheater and almost breeze past a door hidden in a recess. I hadn't noticed it before, when we were carting Artemis and Antonio out of here as fast as we could.

Or before, when I took a moment to remember the horrible feelings I held every time we came here. I just wanted to understand it, and Tem's reaction to seeing me for the first time in nearly a decade. But instead, if left me more confused.

The door is stuck. I kick at it until the hinges fail with a loud *crack*, and a cloud of dust puffs out of the room.

It's a storage closet, from the looks of it. Small, cramped, dark. There are boxes stacked pretty much everywhere, leaving only a narrow space to step into the room.

Which I do, because I am the cat that curiosity will no doubt kill one day. But Kade used to say I had nine lives. A few are surely gone after a harrowing deployment, though. And now the recent interactions with Gabriel.

I shiver.

It's not cold down here by any means, but... I don't want to think about where Gabriel made me go. While I was in an in-between state.

Instead, I flip one of the lids off a box and pull out the first folder my fingers brush. I steady my light, aiming it at the first page. There are two photos—one professional shot of a young woman, some sort of portrait. The other, she's naked.

My throat closes, and nausea rolls through me.

It's a personal record on the first page. Age, weight, height... hair color, eye color. Address. Even her parents. Behind it are handwritten notes.

Patient 52Y presents as a virgin. Hymen is intact. Patient required sedation for further examination...

I snap it closed, then grab another file.

Another woman, then another. Finally, I just... I stop.

There's got to be fifty folders in this one box.

And there are a dozen more boxes.

My stomach cramps. I stumble out of the room, just barely rounding the corner when my dinner reemerges. Onto the floor.

I can't even remember the last time I puked, but I do now remember why I try to avoid it at all costs.

Except for the horror my imagination is creating and running away with, it's hard not to stay hunched. I wait for the second wave of nausea to roll through me, and I swallow sharply a few times.

They're just boxes.

Even if they contain ghosts... we're compartmentalizing.

Boxes.

Paper, cardboard, dust.

I carry them out three at a time, my muscles straining. I

put them in the bed of my truck, parked in Artemis' usual spot. I didn't want to drive her car again and incite the Hell Hounds. That Malikai is one angry fella...

No, thanks.

I make four more trips, filling the truck bed completely. I roll the cover across it and grimace. It will protect the pages, and the sky overhead is clear. The stars glitter brightly, all signs of the sun long gone. There's no chance of rain, although wind could do a number on it.

The last thing I need is to lose this miraculously found evidence of Terror.

On the way home, I'm rerouted. Road closures near the center of town, with firetrucks lining the sides of the street. I coast through an intersection and look left toward the university. Just beyond my vantage point, smoke catches a familiar orange-and-yellow glow of flames.

Someone in a high-vis orange vest spots me and heads in my direction.

I roll down the window. "What's up, man?"

"House fire," he explains. He has a tattoo on his face. A black X marking out one of his eyes. "There's some worry about the gas line, so the trucks have been ordered back."

A slither of unease worms through me.

"Okay." I motion in the direction I need to go, which luckily is far away from here. "I didn't mean to rubberneck."

The guy breaks out into a smile. "Nah, man. Totally fine. It's quite the show."

Right.

I wave and raise my window, letting my foot off the brake. For a second, I imagine him darting in front of my truck. But instead, he takes a few quick steps back and watches me continue down the dark, nearly empty road.

Something isn't right—but I don't have the capacity to deal with it.

My phone beeps. It's a special noise that I reserve for the reminder I set up on new numbers, and I sigh.

One hand on the wheel, with the other I dial the familiar, memorized number. I've been reciting it from heart since I was a kid.

The call goes through, and I pull over outside of Tem's building. The last thing I need is for the call to drop when I go into the garage.

"Hello?"

"Hey, Mom." I force a smile, knowing it'll translate into my tone. "How are you?"

"Reese?"

I sigh. "Pretty sure I'm your only kid?"

"You missed our last call."

Oh. Guilt rattles me, and I run my hand down my face. "I was in the hospital. I'm sorry I didn't call."

"You're okay now?"

"Totally fine," I lie. "You know they've got experts on staff."

She hums. "The military usually informs us when our son is injured."

"I told them not to. It laid me up for a few days, is all. I wanted to let you know that we've got new orders, so I might not be around for a while."

"I don't suppose you can tell your dear old mom about it?"

I settle in. This guilt is normal—I've been lying to her for years. So I tell her a story from when I actually *was* deployed, a mission laid out by command and painted to be a totally normal, run-of-the-mill day.

It wasn't quite that peaceful, but I give it the same

coloring our superiors did. A two-day transport, there and back, on a road that's already been carefully monitored and swept by a different team.

Eventually, the clock ticks over to a new hour, and I groan. "I'm sorry, Mom, I've got to head out."

"I appreciate you calling," she tells me. "It's late here. I was on my way to bed."

I time it that way. Doesn't mean I feel good about it, though. "Okay, I'll let you go. Love you."

"Love you, too, Reese."

The line goes dead, and I throw the phone onto the passenger seat.

I hate my mother.

I hate her with as much love in my heart that I can muster, because she is just as much at fault for my shame that my father is. I tried abandoning her, but I couldn't do it. At the end of the day, she's the only family I have.

My father was written off a long, long time ago. Almost five years ago, he left Mom and moved straight into the house he bought for his twenty-year-old mistress. I only found out when Mom called me crying after he had already gone.

He's the real piece of shit, and not just for cheating on my mother and then leaving her for a younger woman. The girl is younger than *me*—something that causes no shortage of revulsion. But he was also heavily invested in Terror. And that, really, was the end of our relationship.

I park next to Tem's car in the garage and head up.

My phone rings almost as soon as I step out of the elevator. I have a new number—not that I need to hide from anyone, really, it's just ingrained habit. I contemplate not answering. Who would be calling? Tem's cell is programmed in, as is Saint's. And, grudgingly, Kade's.

Well.

Only way to solve the mystery is to answer it.

"Hello?"

"Reese." Antonio's voice fills my ear. Recognizable even though my conversations with the man have been limited. "I can't get ahold of anyone else. I need you to come back to Bow & Arrow. *Hurry*."

"What's happening?"

He makes a strangled noise. Then, "Cyclopes."

The line goes dead.

24 ARTEMIS

"ANTONIO CALLED." Saint holds up his phone.

I wriggle back into my leggings and push the thick curtain of hair out of my face. It wouldn't be *unusual*, exactly, since they know each other. Antonio has been a fixture in my life, and Saint was forced to come along with me on some nights. Not saying they got close, but...

"Four times," he adds.

I pause. "Did he leave a message?"

"Yeah." He taps on his phone, and a minute later, Antonio's voice plays between us.

"Saint. Antonio here. I hope you're with Artemis. Something strange is happening in North Falls... I'd feel better if we had some extra bodies. Call me back."

I take the phone from him and redial.

It goes straight to voicemail.

"Okay..."

I shift my weight, then look up at Saint. He didn't have much adjusting to do—I was the one completely naked by the end of it, and he only lost his shirt and his pushed-down pants. His shirt is back on now, hiding the tattoos that decorate his chest.

Shame about that.

There's a dragon, of course, that matched Nyx's. The galaxy. The hourglass brand front and center. A snake, flowers, geometric lines, a skull.

"I don't suppose you have any guns here?"

He must be worried—he doesn't even crack a smile. Instead, he turns and disappears into the back room. I follow, still straightening my shirt. My lips are puffy from the intense kisses, my skin tingling with residual arousal.

The back room has a cot set up in the corner, with a pillow and folded blankets neatly stacked at the head of it, but the majority of the space is taken up by his desk. Where he draws, I imagine, and creates the visually stunning tattoos.

In the supply closet, he taps in a code to a tall safe against the back wall. The interior automatically lights up when it cracks open, and he removes two handguns. One for me, plus two magazines, and another for him.

"What, no rifles?"

He grimaces. "You're not concerned?"

"I'm trying not to think about it."

"We don't have a vehicle."

Oh, shit. "And I don't have my phone."

He tosses me his. "Call Reese."

I unlock it, and it immediately fills with Reese's contact info.

Oh—he's calling me. Well. Not me. Saint.

Because he wants to talk to Saint, or because I don't have my phone on me? Do these guys talk to each other when I'm not around?

I knew Reese and Saint were hitting it off, but this feeling in my chest is unusual.

Jealousy?

Fuck.

"Are you going to answer it?" Saint looms over my shoulder.

"Uh—" I mean, *yeah*. I accept the call and hand it back to him wordlessly.

"Reese?" Saint quirks a brow at me, but I just shake my head. He puts the call on speaker phone.

How the hell would I explain my weird reaction to Reese calling him?

"Did Antonio call you?" His voice comes through clipped, almost hurried.

"Yeah, we missed it. I'm with Artemis." Saint clears his throat. "You heading to Bow & Arrow?"

"He asked me to."

"Swing by Starlight and pick us up."

Reese makes a noise of agreement. "Be there in two minutes."

I lace my boots and tuck the gun in the waistband of my leggings, stashing the extra magazine in my hoodie. My adrenaline is picking up, but it isn't quite the rush I need. My attention homes in on the craving inside me.

There's a low chance of me ever being normal again.

Saint locks up behind us, and I glance both ways down the empty street. It's usually busy, but today is quiet.

I take a deep breath and pause.

There's smoke on the air.

"Look." Saint points.

Behind Starlight, thick white smoke rises. It shouldn't be visible against the dark sky, but light from the city catches in its plumes.

"What's burning?" I question.

Reese's truck comes swinging around the corner, and he slams to a halt at the curb in front of us.

"No time to figure that out." Saint ushers me around and into the middle seat.

This is a bit of déjà vu. Reese rescuing us, the darkness pressing in on his truck. At least we're not feeling the stranglehold the Cyclopes had in West Falls.

And yet, as soon as I think that, I take in the sharpness of Reese's gaze.

"What?" I question.

"Antonio said something bad was going down at Bow & Arrow." His attention shifts to Saint. "You guys armed?"

"Yes," I respond. "He left Saint a voice message, but he just said something strange seemed to be happening."

"Because he couldn't reach anyone," Reese retorts.

He drives faster than I've experienced from him, flying toward North Falls. I hurry to buckle my seat belt. Saint takes over before I can click it in, securing mine first and then his.

"You talked to him?" Saint asks Reese. "What did he say?"

"Something about the Cyclopes."

A chill skates down my spine.

Saint and I trade a look. There's an obvious connection between the Cyclopes, Gabriel, and Kade. So who's running them toward North Falls? That section of town, historically touristy, has been neutral for decades. Gangs stay away because it brings money in, and their activity would scare the crowds away.

But as we move toward winter, something in me alarms that the new gang doesn't really give a shit about previous rules.

"I need to call my brother," I whisper.

Saint nods and wordlessly hands me his phone. I hold on to it for a long moment, then shake my head. He can't always come straight to my rescue, right? Apollo has always done that for me. With Wolfe and Jace, they've done their best to protect me from every bump in the night.

It's just their way. They knew my past—they were there to receive me when Apollo brought me back to the Hell Hounds' compound, after all—and they've always been careful to steer both the Titans and Hell Hounds away from human trafficking.

They didn't tolerate it because of *me*.

But their attention couldn't remain locked on it. At the time, they were under Wolfe's father's thumb. They were teenagers... we all were. And because their lives were dictated by someone else, I was left on my own for a lot of the time.

Hidden away, even.

That was a dark time. I'll admit—I spiraled. I didn't know what I had done to deserve it, I was grappling with my parents' role in it and also survivor's guilt. While I got out, and everyone else in that outpost location, the boys and girls in Terror were still there.

After, when Terror was dismantled, the building sat empy for almost two years.

Until I bought it. And transformed it.

But did I really? Or did I just put a pretty mask over it?

Reese finds my hand and squeezes my fingers. I don't know how he knows I need it, but I cling to him and focus on reality. The truck, the wind slipping in through his open windows, the increasing smell of smoke.

"Did you see a fire on your way over?" Saint jars me from my thoughts.

Reese dips his chin. "Before Antonio called me. A line of fire trucks was parked at the top of Main Street, redirecting traffic away. A guy told me to keep moving."

He doesn't sound confident in that.

"Why would fire trucks be parked away from an active fire? He gave some bullshit answer about a house fire getting too close to a gas line."

Saint scoffs. "An underground gas line?"

"The last time that happened..."

Well, a fire started in the basement of a house right near Sterling Falls University. They couldn't really save it then either, but I think that was more due to the arson than anything else.

"Let's figure out what's going on at Bow & Arrow, first," Reese mutters. He suddenly straightens. "Wait."

"What?" Saint questions.

"I, uh, have something valuable in the back of the truck. Is there somewhere we can stash it?"

A headache has been creeping over me, but it pulses pain between my eyes. I pinch the bridge of my nose and focus on taking a deep breath. Suddenly, all I can think about is heroin. The rush, sure, but also the way it takes the pain and floats it away. I've been going cold turkey—halfway out of necessity and also because *fuck that*. Gabriel had me unconscious again. He manipulated Reese by using me.

Nearly got me caught... although that's more my fault than his.

My body feels like it's gone through a meat grinder, but I somehow stay upright. Even when my skin gets too tight, and the world seems to narrow down to how I feel. Clammy, aching.

It could be blamed on low blood sugar. A little tremor runs through me.

"...Apollo's house."

I lift my head. They want to make a detour all the way across town? *Absolutely not.* I don't know if I can last that long. Already, my mind keeps ticking back to finding Gabriel. I could sneak away and beg him for more.

You cannot do that.

"We don't have time for that," I say. "Park it on a side street in North Falls. No one will know the difference."

Reese grunts, but he doesn't argue. And he doesn't turn away. If anything, he just presses down harder on the gas pedal. The truck engine whines as our speed climbs, and I swallow down my nausea.

Damn body.

Damn drugs.

I touch the cool metal of the gun at the small of my back, then make sure my shirt and sweatshirt cover it. We park two blocks from Bow & Arrow and hop out. I stagger and catch myself on the door, but neither say anything.

Which is good.

I can't come up with yet another lie right now.

And I don't know if I'll be able to hold up to whatever we're about to face in my club.

25 SAINT

WE MAKE good time to the club, but Artemis stops dead when we step onto the sidewalk. I almost bump into her, and Reese into me, but we both manage to avoid the collision.

"What is it?" he asks.

I spot it a second before she says, "There's no line."

The front of the club isn't *empty*—there's just no one stopping people from entering.

She throws her shoulders back and heads for the front door. We join the masses slipping in, and I try to keep track of both her in front of me and Reese at my side.

What's normally a relaxed-but-energized crowd is... *not*.

"Come on," she calls over her shoulder. "I need to find Antonio."

I reach out and grab the back of her shirt, covering the handgun stuffed in her leggings. No need to freak out her patrons, right? Although from the look of it, no one is paying a cover. Definitely not the people who've followed us inside and are dispersing.

She immediately turns for the stairs that lead to the

rooftop restaurant. Reese and I are at her heels. She bursts through the door, then cuts across the empty space and into the kitchen. It seems like they all left suddenly—the normally spotless kitchen has remnants of food, utensils, and pots and pans spread out. The dishwashing rack is full of dirty plates.

It may as well be a ghost town.

"What the hell is going on?" Tem murmurs.

She steadies herself on one of the counters. I eye her. Her face is pale, almost green-hued. She wipes her brow with the back of her hand, but doesn't say anything about it.

I trade a look with Reese. He's more looking around than at Artemis.

I don't know what happened—but I do know it's probably not good.

Tem's people are loyal. They wouldn't leave unless they had to.

"Antonio!" Artemis suddenly calls.

Her volume makes me flinch. She rushes down the hallway and stops at his office.

The door is open, the desk wiped clean. Literally—there's nothing on it.

"He had a computer," Reese mumbles behind me.

Artemis whirls around. "How do you know?"

"I was here... an hour ago? Maybe two. I sat in that chair." He points to the one across from Antonio's. "We had a conversation and then I left. When he called me back, I figured it was in regard to... that."

I narrow my eyes.

Artemis seems to be of a similar mind, because she crosses her arms. "What was the conversation?"

His expression blanks out. "Don't ask me that."

"Why not?"

"Leave it, Tem." I pull her from the office and close the door. "Check yours."

When she twists the knob, the door swings open under her hand. Not locked. And similarly cleaned out.

"We just replaced my computer and his." Her voice is tight. "The sheriff failed to return what he seized."

From the warrant...

"Nadine wasn't much help," she adds. "I went to her office to try and get some answers, and she was pretty vague. The warrant itself was for our hard drives, but there wasn't a clear answer why that would be related to one of my brother's informants. Or his murder."

"When did you see her?"

"Before..." She gestures vaguely at her collarbone.

The tattoo.

Ah.

"Oh!" She perks up. "I did take photos of her recent emails. And the deleted ones. I don't have my phone on me, but we can check it later."

Reese looks like he's going to say something. He opens and closes his mouth and finally shakes his head. "Never mind."

"That doesn't help us find Antonio now," I point out.

She frowns. "Maybe he's trying to find someone in the club. We should search it."

Unease snakes through me. "There's no one manning the doors, Tem—"

"I know that." She flicks her hair over her shoulder. There's a tightness to her that I didn't see before, but it seems like she's stiffer than ever. "But he wouldn't leave. And he said something about the Cyclopes? In Bow & Arrow?"

“He said something strange was happening in North Falls on our voicemail,” I say.

“And yes, he mentioned Cyclopes to me,” Reese adds.

She pinches the bridge of her nose.

“You okay?” I stare at her.

I mean… we just had a moment. A long moment. To go from that to this, rather abruptly, has got to be unsettling.

“I just have a headache. It’s fine.” She glares at me. “Help me find Antonio.”

Reese sighs. “We will.”

“If we had cameras…” She casts another glance at Antonio’s office, then grimaces. “No, it’s fine. We can find him the old-fashioned way, right?”

“Right,” we echo.

We go out into the club, and she yells over the music, “I’ll take this level!”

Then she’s gone, worming through bodies and disappearing from sight.

What the fuck?

“Keep an eye on her,” I bark at Reese.

Then I continue down the stairs and into the mob on the dance floor.

26 ARTEMIS

THERE'S no sign of Antonio. Every passing moment I don't see him, my pulse jumps higher, until it feels more like a hummingbird's wings than a heartbeat.

I wanted people to feel like they could get lost in Bow & Arrow. The hallways are dim and twisting, all glittering dark marble with gold and silver veins. The sconces on the walls cast low, warm light on the floor in shallow half-circles.

There are too many people here. The music is too loud.

I haven't seen a single person I recognize—and that's shocking. I know a lot of people, both from years owning Bow & Arrow or from attending Olympus religiously.

The hallways, while somewhat of a maze, always lead back to the main dance floor. Some of the halls split off into smaller rooms. Quiet ones. Although they're regularly patrolled to make sure nothing bad happens in them—like wandering hands, for example—now they're filled with writhing, naked bodies.

I shudder and turn away instead of trying to stop it.

I'm picking my battles.

Gabriel appears in front of me.

A flicker of fear skips like a stone across my body. He appraises me, his head cocked.

There's a pause in the music. The end of one song, and a breath before the beginning of another.

"You don't look so hot, Artemis," he says in the quiet. His solemn expression suddenly cracks, a grin splitting his lips. "I've missed your visits. You've been so, so strong. That's got to be tough, don't you think?"

I grit my teeth. "I'm fine."

The next song begins.

"*Fine* is a boring word. How do you feel?"

I can barely hear him. Wordless music, a heavy electronic beat, scrapes at my brain and vibrates in my chest. It makes me feel worse, honestly, but I can't do anything to stop it. I won't show weakness in front of Gabriel.

He inches closer, until his mouth is at my ear. "Do you want to climb out of your skin? Have you been able to keep food down? Pesky nausea. It's okay to be in this position. It's okay to fail."

"What happened to you, Gabriel?" I exhale. "How did you become this?"

His lips move at my ear. "I blame you for what happened, but it was the waiting that killed me. Can you imagine that? Just lingering on the edge of living for *years*, to no avail? I like to think I didn't waste them—it was a good cause. But when I finally woke up, I was angry. At you, at Antonio, at everyone who let Terror remain. I simply found someone who understood—and fed—my anger."

Who?

He crowds me back against a wall, just as a group of men and women come rushing down the hall. Only one man does a double-take but quickly averts his eyes at

Gabriel's bared-teeth hiss. I force myself to meet Gabriel's gaze when his attention returns to me.

The unfortunate part is that he's attractive. Dark hair that's starting to grow out a bit, so it falls into his piercing blue eyes. Pale skin with just a glimmer of a tan. My heart hurts, knowing what he went through.

Not just in Terror, but out of it. Because his trauma clearly didn't end. Of course it didn't.

"I'm sorry," I tell him over the music. "It doesn't make it better—"

"It doesn't." He withdraws a syringe from his pocket. "This, though? It makes me feel a little better to watch you deconstruct."

I'm not going to take it. I don't even focus on it, the amber liquid somehow magnified and illuminated in the dark hallway—or maybe it's just my imagination. And my fixation.

Shit.

"I'm going to get better," I tell him. "And then what?"

"You'll get better when you hit rock bottom. Which is what, exactly? What does rock bottom look like for the most independent, fearless woman I've ever met?" He reaches out and traces the capped point down the side of my face. "It looks like fear. It looks like loneliness. It looks like your lies isolating you to the point where you don't think you can tell a single person the truth."

He exhales.

"It looks," he continues, "like shame. Your shame is so colorful, Artemis. You've overcome so much. You were sold to the highest bidder time and again. You were dressed in gold chains they called lingerie, and you don't seem to care that one of your rapists has been living under your roof."

I stiffen. "Reese—"

"Say it with me." Gabriel leans down. "He *fucked you* and didn't give you a choice."

"He didn't have one either."

"That's what I told myself, too. Those times when I just really wanted to disappear into the moment and pretend it was normal." His eyes are cold. He's so far removed from this conversation, I don't think he even cares about the buttons he's pressing. He just wants it to hurt in any way possible. "Did you fall for Reese as a fifteen-year-old? Develop an unhealthy attachment?"

"No—"

"No," he repeats. "I don't believe you, Artemis."

Did I?

I press my hands to the wall to keep from snatching the syringe from his hand.

"He was the only one to offer you kindness, wasn't he? Outstretched hand, a smile. And then, even if he said he didn't want to, he fucked you." He shakes his head. "I've been there, Artemis, remember? I know exactly what kind of sick games these people will play to get inside your head. Fucking a shell of a woman isn't enough. Stealing our virginity wasn't enough."

"You're wrong."

"I'm *right*," he counters. "But you don't have to let that betrayal crush you. It's all stuck in your head now, isn't it? Every time his parents brought him to Terror, every time they watched from the corner—how twisted was it that they *watched* their son fuck a girl they bought?"

"Stop saying that." I inch past him.

"And now he's getting the milk for free," he says.

I freeze.

My relationship with Reese now has no bearing on our past.

The biggest lie I've ever told.

"He still calls his mother," Gabriel adds.

I know that.

I saw the records myself, passed from the sheriff to Kade... and then to Gabriel? I don't care that Reese still talks to his mother. I don't care that he didn't immediately cut them off once he could support himself.

There's a reason I never asked about his parents. Their judgmental gazes burning down on us. The so-called lessons he was supposed to learn in Terror, with me.

But all those reasons seem to pale in the face of his continued relationship with his mother.

I should've asked.

I still can.

But I won't. Opening that can of worms might give him the idea that he can pry right back. And then I'll have to explain about my parents. Or worse.

"Why are you doing this?" I finally ask Gabriel.

He makes a face. "I want you to reach out and take this." He taps the syringe against my forehead. "I want you to give in to your baser instincts and feel wild with the need to inject this into your blood. Does everything hurt? Do you have a headache no amount of aspirin can shake? Do your bones feel like they're grinding together?"

I grit my teeth.

The answer is *yes*. I've been withdrawing from heroin for what seems like ages, and I still haven't shaken the symptoms.

"No one noticed." He reaches out and curls a lock of my hair around his fingers. "No one noticed when you were high. They didn't say anything when you were struggling. They don't see that you've been losing weight, not eating, disappearing for hours to come find me and shoot up. Why has not a single person in your life said anything about it?"

My eyes burn.

Damn it.

I blink rapidly, but my chest is too tight. Panic claws at me.

"You're probably wondering how I am *so* right," he guesses. "And you're thinking to yourself—why is it that the people who claim to care are so fucking ignorant? Maybe it's because they don't actually care at all."

I think of Reese holding up the empty syringe in Emerald Cove, his worries fading as he accepted my lies about Gabriel planting evidence. Kade lifting me out of the bath, then letting me walk out.

Saint, not asking a single question about *me* when I burned down Kade's house. Not noticing the track marks on my arms when I was bare-chested in front of him for hours. Not seeing me, not caring enough to not tattoo the guy conspiring with *Gabriel.*

My brother has let me avoid his calls. Hasn't gone through Saint.

Antonio let me stay away, even though he, of all people, would know immediately.

Tears drip down my cheeks.

"There." Gabriel leans in and licks them away.

I shudder, but I don't move. Not until he offers up the syringe on an open palm.

"It'll make it hurt less."

I take it.

I hate myself.

He steps away, but I'm already moving. *Rushing.* Down the dark hall, into the women's bathroom.

My hands shake. I stumble into the last stall and sit on

the toilet. I use the hair tie around my wrist as a tourniquet, sliding it up my arm. Every breath comes fast and shallow.

I can barely see through my tears, but there's something else.

Excitement?

I'm going to be sick.

I tap the vein and bite the cap off the syringe. The needle is exposed, gleaming in the low light. The bathroom aesthetic matches the rest of the club. It's supposed to be moody. Black marble walls, a chandelier over the sinks. Recessed lights over each stall.

It's by that light that I slide the needle into my skin.

My heart skips at the sting of it, and I pause. It's almost as good as the rush I know is coming. I pull back on the plunger, and a thread of red blood is dragged into the chamber. It tells me I successfully hit the vein.

Wait.

For no other reason to prove that I can.

Three.

Two.

I hit the plunger before I can think *one.*

27 REESE

"COME ON, COME ON." I follow one of the never-ending hallways, hoping it'll spit me out in familiar territory.

While I've visited Bow & Arrow before, it was always relatively simple to figure out where I wanted to go. One, I sought the attention of Artemis—and in the quieter spaces of the VIP lounges seemed like the best idea. Two, there were always people around to ask.

Now, the club is overcrowded, and a thread of chaos shivers through the masses. The music pulses louder, the dancing becomes wilder. The shift started minor, almost miniscule, and now seems too much.

There are no employees either. We witnessed everyone coming in at liberty, but it's taking a turn for the worse, their collective behavior becoming more violent.

Did all Tem's employees abandon ship?

Did someone call them away?

There are usually waitresses, for one. Bouncers. Bartenders. I spot a patron behind the bar, drinking straight from one of the bottles while others cheer.

I clench my teeth and force my hands to remain at my sides. Reaching for a weapon right now would be stupid—the last thing we need is a stampede of people.

There's danger here, yes, but there's one objective: find Antonio.

The older man said there were Cyclopes here, and yet...

"You lost?"

I spin around. A woman stands in the middle of the hall, her hands on her hips. Her hair is long and blonde, her makeup exaggerated. There's a sharp X over her left eye, either a tattoo or drawn in eyeliner. Long black lashes, deep-red lipstick, that kind of thing. It seems more like a costume than anything Artemis wears, although I've seen her do a similar style.

Maybe I'm biased?

"I got turned around," I say.

She motions me closer. "It's okay. I'll lead you out."

"Thanks."

I follow her back the way I came, and she takes an unexpected right. The hallway is almost totally dark at the entrance and completely hidden in shadow.

Her phone's flashlight clicks on a second later. "Bulb must've gone out. This way. Watch the steps."

Down four, then on a smooth path again. The hall curves, and suddenly I know exactly where I am. The door to Artemis's apartment is just around the corner, and it leads into the service hallways. Which means I'm between the dance floor, which is set down a level from the street entrance, and the third floor with the VIP lounges.

"Thank you, I've got it from here."

She whirls around. She's right under a light, and it highlights the X. She blows me a kiss and saunters away, while I try not to cringe. The realization clicks.

She's a Cyclops?

Wasn't I just saying there were no signs of them?

But they *are* here—and they're here as part of the crowd.

Until when?

What's the signal?

"Oh, good." Gabriel comes up behind me, slinging his arm over my shoulders. "Benny did her job. She'll get a gold star for that one."

I try to shrug him off, but he holds tight.

"Hey, hey," he chides. "I'm not gonna hurt you. Just the opposite, in fact."

"The opposite of hurting me?" I scoff. "How's that?"

"I'm going to point you in the direction of a certain foxy lady... Oh, I'm sorry, *golden girl*. She might not be too happy to see you, though." He pouts. "I hate it when Mommy and Daddy fight."

"Gabriel," I warn.

He drops the pout and grins. "You're so easy to manipulate, Reese Avery. But you're not the only one. So run along and find Artemis, and then you two should get out of here while you still can."

He gives me a push.

I glance back, but he makes a shooing motion.

"Try the women's bathroom," he suggests. "Maybe. Better hurry, though..."

Well, shit. What the hell does that mean?

So much for finding Antonio.

I hate to say it, but I agree with him on one thing. I'll pick her—and protect her—any damn day.

28 SAINT

THIS IS GOING WORSE than expected.

Someone looms in front of me with a tattooed X over their eye. They don't seem like they belong in Bow & Arrow. They don't belong in Sterling Falls. But the guy's gaze skates past me, and then he's moving on.

Whatever they're searching for, they clearly haven't found it.

I glance up.

I don't know what leads me to, but my attention flicks to the VIP section two stories above, which has a wall of glass to overlook the dance floor I stand on.

And there's Kade.

My stomach knots the instant he locks eyes with me.

It should be impossible—we're so far away. I shouldn't be able to tell he's looking at me. But then he tips his head to the side, and I blow out a long breath. I push through the crowd, heading for the stairs that will take me up.

I'm not sure what good it's going to do.

Is there anything I can say that will convince him to retreat? To leave Bow & Arrow alone?

He meets me on the stairs. The bouncer who usually mans the VIP lounge entrance is gone, the path clear. He bodily herds me away from it, though, and into an alcove. His black t-shirt is form-fitting, and the open jacket doesn't conceal the gun strapped to his hip. Black pants, black belt. There's a black bandana loose around his neck, like it was once pulled up over his nose to hide his identity.

"What the fuck, Kade?" I glare at him. "What's going on?"

"This is one of the pillars," he says.

He's so fucking calm.

"Did you know that before? When—"

"Before what?" He tugs the collar of his shirt, baring the tattoo I gave him. "Before this? Yes. Before I caught you ogling my dick? Yes. It's been set in motion for a long time now. This is just one thing that has to happen."

"Because you want to take over the town."

I'm such an idiot. I knew it, didn't I? We all knew the Cyclopes had their sights set on taking over more ground than West Falls.

They shouldn't have been allowed to enter the city in the first place. That's a failure on Jace King's part. And Wolfe. And Apollo.

But they're not here...

And somehow, I surmise that, too, was part of the plan.

"This is Tem's club," I say quietly. "You're hurting her."

"She will understand." He sighs. "It's not my plan, okay? I'm just following along."

He sent a bomb to the Hell Hounds. He somehow managed to get the Olympians out of Sterling Falls, and he's using their absence to take over everything.

"Did you see our handiwork at City Hall?"

I pause. He pushes me up against the wall, and I

fucking let it happen. Mainly because I want to see what he's going to do... and I need him to keep talking.

"I'll take that as a no. The poor sheriff. He thought compliance would keep him safe. But we burned it all down."

My shoulders inch higher. "Is that what you're going to do here?"

Kade makes a show of looking around.

I growl.

His smirk gives me anxiety.

"No," he finally says. "I'm not going to burn down this club. Gabriel might have other ideas. He's been toying with Artemis. That was part of our deal, you know? He gets her, I get Reese."

"Bullshit."

He appraises me. Dark eyes, dark hair. He's taller than me. He smells like citrus.

Why am I smelling him?

He inches closer, until we're practically touching. "What would you give me to stop all of this?"

"What do you want?"

"I want you to admit you were ogling my dick." His gaze drops. "And that you're a little turned on by me."

"I'm straight." I shake my head. "Fuck off."

"I'd like to fuck *you*, if we're being honest." He puts his palm on my chest, right over that damn brand. He pushes, and I hit the wall.

My dick wakes up.

If I could think of literally anything except how one single point of connection has my cock rising in my pants, I would. But that and his fucking arrogant smile are all my mind can latch on to.

He slowly looks down between us, and that smile widens into a full-on grin.

"Hmm." His other hand grips the front of my jeans. His fingers slip inside the waistband, and he uses it to tug my hips forward. Into his. He's hard, too, and the way his tented jeans rub...

"Jesus," I grunt.

"I thought so." He shoves me back. Harder.

I hit the wall again, not just my shoulder blades but my ass, my head. He presses into me, pinning me to the wall the way I would Artemis.

Or Elora.

My throat tightens, and I shake my head.

He grips my jaw. "Stop."

I lock my gaze on his. My body stills.

"Good," he whispers. He leans in, and his lips brush mine. "Saint? I don't think you're straight at all."

Holy fucking shit.

He kisses me once, the softest peck, then again. And again.

Teasing, featherlight contact.

Until my resistance crumbles and I lean forward to meet him.

His hold on my jaw doesn't loosen. If anything, he uses it to angle my face. It's like I give him an inch and he takes it as permission to run a mile. His lips press on mine, sliding, inching. His hips keep me against the wall, and my cock leaps in my pants.

He has to feel it, just like I can practically feel the pulse of his against my thigh.

While it should embarrass me, I don't seem to care at the moment.

He pries open my mouth and infiltrates it with his

tongue. I groan into his mouth as his other hand comes between us. He lifts my shirt, running his fingers across my abdomen. It's a rather maddening path.

This is insane.

I pull away.

"Good," he repeats, his pupils dilated.

I'm sure mine look the same.

"Hold on to that feeling."

"W-what feeling?"

"This one." His hand leaves my abdomen and cups my dick through my jeans.

I jump.

"I did that to you. Say it back to me."

"I—"

"Who made you hard?"

What the fuck is his problem? I shove at him, but he's got the leverage. He barely moves. He doesn't seem to care about the lack of privacy either. This alcove doesn't have a door. We're not enclosed—anyone could see us.

"Who. Made. You. Hard?" He leans in and nips at my lower lip. Bites it.

Pain and pleasure. A terrible, heady combination.

A drop of blood spreads across the tip of my tongue.

"Should my next question be, who can make you come?" There's a challenge there.

He squeezes, and I grunt. He's serious.

"You," I finally spit out. "You made me hard."

"Good boy."

Fucking hell.

He smirks. "Like that?"

"No."

"Liar," he whispers.

He finally releases me and adjusts his pants. "Baby steps. That was just a taste of what I want to do to you."

I swallow and rake my fingers through my hair. I don't know if I can *do* much more—I'm not convinced I want to. My dick, however, is fully on board with more touching. Which is not great.

And worse, the guilt that usually comes with attraction?

Totally absent.

"Now," Kade says. "Things are about to get messy. But remember what I said?"

"Hold on to the feeling," I repeat. "What do you mean by *messy*—"

He winces. "This might've been a little distraction."

"What?" I shove past him.

This time, he moves aside. I burst into the hallway and take the stairs down, to the first landing that gives me a view of the club.

The empty club.

The music still thunders, the colorful lights swinging across the floor and walls, but the whole place seems to have been evacuated.

The DJ is gone, even.

But as I watch, people enter.

They're forced in by armed men with bandanas hiding the lower half of their faces. People I recognize, some I don't.

Nadine Bradshaw, who holds a seat on the city council, and her brother. More city council members, people from the sheriff's office. Deputies in uniform, secretaries, detectives in plain clothes.

It's hard not to get to know all of them in Sterling Falls. It's such a small town.

Antonio and the two club bouncers are brought in from

another door. Sam, the manager, and the head chef who runs the kitchens.

Fighters at Olympus—the regulars I can recognize from years of studying my opponents. Hercules, Minos.

Jeffrey Thompson, the mayor, who has always held a sham position in Sterling Falls.

The Sterling Falls University president and two of his colleagues.

"Go join them," Kade says from behind me.

I glance back. "Where is Artemis?"

And Reese?

"Gone." He tips his head. "Part of the deal. They're separate from this."

And I'm not.

He steps forward. "Go stand with Antonio. You think Artemis would break if he died? Then protect him."

There's a silent plead there, I think, although it's hard to tell by his tone.

Either way, I'm not going to fight it. My arousal sufficiently doused, I go down to the bottom floor and make a beeline for Antonio. The older man's eyebrows hike slightly at the sight of me, but I shake my head.

Both in not knowing where Artemis is, besides *gone*, and what's happening.

I know most of the people in this room.

The only ones missing are Jace, Wolfe, and Apollo, and then Artemis and Reese.

And Gabriel, although I have a feeling he's lurking somewhere.

"I met him," Antonio says, just loud enough for me to hear over the music.

I jerk to attention. "Who? Kade?"

"No." He shakes his head. "Graves."

The music pouring from the speakers stops. It was loud —but now my ears faintly ring with how silent it is. I glance at Antonio, not liking this a single bit.

Graves. The name sounds vaguely familiar, in the way an old friend's sibling's name might be. I can't immediately place it, though. And it isn't until a collective murmur bleeds through the crowd around us that I realize Kade has made himself visible on the landing.

Gabriel stands beside him.

They're dressed similarly. All in black, bandanas slung around their necks. Their men around us, now that they're closer up, all have the X tattooed over one eye. The upper lines cut through their eyebrows, and the bottom points end just above their cheekbones.

A sign of fealty?

Cyclopes.

One-eyed monsters. *Giants amongst men.*

It's kind of ironic that their name choice indicates single-mindedness. That, in Greek mythology, while the monsters were great, they were also aggressive. They lacked focus.

Somehow, I don't think Kade and Gabriel met and decided to form a gang.

No... this is something else.

Graves?

Graves.

Graves.

Come on, Saint, fucking think harder.

I snap my fingers.

Wesley Graves.

He's better known as Kronos. Or, he was before I killed him last year. So... what kind of connection does this guy have to Kronos? Besides the last name.

Cousin?

Father?

Son?

Brother?

Kade said I should join these fuckers and protect Antonio—but if this Graves guy knows I killed Kronos, then I think I'm in more danger than even Kade realized.

29 ARTEMIS

"LET ME HELP YOU." Reese kneels beside me.

How long has he been here?

He carefully takes the syringe from my fingers. He slides the discarded cap back on it and tosses it in the trash, then returns to my side with a wad of toilet paper. He holds it to the crook of my arm with one hand, supporting the back of my head with his other.

"Stay awake." His low voice conveys the order, but also concern?

I don't know why he'd be concerned.

I'm fine.

"Artemis."

I focus on Reese. We're standing. Moving. Our footsteps are mere whispers across the tile. I wrap my arm around his waist because I can't really feel my legs, and I'm not sure how I'm walking. Everything is coated in honey. He gets me out of the bathroom and down the hall. My eyes shut, and the next thing I know, we're in his truck. He's got my seat belt buckled around me, and my fingers dig into my thighs.

"Talk to me," he says. "How bad is it?"

The urge to lie, to downplay it, surges through me.

Not bad, I almost say, but the words don't come.

He found me on the floor of a dirty bathroom, shooting up heroin like my life depended on it. I'm sure when this floating sensation leaves, I'll give a shit. I'll probably be embarrassed. The worst part is, the rush wasn't as good as I was hoping. Imagining. It hit me hard enough to feel, and it took away the pain just like Gabriel said it would.

But...

But.

There's another part of me that wants more. I want adrenaline and euphoria. I want to feel like I can orgasm from a single swipe of a finger across my nipple.

I don't.

That's not to say it isn't good, but it's far closer to what I'd imagine *normal* feels like. If normal means I can barely keep my eyes open and my skin tingles.

Reese takes me far, far away. The window is open a crack. The cool night air flows over me, sweeps through my hair and lifts strands from my heated neck. I lean my forehead against the glass, groaning at how cool it is on my fevered skin.

The stars are out tonight, but there's also something else.

Smoke, a little voice in my head whispers. The smoke from an earlier fire... or maybe it's still burning? I don't know how long it took for Kade's house to burn out, all I know is that he didn't call the fire department. It didn't leap houses, it just consumed what I meant it to.

For a brief moment, the fire conformed to my will.

I don't think that would happen again, though. And I don't think it's the case this time.

My brother and I nearly burned to death in an explosion. It didn't listen to my *will* that time either. The bomb was set to ruin the center of Sterling Falls, so of course we tried to stop it.

And accidentally detonated it.

But hey—no harm, no foul. Right?

Speaking of Apollo. I haven't heard his voice in so long. Tears burn at my eyes, falling down my cheeks. I swipe at them, patting my cheeks, until Reese catches my hands.

"Hey, hey. Don't hit yourself."

There is a sob *right there.* I have a lump in my throat, my chest is tight. My breath comes in panicked little gasps and pants. My eyes fucking sting. All the hallmarks of needing a good, soul-deep cry, and I've got nothing.

I miss him.

Apollo makes everything better.

And yet... he's not here. He left Sterling Falls, he left *me*, alone with monsters lurking in the shadows. Why didn't he bring me and Saint with him?

Why did Jace ever put Saint and me in the same room?

They'll be so embarrassed.

No, no, no.

Wrong.

They're going to be so *ashamed*, and while shame and embarrassment are similar, one is infinitely worse to stomach. One will bring back all the memories of that stupid brothel that Apollo tries desperately to avoid. Killing people at sixteen...

The Hell Hounds' leader, Cerberus, had to know he hit the jackpot when he learned of it.

How Apollo felt about that night, however, has remained a mystery.

I could only conclude he hated it, and me for forcing his hand.

"Don't tell my brother," I whisper across the near-silent truck cab.

He scoffs. "I know he and I haven't had more than a single conversation, but trust me on this: he'll kill me."

"He'll kill *me* if you do." I wipe at more tears. "He'll disown me."

"Artemis. He won't." There's something in his voice. He brushes the backs of his fingers down my arm, and goosebumps rise in their wake. Then does it again.

I look at him.

His expression is pained. "Everyone will understand. I don't know how it happened, but..."

I huff my disbelief. "You went from telling my brother to *everyone*—?"

"You're right." He pauses. "I was making assumptions that they would eventually find out. But they won't if you don't want them to. Your brother, though, will understand... if it happened how I'm guessing. Will you tell me about it?"

He pulls over, kills the engine, and twists to face me.

Full attention.

I swallow. My tongue suddenly feels like it's too big for my mouth. I'm going to stumble over my words—if I can even force them out. I have to try, though. Something about Reese's expression conveys that I don't have a choice.

"You caught the nurse who was giving me heroin," I start.

"Saint did," he agrees. "But I was there."

"Right." My heartbeat quickens. This is worse than adrenaline—it's fear. "Saint was gone, and I think you were sleeping? Gabriel came in when I was going through withdrawals. He gave me more—not enough to put me out, you know, but enough to feel it—and then told me I knew where to find him."

We're all mad here, Gabriel had said.

I thought I dreamt it, but then I showed up at Madness, and it was a downhill slide from there. What would've happened if I resisted that first time? If I didn't let him show me how to inject it, if I didn't give in to that delicious rush the first time?

If I didn't stare him down across the table and let him compress my finger on the plunger?

Maybe I wouldn't be here.

Or maybe I would.

Maybe Gabriel would've kept trying, kept picking at me, until I gave up. He did it tonight, didn't he? He knew I was fighting the addiction, and he shoved me into the darkest spot he could before offering the one thing to take the pain away.

I hate it.

I hate *him.*

And mostly, I hate myself.

"I found him," I finish lamely. "I wasn't strong enough to resist. I'm still not."

"It's not your fault, Tem," Reese says carefully. "But we should get you some help. If you're open to it."

The truth, this time, is easy to admit: "I don't want to be like this forever."

He nods. I reach for him, and he takes my hands. He's steady where I am weak.

"Yes. I want help."

He tips his chin toward the truck's windshield. I follow his gaze, my brows furrowing at the familiar sight.

We're at the marina.

"Come on." He gets out of the truck. He circles around and helps me down.

He guides me to a speedboat at the end of a dock. Its navigation lights are on, and a man sits on the deck. It isn't until we get up next to it that I recognize Bobby, the houseboat owner. He's wearing a dark-blue windbreaker and white pants instead of his usual eccentric get-up, his long hair caught back in a bun and black cap covering it.

"Hello, wayward travelers," Bobby greets us. "Are you ready?"

My stomach twists. "Ready for what?"

"Tem." Reese releases me. "You're free to stay here. I don't want you to think I'm pushing you. But..." He runs his fingers through his hair, and it seems to be a sign of distress.

Should I be stressed, too?

I can't feel anything, but... *maybe.*

"I hate that Gabriel got to you," he confesses. He grips the back of his neck tightly, the cords of muscle on his forearms standing out. "Let's make it better."

All at once, it clicks into place. There's only one place I can imagine would get me out of Sterling Falls but keep me safe from *everyone*. Kora spent time there. Kade mentioned checking it out in an effort to cover his bases about Reese.

Which would lead me to believe that Reese knows about it, too.

The island itself is fine—small, unassuming—but the trauma rehabilitation center that takes up almost half of it is the important note.

This isn't quite trauma... but maybe it would be good to get away.

I can't even face Antonio like I am. Haven't admitted to anyone my issue, didn't do a thing to get help. Not from my brother, Saint, Kade, Antonio... the list goes on. There are so many people I *could've* reached out to, and yet, I am totally alone.

Especially as I nod to Reese and climb onto Bobby's boat.

He follows.

I glance back at him, but he just scowls. Like I'd be a fool to think he would let me travel alone.

"This isn't forever," he assures me.

Bobby hands us life jackets and points to where we can sit. I strap it on and fiddle with the buckles, while Reese takes the seat across from me. Bobby makes quick work of freeing us from the dock and firing up the engines.

We drift out a foot, then two, and Bobby puts the engine in gear. The water churns at the stern, and we pick up speed. I shiver.

"It can't be forever," I finally reply. "With Gabriel and Kade—"

"The town isn't as important as you," he interrupts. "I know you care. I know there's a lot at stake. But I'd rather you be alive and sober. *Healthy*. If I could stay with you, I absolutely would."

"How did you arrange this—or when?"

He sighs. "You slept for a bit after I put you in the truck. I asked Kade who could get us out of the city."

"And Kade was more than happy to help?"

He frowns. "He gave me Bobby's number, but he didn't want to know anything else. Yes, he was happy to help. I think he and Gabriel have some sort of... pact? About the two of us."

Great. I don't remember falling asleep, but there are lags in my memory. Time gaps. Going from leaving the bathroom to being buckled into my seat.

I nod slowly and turn my gaze to the open water.

No one stops us. No one shouts out. It seems like all the efforts of the Cyclopes have left the marina wide open.

Either that, or Kade paved the path for us. And knowing that Reese asked Kade for help, I fear it's more than likely the case.

Which begs the question... do I owe Kade for making this easy? Or is he simply trying to right a previous betrayal?

I reach for Reese. He moves to my side and takes my hand, wrapping his free arm around my shoulders.

We stay like that until we lose sight of land.

30 KADE

GABRIEL INCHES UP BESIDE ME, smirking to himself. He sometimes seems so sane, and then it all just vanishes in an instant. Like the sanity is a mask, and sometimes he can't help but drop it.

Sometimes I consider it to be the reverse—that he's actually a rational person, but he can't let anyone get too close to him. So he acts mad, and his antics keep everyone at arms' distance.

"You got Artemis and Reese out?" I confirm, because it bears asking a second time. Or third. I already know based on Reese's text.

They had to leave Sterling Falls. It was logic on Reese's part, although I assume Artemis fought him on it. But as soon as he asked for a path out...

Bobby was ready and waiting. They're in my speedboat, but I trust the eccentric man to captain it well. He'll bring them wherever they need to go and return to Sterling Falls. But he has his orders: under no circumstances should he share where Artemis and Reese go.

I promised I'd kill him myself if that secret slipped.

Sterling Falls, though...

The pieces have been moved across the board, our traps set. The only *ask* from Gabriel and I was for those two. I don't know if Gabriel wanted Artemis to be safe or to suffer, but it doesn't matter.

Alive is alive is alive.

"Out," he confirms. "He carried her away. Poor broken little bird."

I glance at him. "What did you do?"

"Addiction is a strange thing, don't you think? It has a hairpin trigger. Anything can set it off... sadness, loneliness, fear. Sometimes people don't want to feel emotion. Some think they can't feel *without* it." He taps his chin. "Which do you think Artemis is?"

I go still. "What are you saying?"

"Heroin comes from morphine. Did you know that? I found it fascinating. We give morphine to people in hospitals... all it took was a twist on genetic makeup. Well, I don't know for certain. I'm not a chemist."

"Gabriel." I clench my fists and force myself to release them, finger by finger.

"I broke my favorite toy," he says sadly. "She was fighting it. I just convinced her that everyone had abandoned her except for the drug. I don't know if that's how it is for everyone. Some never wake up."

His gaze hardens, but I ignore it.

He got Artemis addicted to heroin?

How the fuck did I miss it?

I blow out a slow breath, my need for control superseding losing my shit on him. I would if I could—if this was a regular night, I'd beat him black and blue. But tonight is important. Even having this conversation in sight of the railing, and the people below, seems too public.

One wrong expression, and everything could fail.

The Cyclopes look up to Gabriel and me. Whether they follow one of us or both, we cultivated our places in the hierarchy. To see us fighting would only cause a ripple of dissent.

And with dissent comes weakness.

With weakness comes anarchy.

Gabriel bounces on his heels. "It was such a fun experiment. She hid from everyone. You didn't notice? Can you think back and spot her lies?"

"Shut the fuck up," I growl.

He hums.

Still bouncing.

Still *happy*.

"You thrive in this sort of chaos, don't you?"

He lifts a shoulder. "I grew up in chaos, Kade. Stability gives me hives."

Almost against my will, I find myself analyzing Artemis's movements over the last few weeks. Besides the fact that she was avoiding me because I gave her to Gabriel to save Reese...

She burned my house down, which was a bit irrational. Granted, I think she has something going on with Saint. It could've been a territorial thing—and that's why I didn't push her too hard when I met her at Madness.

Also...

The bathtub.

Obviously.

Saint and Reese weren't home when I arrived at the condo, and I let myself in. They arrived back sometime between me discovering Artemis in the bathtub with her clothes on and me picking out new clothes from her dresser.

However, I didn't mention it.

And if I saw any marks on the inside of her elbows, I might've brushed it off. I should've pushed harder. Peeling off her soaking-wet, *freezing* clothes wasn't a sexual act, though. I wasn't staring at her chest—I wanted her covered.

I heave a sigh.

Keeping tabs on her was a side project, but even I'm man enough to admit that I was distracted. Not only by Saint, although he's a delicious factor, but by my job. It's the whole reason I came to Sterling Falls.

Imagine entering the city with one purpose—and a secondary motivation on the side—only to find... *Artemis*.

What started as a simple exploration of what Sterling Falls had to offer became so much more. An addiction in and of itself.

"They're better off gone," I murmur, more to myself than Gabriel.

He nods along anyway.

Movement on the stairs above us draws our attention. I automatically straighten, and so does Gabriel. His spine snaps straight instantly, all signs of mania gone.

The truth is... this wasn't my idea.

And it wasn't Gabriel's.

I elbow him, and we step up to the railing. He makes a motion, and the music abruptly cuts out. Saint has made his way down to Antonio. The crowd around them immediately spots us, and a rushing whisper, like an ocean's tide, sweeps across them.

Gabriel leans on it, frowning down at them.

I glance back just as Marcus Graves steps into view.

31 ARTEMIS

I TAKE A DEEP BREATH. Fear rattles me, but I've never let that stop me. Not when I was on my own last year, or when I was in the depths of Terror. I survived it all—why should this be any different?

"What are you going to do?" I ask Reese. Because what I *do* know is that he's going to leave me here.

He sighs. "I don't know. I need to get back to the truck and stash it somewhere safe."

Because... he said there was something valuable in it. It's why we parked far from Bow & Arrow. I don't even remember the walk to his truck.

"What did you find?"

He shakes his head. "I don't want to say."

Bobby pops up onto the deck. "It's just ahead. We'll be there in a few minutes."

"Thanks," Reese murmurs.

The wind lifts my hair. I pull it over one shoulder, quickly braiding it and looping my hair tie around the ends. The hair tie I resorted to using as a tourniquet...

Shame smacks me in the face.

"Can you get to Emerald Cove?" I ask.

He raises a shoulder. "I think I should find Saint."

Fuck. How the hell did I forget that we left Saint at Bow & Arrow? Gabriel was there—would he do something to him? I grab Reese's arm, panic surging.

"Kade will keep him safe," he says, although there's a note of uncertainty there. "I'll go back and find them both. Kade owes us answers anyway. And… there's something else I have to do."

"Go to my brother's house if you need a safe place," I advise. "It's between the Hell Hounds' compound and Olympus, but they kept it in Kora's name. It should be off Gabriel's radar. Do you have a pen and paper?"

As far as I know, Kora Sinclair is a foreign name to him and Kade.

"Hang on." He goes to talk to Bobby and returns with a tiny notepad and pencil. "Here."

Almost a lifetime ago, we had a friend named Daniel. He helped us on many occasions, but the most important time was when we had to save Kora from a certain madman. His skills on the computer are nothing to sneeze at. But because of his cautious nature—actually, he'd probably get along well with Reese and his love of burner phones—we developed a method of getting in contact with each other.

Correction: *he* developed a method for me to get in touch with *him*. He laughingly said I was one of the easier people to find, thanks to a digital footprint the size of Alaska.

I blame online shopping.

"Follow these instructions. Daniel can get you guys set up, just in case the sheriff…"

Well, I think we can probably count on the sheriff folding under new pressure. Or bribery.

"Daniel," he repeats. "Is he in Sterling Falls?"

"He used to be." I sigh. "He moved away after the war ended. He prefers digital carnage to actual blood, and it was a lot to handle. Being there kept triggering him."

Reese accepts that with a quick nod.

I feel oddly out of my league here. The last time Sterling Falls fell to pieces, I was there. I was part of the shadows. Now I'm effectively being taken off the playing board altogether.

We sit in silence until we're secured to the small dock. Reese and I both hop onto the moving dock. It lifts and falls gently with the rolling waves coming in, but this side faces land. The ocean isn't at its fiercest over here.

Up a sloping gravel path that leads from the dock awaits a parked golf cart. Its headlights are on, pointed diagonally and illuminating a thick cluster of trees. The electric vehicle has two bench rows, no sign of actual golf clubs, and a woman and man stand in front of it.

"How did they know we were coming?" I whisper.

Reese eyes them, then me. "Maybe they saw the boat?"

Bobby joins us on the dock. "I had to let them know we were coming in. Isle of Paradise can be a bit... finicky... when boats show up in the middle of the night."

Oh. I'm not going to ask how he knows that.

Has he delivered others to this island?

"Okay."

I face Reese. "I don't know if they allow visitors, but if you can get a call through..."

He grips my hands, squeezing tightly. "This is *not* me abandoning you. I will be right here when you're ready to come back. You're a warrior, and this is just another battle you will overcome."

He makes it sound almost *easy*.

He kisses my cheek. "I choose you, Artemis Madden."

My heart skips, and I turn my head fast to catch his lips with mine. I don't know what awaits me on this island—all I know is that *paradise* is about as far away from it as possible. I kiss him like I'm never going to see him again, then pull away before it can get too intense.

"Good," I whisper. "Remember that in a few weeks."

"I'll remember that every day for the rest of my life," he says.

Shaking my head at him, I head toward land.

Toward the people waiting for us.

My hands shake.

"Hello," the woman greets me. "Can we help you?"

I nod carefully. My throat is tight, my mouth dry. I don't know how I can possibly force out the words—but then I do, I speak, and they float between us.

"I want to get sober, and I can't do it alone."

No going back now.

32 SAINT

"YOU MIGHT BE WONDERING who I am and why my men have gathered you here."

The man looks around carefully from his position above us. He wears a black suit. His white shirt is partially hidden under the buttoned jacket, and a slim black tie is knotted at his throat. He gives off regal vibes in the strangest of ways. Like he has any right to stand in Tem's club as if he owns it.

The mayor scoffs from the other side of the crowd. "Gathered? That's a nice way to put it. Your men rounded us up—"

A Cyclops jabs him in the back with the butt of his gun. The mayor staggers forward, then glares back at the man who struck him.

A chill rushes through me.

The man above, standing to the side of Kade and Gabriel, is closer to Antonio's age than ours. His hair is mostly dark, perfectly styled with a single curl hanging down in the middle of his forehead. He reminds me of a 1950's rock star. Somewhere between attractive and average, but the magnetism is hard to miss.

The one above us continues as if there wasn't an interruption. "You can call me Ouranos. And I am here to save Sterling Falls."

I bite the inside of my cheek. I *like* Greek mythology. Studied up on it quite a bit when I was first starting to make masks for Olympus. Ouranos is the father of the Titans, but he seems too young to be Kronos' father.

Brother, then?

"We're fine on our own, thanks," one of the aldermen calls.

Ouranos cocks his head. "You call this *fine*?"

He leaves the staircase landing and heads down. Kade remains immobile, but Gabriel follows behind him. I meet Kade's gaze. Any heat or passion is gone, replaced with a cold façade.

At least, I hope it's a mask and not the truth of him.

Ouranos reaches the dance floor and strides toward the alderman. There are four of them here, including Nadine Bradshaw. I only know one who's out of town...

"Is fine all you hope for Sterling Falls, Baron?" Ouranos questions.

Alderman Baron—whose name I didn't know, and certainly didn't expect *him* to know—gapes. He's more shocked than me.

Antonio's hand wraps around my wrist.

"Fine is not a benchmark of success. *Fine* is a failure."

Up close, I can make out the silver hairs at his temple. His face is clean-shaven, like Gabriel and Kade. His jaw is steep, his face narrower than what might be classically handsome, and his nose has a bump just after the bridge it that makes him stand out.

"Hold him," Ouranos says softly.

Two of his men grab the alderman from behind, one on

each arm. They were there too fast, almost anticipating their boss's order. Or perhaps not trusting the Sterling Falls' native to behave. Baron immediately struggles, yanking to no avail.

"You are a failure to this town." He lifts his chin, and they shove Baron to his knees. One of them offers a handgun, which Ouranos takes.

Antonio's grip crushes my wrist. I grasp at him back, my body tensing.

The gunshot is not unexpected, but it *is* jarring. I shield Antonio with my body, half turning away. If there was any hope that this was a ruse, it's now gone.

Baron drops, released by the Cyclopes holding him.

Ouranos hands his weapon to one of them, producing a handkerchief from his breast pocket and wiping each finger individually.

He moves through the crowd. I keep Antonio behind me, but everyone shifts out of his way. Not a single person seems to be able to meet his gaze.

He stops in front of Nathan Bradshaw.

The sheriff has never been my favorite person, but right now, I'd prefer he live to see another day. He's in his uniform, although his hat is missing.

"Sheriff Bradshaw," Ouranos says. "You seem to have deals with everyone in this town."

Nathan straightens.

"Loyalty test," Antonio breathes.

Great.

"Tell me. Who do you trust more? Kade Laurent or me?"

The sheriff eyes him, then shakes his head slowly. "Couldn't say, sir."

Ouranos laughs, then claps his hands. "*Sir*, I love that.

Such respect already? What have I done to deserve such a thing?"

Bradshaw glances down at the blood speckled across his white shirt.

"Ah. *Murder* bends your will? Not money." He looks pointedly up at Kade, still on the landing. "Money is attractive to you, isn't it, Sheriff?"

He grunts.

"Well, let me tell you all something." His gaze sharpens. "I will not *pay* you to be on my side. You either are, or you won't be leaving this room. And that applies to you all. Sterling Falls' bold leaders and businessmen."

I think I'm here by mistake. The only thing that keeps me focused is that Kade said to protect Antonio. And the older man was led into this room by the Cyclopes, which means he was rounded up.

He's included in this.

Ouranos stares down the sheriff until the latter breaks it. His gaze drops to his feet, and he mumbles something too low for me to hear.

"Good," Ouranos says. "Please know, Sheriff, that I don't believe a word out of your mouth. But it's no matter. There are always weak points."

He nods, and a Cyclops shoves the sheriff's sister forward by her hair. He pushes her toward Nathan, stopping just out of his reach.

"Now." Ouranos holds his hand out for the gun again. "Who do you trust more? Me, or your sister?"

The sheriff blanches.

"Do you trust me not to kill her?" he continues. "Or do you trust that she'll survive?"

"I—*you*," he says.

"I want you to remember this moment when you

consider going against me," Ouranos says. "Nadine. An alderman. Alder*woman*? I must say, I don't know what's politically correct. Correctness when in terms of politics doesn't hold my interest."

She nods, but her whole body trembles.

"Oh dear." He rubs her upper arm. "Did that frighten you?"

She continues nodding.

"Ah. Sensitive soul." He glances at her brother again. "I don't think it would take much at all to make you scream. Gabriel?"

Gabriel appears at his shoulder.

"Perhaps Nadine could test out that new cocktail," Ouranos suggests. "And then her brother would surely come to heel."

"No—" Bradshaw takes a big step forward, only to be blocked. "No, I'll listen. I agreed."

"Relax." Ouranos keeps stroking Nadine's arm. "She'll be okay. It's just to make her sleep."

Gabriel seems to have come prepared. There's a syringe in his hand, the cap off and needle tip catching the light as he pushes out a drop of liquid. He approaches Nadine, whose chin wobbles.

Did Artemis look at him like this? With such fear?

My stomach twists, and I risk a glance at Antonio.

He was there—he witnessed Gabriel's cruelty first-hand.

The room is completely silent as the Cyclops manhandling her straightens her arm away from her body. Gabriel slides her sweater up, and his body blocks what he does next.

Inject her, I can only imagine.

"Don't..." she says weakly.

They release her.

She staggers, then goes to her knees. Gabriel falls with her, cupping her cheeks.

"Sweet dreams, Alderman," he coos. "We'll talk about it when you wake up."

When she falls unconscious, mayhem erupts.

A few bolt for the main exit. I grab Antonio and haul him with me into one of the many hallways.

Like *fuck* are we going to be put through some loyalty test.

A gunshot rings out, then another.

Bloodbath.

"Faster," I grunt at him.

The nightclub manager, Sam, is with us, as is the chef. I don't know what happened to the two bouncers.

"There," Antonio wheezes, jerking my arm to the left.

There's a service door his waitresses use when things need restocking. I yank it open and shove him in ahead of me, then Sam. Artemis would probably kill me if I left her. I push the door open wider for the chef, still coming down the hall, when a Cyclops spots us.

He shoots without hesitation.

The chef screams and falls.

Fuck.

I slam the door shut and lock it. I have to—it's that or we'll all be caught.

Antonio and Sam are halfway down this hall, waiting for me, and Sam lets out a choked moan when no one follows.

"He got shot," I tell her. "We need to get out of here."

The real question: did they surround the outside of the building in anticipation of escapees?

I pull my gun and check that it's loaded. I keep it out,

pointed at the floor. My finger is straight along the barrel, and it'll stay there until I see something worth shooting at.

But for now, we're alone.

We make it to the door that exits into the alley, only to find chains looped around the handles. A fat padlock holds it shut.

I hesitate. "I could shoot it, but it would definitely draw attention."

Sam and Antonio trade a glance, and Antonio finally nods. "There's another exit through Terror. It goes under the building beside Bow & Arrow."

Fuck it. "Let's do it."

We hurry to the entrance to Terror. My skin crawls as soon as the metal doors shut behind us. Tem's stories merge with what I'm seeing, and it brings this place to life in a very visceral way.

My heart aches for her.

She got out. I hold on to that and follow Antonio and Sam. Our pace isn't fast, but only our footsteps sound in the empty space ahead and behind us.

As we travel, I turn my attention to Ouranos.

"How did you know his name?" I suddenly ask Antonio.

The older man stiffens.

"Come on," I press. "He doesn't strike me as the sort to introduce himself one way to you and another to everyone else."

He sighs. "Fine. It was a long time ago, understand, but he still resembles the boy he was."

"You knew him before?"

"His name is Marcus Graves. He's a judge in Emerald Cove. His appointment was a big deal... news traveled even to us in Sterling Falls. To those who paid attention anyway.

The district he was appointed to covers both cities. It made sense to remember his name... in case."

Sam bites her lip. "He presided over some of the Terror stuff."

My steps lurch. "Excuse me?"

"Not everyone was killed, you know. The takedown was partially an inside job by the Hell Hounds—it seemed to be a scandal at the time, since Terror was also funded by them—but I remember him from testifying against some of the guards."

Antonio nods slowly. "I would've had to testify, too, but Artemis kept me away from it."

I squeeze his hand, then hers. I'm not sure who I am, being Mr. Sentimental, but it seems to help steady both of them. I have no idea of Sam's history—but if she had to testify, it means she's no stranger to this place.

"I'm sure she wanted to protect you. Now let me. We need to keep moving."

It takes almost ten minutes to reach the heavy metal door. Unlike the Bow & Arrow doors, this one isn't blocked. I make them wait, spines pressed to the wall out of sight, and take the first two steps out into the open alleyway.

There's no sound, no movement in the darkness.

"Hurry," I whisper-yell.

We need to get out of here before they decide to search farther out from Bow & Arrow. If they care at all that we've escaped.

33 REESE

BOBBY DROPS me off on the dock closest to the parking lot, and I jog toward the truck. My phone is off, although I'm too conscious of it in my pocket. And the way to contact Daniel, which includes using a public computer—or a borrowed one, she scribbled—and messaging a public forum with a set of phrases.

It seems a little weird, but I think I need all the help I can get.

Once I'm in the truck, engine rumbling, I turn my phone on and dial Saint's number.

He answers almost immediately. "Where are you guys?"

My gut churns. "Can you meet me at Apollo's house?"

"Yep."

"Okay. Turn off your phone after you hang up."

The line goes dead, and I follow my own instructions. I'm tempted to chuck it out the window, but it's currently my only lifeline to Artemis.

I can't believe I just left her there.

What the fuck was I thinking?

Heroin, Reese. She's addicted to heroin.

Of all the fucked-up things I thought Gabriel did to me, it pales in comparison to the iron grip he has on her. Addiction is no joke. And it seems like, even when she fought it, he was there to twist the knife and drive her right back into it.

I squint at the address at the top of the page. She said it was between the Hell Hounds' compound and Olympus, so I head in that direction. It's slow going on the curving road from South Falls. There are no streetlights out here, and my truck takes the turns precariously.

I hold my breath past the Hell Hounds' compound. The *last* time I came this way, Artemis was unconscious in the back of her car, and I was surrounded by bikers.

And then Kade saved my ass, intentionally or not.

There's no sign of them now. I even peer down the long gravel driveway to catch a glimpse, but it's so dark, I can make out nothing.

Finally, I find their driveway. I pull in and park in front of the large white house. It has a wraparound porch and double front doors. I kill the engine and head up the steps.

Key in last hanging plant on left, she wrote. *Security code is 5674663.*

After a minute of feeling around the soil, I find it. I unlock the door and type the code in at the security panel.

This is weird.

I clench the key and move deeper inside.

"Hello?" I call. "If anyone is here, Artemis sent me."

Nothing.

Still, I check all the rooms. Everything has been left orderly and neat, like they prepared to be gone for a while. One of the bedrooms upstairs has an extra-wide bed, three different matching comforters, a million pillows, and two closets.

I guess I don't really want to know.

Instead, I go downstairs and await Saint.

SAINT DOESN'T ARRIVE ALONE.

Antonio and Vittoria accompany him in her car. They're both in the backseat, hunched together, but the glow from the porch light illuminates their faces.

I hurry down the steps and open the back door, offering my hand to help them out.

Vittoria takes it and allows me to guide her out, with Antonio close behind.

Saint frowns at me.

"What?" I question.

His gaze moves past me to the doorway, then back. "Where's Tem?"

I should've expected that to be the first thing out of his mouth. "That requires more than a simple answer," I say carefully. "But I have some stuff in the back of the truck; can you help me bring them in?"

His gaze is skeptical.

Can't blame him for that either. If I got such a non-answer, I'd be pissed. Yet he follows me to the back of the truck while Antonio and Vittoria head inside. We carry the dozen boxes up into the living room, stacking them against the back of the couch. It isn't until the last one is inside, the door closed and locked behind us, that Saint plants his hands on his hips.

"Answer time, Avery."

I grimace.

Antonio and Vittoria watch us from the other couch.

"Let's sit," I mumble.

I didn't think I'd have to be the one to break the news to them. My other option, though, would've been to let Artemis live through it. If she could even find the words to tell them.

No, no. It's better this way. She's getting help.

"Gabriel was keeping her unconscious in the hospital with heroin," I start. "Saint figured out the nurse was giving it to her through the IV, and she woke up once it worked its way out of her system."

Saint narrows his eyes.

"However... Gabriel planned for that. He snuck in at some point during our stay and gave her more at the height of her withdrawal. He told her where to find him for more."

I focus on Saint, because the heartbreaking expressions on Antonio's and Vittoria's faces are almost too much to take.

"For the next few weeks, she would meet him and..." I rub my eyes. "He taught her how to inject it. Gave her pre-made syringes. And when she would resist, he pushed her into thinking she was all alone."

"She wasn't." Saint's voice cracks. "She's not alone."

"I know. I told her, but amidst this, we were dealing with Kade's betrayal, and..."

Saint blushes. I don't think I've ever seen him turn so pink so fast.

I point at him. "What is that?"

"What?"

"Why are you embarrassed?"

He glowers at me, but even the tips of his ears are changing to red. "It was my fault with Kade's tattoo, that's all."

I roll my eyes. "And that prompted her to burn down his house. It seems to line up with what I've heard about heroin withdrawal. It can make even rational people do stupid, spur-of-the-moment shit."

Saint shifts in his seat. "He deserved it."

"Yeah."

Antonio clears his throat. "You still haven't said where she is now."

Right.

"There seemed to be only one place *to* go." Pause. "I brought her to the Isle of Paradise."

Saint swears under his breath, and Antonio seems equally stricken.

"She's okay there," I say. "Gabriel would've kept hitting her where it hurt—now he can't find her."

Vittoria nods at me. "You did the right thing, Reese. Getting her professional help while all of this is going on..."

I focus on them. "Not to sound too abrupt, but why are you two here? What happened after I spoke to you on the phone, Antonio?"

"Maybe a drink first," Antonio suggests.

Saint and I jump up and both go into the kitchen.

I elbow him. "Do you know a Daniel?"

He eyes me and nods.

"Tem suggested I contact him."

"You should," he says. "He might not come back for anyone except her or Kora."

"Have you talked to Jace?"

He bites his lip and checks that Antonio and Vittoria are out of earshot. "We made a run for it. Before you texted."

My eyebrows lift. "And?"

"The road out is blockaded."

Shit. "How the fuck did that happen?"

Saint leans his hip on the counter while I rummage for alcohol. Not sure that's what Antonio meant, but it sure as fuck seems appropriate.

"Jace, Wolfe, and Apollo used to monitor it. They had a toll booth—not much, really. It slowed people down enough for them to catch their plates, which they'd keep track of. It was a fascinating subset to their business. I think the Cyclopes somehow got into it."

I run my hand down my face. "Okay. So it's a good thing we got out by boat."

Saint shakes his head. "I think you were lucky the marina wasn't under lockdown... but Kade had something to do with it, I'd bet."

"What?"

"He said you and Artemis weren't part of the deal. Right before his freaking boss showed up and killed Alderman Baron."

I frown. The name isn't familiar, although the term *alderman* is. It's essentially the title for those on the city council. They each have different wards.

"Then he made sure the sheriff was completely on their side by drugging his sister in front of us," Saint adds. "So I'm pretty sure we can count on the police to turn us in on sight."

"Turn *you* in." I'm not part of the deal, Kade said?

This cannot go back to saving his life. It was a fluke. Something I didn't want to be held over my head. He was convinced he owed me this blood debt.

And now...

"What's this guy's name?"

"Justice Marcus Graves," Antonio says from the doorway. "Otherwise known as Ouranos, as he's chosen for himself."

I stiffen. "From Emerald Cove?"

"You recognize the name?" Saint steps toward me. "How?"

"I—" I grimace. "He's a justice. Which means he's not on some lower circuit. He rules on federal cases from Emerald Cove. While he didn't directly oversee trials where Cyclopes were defendants, they almost always got a lighter sentence than some of the other organized crime groups in town. Sometimes they were moved up to his circuit, and they were usually sent to a private prison out of town."

"And you know this because..."

"I ran with the Cyclopes. Not on Kade's level. I was doing jobs that felt harmless at the time, and it kept my lights on. They kept trying to dig me in deeper, and I finally heard a rumor that they intended to move on Sterling Falls. I left before I could meet the boss, although everyone on my level was excited to finally see the infamous Ouranos."

Not the whole truth, but they don't need it right now.

I'm ashamed of how I handled myself in Emerald Cove. I was running from my past, and that's the only excuse I have. But it's true—I didn't know Kade was involved, and I certainly didn't know Ouranos was Marcus Graves.

"We need to get ahold of Apollo," Saint says suddenly. "And Daniel."

"Tem said I needed a public computer."

He makes a face. "She's careful."

"We should be, too," I point out. "We don't know what kind of tech access Graves has."

"Kade—"

"We can't rely on him to protect us," I argue. "Why

didn't he warn us? Why didn't he say anything when they set up the blockade on the *only* road out of town?"

He blows out a breath. Then, "*Fine.*"

"Fine," I repeat.

"What's in the boxes?" Vittoria suddenly asks. She brushes past her husband and easily locates the liquor cabinet. We watch her crack open a bottle of vodka and pour it into four glasses. "Reese?"

I wince.

"It's something bad," Saint guesses. "How bad could dusty old boxes be?"

"Bad," I say under my breath. "Real fucking bad."

I gulp down the vodka Vittoria hands me. She, Antonio, and Saint follow suit.

Then... well, the only thing left to do is show them the evidence from Terror.

34 ARTEMIS

I EXPERIENCE five days of agony. I sweat through who knows how many sets of sheets, and patient hands maneuver me out of the way to periodically change them and my clothes. I don't really register who's in the room with me, the pain is so great. There's a bucket for me to throw up into, and a bathroom attached that I've unfortunately rushed to more than once.

That bone-deep ache only grew worse the longer I went without the drug.

If I could split open my skin and pull out my intestines, I think it might hurt less.

And the worst part is that I haven't been able to sleep more than a few hours. I roll and thrash in bed, I press my fingers to my throat to make sure my heart still beats. I cry.

Every so often, my muscles cramp and refuse to loosen.

On the sixth morning, a little of the fog has cleared. I'm able to thank the woman who comes in with a broth for me to sip.

And by the eighth, I'm able to shower. I groan when I

wash my hair, and again when I'm able to brush out the tangles. The bristles against my scalp is heavenly.

Once clean, I put on light-gray sweatpants and a plain white, long-sleeved t-shirt. White socks. Slip-on gray shoes. Very fashion-forward. The woman knocks, returning after a moment of privacy, and motions for me to join her.

Her name is Mary Catherine. I focus on the pale-yellow and green tiles that break up the monotonous cream ones, while she chatters about nothing important.

Just filling the silence, I think.

"You'll be moving to our main house after assessment," she says.

I straighten a bit. "When is that?"

"Now."

Oops.

She opens a door and motions for me to enter ahead of her. I tuck my hair behind my ears and creep inside. It's... well, shoot. It's a therapist's office, clear as day.

There's the comfortable-but-professional chair. There's the couch.

An older woman enters from another door, and she smiles widely. It's toothy, but not in a bad way. Her hair is a mix of blonde and gray. Her dark-purple cardigan looks perfectly cozy. Jeans and tennis shoes complete the ensemble, plus a gold necklace and earrings.

"I'm Dr. Hawthorne," she introduces. "What's your name?"

My eyes widen.

"I didn't tell anyone my name?"

She shakes her head gently. "Our initial hold for drug users is a week. If you elect to leave, we don't keep records. This is day eight, so you are free to go if you want."

She pauses.

I don't say anything.

"Our systems are not online. Everything is handwritten, including if we reach a diagnosis or prescribe medicine. This makes us an attractive option for those who might not want to be found. Domestic abuse cases, et cetera."

I nod along.

"So. Let's start at the beginning, shall we? Would you like to take a seat?"

I eye her. "Is there any reason you'd bar me from leaving?"

"Only if you tell me you're an imminent threat to yourself or others."

"Okay." I sit on the couch and immediately tuck my legs up under me. "I've just got to preface, Doc... I don't think you're going to believe me."

She sits, her full attention on my face. Her gaze is warm. "Try me."

DAY... ten?

The withdrawal symptoms are manageable enough, so I move to the main house. Mary Catherine warns that I'll have a roommate. They do night checks. There are a number of safety precautions, but it's all for the security and wellbeing of the residents.

I hesitate to call myself that.

I'm more like a temporary guest.

It doesn't matter, though. I keep that note to myself, a tiny imaginary asterisk following the word every time she mentions it.

**Not you, visitor!*

Besides therapy and meals, there's a relatively limited

number of activities. I'm not allowed to go into town alone, although Mary Catherine seems to have designated herself as my best friend. She promises me that we'll go as soon as it stops raining outside.

There's no rain.

There hasn't been rain.

I don't say anything, though, and just smile along.

That afternoon, I find myself alone. I wander the halls, not quite lost... just exploring. Content to figure it out as I go. There are lines along the floor, and all the rooms are numbered. It's not really rocket science.

One of the doors is open, and my attention snags on a pair of bright-blue shoes sitting on a desk. The rooms themselves lean more minimalist—a desk and chair, a bed, two pillows and one blanket per person—but I've seen how *residents** make their space feel like home.

The shoes, though...

I'm not sure what happened to my old clothes. I wasn't married to anything I was wearing, and I didn't have a phone to worry about. My cell is probably still in my condo, dead or neglected on the charger.

If I had it, I think they would've taken it away.

We're not really allowed to have laces. That was another thing explained to me by both Dr. Hawthorne—with logic—and Mary Catherine—with horror. Because laces can be used to hurt ourselves if we really want, and she *really doesn't* want that.

This person has shoes with laces, though, and they're not the drab gray I've seen everywhere else in the past two days.

Against my better judgment, I enter the room. I stop right at the edge of the desk and stare down at the bright-blue shoes. They look soft, like fake suede, and the laces are black. There are little lightning bolts on the sides.

Not my color, but cute.

And curious.

When I turn to leave, someone blocks my way. A girl maybe double my size.

"Hi," I blurt out, trying not to seem startled.

"Like them?" She points at the shoes.

Well, she points at my chest, but I'm blocking the desk. So I can only assume what she means.

"They're very pretty."

"They came for Sleeping Beauty."

I squint at her. "What?"

"Gifts come for her, but she doesn't need them. So I took them." She shifts out of the doorway, leaving me a gap to slip through.

"Where is Sleeping Beauty?"

"One-oh-nine." The girl picks up the shoes and cradles them to her chest. "Imagine if one day she woke up and found her bed covered in presents? She'd be sick with it, I think. I'm just helping."

I nod carefully. "You're right."

Remind me to lock my door—oh wait, no one's sent me a damn thing.

I have a pad of paper and pencil in my desk drawer. Dr. Hawthorne has suggested that I write letters to my loved ones. But how am I supposed to begin to explain...? I assume Reese gave a summarized version to Saint. Maybe Antonio. No idea about Kade.

They feel so far away.

My watch beeps. It's not a smart watch, but it has alarms built into it for the daily group therapy, which happens twice a day.

Lucky me.

Putting Sleeping Beauty out of my mind, I leave the girl to her stolen shoes and prepare to spill my guts.

Dear Saint,

I'm sorry.

I kind of just left on you, didn't I?

Part of me hopes Reese explained it all. The details that I told, the stuff that he noticed... Another part of me really, really hopes he didn't. That part—the delusional part—wants you to hear it from me.

How I succumbed to addiction, how Gabriel got under my skin.

I'm sixteen days sober. My headache has subsided, and the bone-deep ache is finally abating. Sleep doesn't come too easily, and much to my roommate's annoyance, I toss and turn for much of the night.

Ah, well.

Sixteen days.

Seems like I've been gone two months, not two weeks and two days.

Am I counting?

Does my obsessiveness show through this letter?

A clock may as well be taped to my head, a calendar printed on the inside of my eyelids.

Sometimes all I can think about is leaving. I get so desperate to escape, I consider jumping into the ocean and taking my chances.

The ocean has always liked me, after all.

Other times, like tonight, the thought of leaving this place petrifies me.

How is Sterling Falls?

How are you*?*

Please fill me in on Reese and Kade—yes, I know, I shouldn't want to know anything about Kade Laurent, but I can't help it. I find myself wondering. Caring.

And Antonio. Give him my love. I'll hold on to my apologies and offer them to him when I see him next.

With love,

Artemis

I HOLD my breath when I reread the letter.

Saint would reply, I think.

But I don't send it, so I guess I'll never know.

35 ARTEMIS

Dear Saint,

It occurred to me that I could write to anyone else, but I most want to talk to you.

How are you? Do you have any new tattoos? Have you put your artwork on anyone more famous than the guys from last year?

I dream in equal parts about you and heroin. If it's you, I wake up crying. Because you're so far away from me, and I can't do anything about it. Or maybe I just won't. *That's what we're learning here, you know? The option to not do anything but exist.*

Unfortunately, I'm making friends. Some of these girls are so nice, I just know terrible things happened to them.

Have you seen my brother?

I contemplated writing to him, but I don't know how much he knows. I don't even know if he's back from Emerald Cove yet. If he isn't, I can't worry him.

I know he'd storm the island if he thought he had to. He's done worse, after all.

Send my love to Antonio and Vittoria.

Tell Reese he'll get the next letter.

All my love,

Artemis

IT JOINS the first in the drawer.

The words I write are like an open wound. It's a new kind of pain that I haven't experienced before. I'm afraid I might get addicted to the bite of it.

What if spilling my mind out across pages is my new form of relief?

Dear Reese,

We talked about Terror today.

I thought of you, but not in a bad way.

It was kind of healing.

—Artemis

I'M SICK OF LETTERS. I take a walk outside, wrapped in a thick red coat. The isle is coated in a fresh layer of snow, and the air is crisp. It's cold enough to sting when I inhale, so I keep doing it. Big inhale, then exhale a cloud from my lips and nose.

I think they give us red coats so we don't get lost.

Someone said Christmas is just around the corner, and I can't fathom that.

We arrived here too fast.

My slip-on shoes don't have enough tread for this walk. The snow crunches under my feet, and I slide a few times on my way through the trees. I just want a break from being inside, and I finally got permission to go into town on my own.

It's been over a month without any incident. I've been walking more, mostly within sight of the low white buildings. I would weave through the tree line, catch glimpses of the ocean through the snow-covered branches, but never went farther.

That darn fear again.

The town—it's kind of laughable to call it that. There's a collection of homes belonging to people who live on the island full time and provide for the trauma center and run the shops. Then, closer, there's one main strip of shops.

A library, a grocery store, a post office.

The letters are in my pocket, sealed and addressed and stamped.

Dr. Hawthorne recommended that I send them, but...

I don't know.

Instead of the post office, I go into the library. I smile tightly at the man behind the desk. His eyes narrow at the red coat, which would appear to be a signal of exactly what I am. Not *who*, but *what*. The category of person.

Which is: trauma-filled.

Laughable.

"Do you have computers?" I ask him.

He inclines his chin and waves his hand toward the back of the library.

"Let me know if you need help," he calls to my back.

I won't.

There's a row of ancient computers against the far wall. I take a seat at one on the end and shed my jacket.

I log in under a fake name and send the message I memorized to an account I'm not sure still exists.

Not two minutes later, I get a reply.

A link.

I click it, and a new window opens.

A chat.

D

That you, T?

T

In the flesh.

D

I made it to SF

Daniel went back to Sterling Falls? My heart squeezes.

T

How is everyone?

D

We're staying on the DL. Holed up at K's.

Down-low. Kora's house.

T

I need to see you guys. This thing has a webcam

D

Ok. Give me a min.

I lean back in the chair and drum my fingers on the

desk. My heartbeat is doing something weird, fluttering in my chest. It takes a long moment to pinpoint that I'm not anxious—it's just plain old nerves.

Finally, Daniel replies with another link. I click it, redirected once more, and hit *accept* on its request for access to my camera and microphone.

It isn't Daniel who fills the screen when it connects, though—it's Saint.

I immediately burst into tears.

Fuck the letters. This is better—and so, so much worse.

"Hey, wildcat," he says softly.

"Hi," I hiccup through my choked sobs. I pat at my cheeks and try to control my voice. "How are you?"

"As good as we can be." His gaze burns into me. "When are you coming home?"

"I—" My mouth dries, and that fear takes hold. "I don't know."

"I miss you," he says.

"Saint, I'm so sorry." I lean forward. "How can you miss me after what I did?"

He grimaces. "Try to believe me when I say: I don't hold it against you. Okay? And what I should've said before we left Starlight is that I've been falling in love with you for the past year. Nothing you could do would dissuade me."

I cover my mouth.

"Do you hear me? I'm in love with you, Artemis. I'm telling you this because I want you to come back, but I want you healthy. Can you do that for me, baby?"

Maybe.

Suddenly, Saint is shoved out of the frame.

Reese fills the space. "Hi."

I smile. "Hi."

"Quick recap, since I'm sure Saint jumped straight into a monologue about how much he cares about you. Ready?"

I settle in. "Ready."

"Kade is unsurprisingly still an ass. He and I have been talking on a secure line, but he doesn't know anything about you. He was pissed to learn that only one of us left Sterling Falls the night Ouranos arrived. Gabriel and the sheriff are now almost always together because of events."

"Wait. Ouranos?"

He makes a face. "Sorry. Turns out, Gabriel and Kade have a scary master holding their leashes. His name is Ouranos... but also known as Marcus Graves."

Why the fuck does that name sound familiar?

I stare at Reese, waiting for it to connect.

My mind has been getting clearer since ridding my body of the drugs, but I still have foggy moments. Like right now, when I *should* know exactly who that is.

"He's a justice from Emerald Cove," Reese says.

I snap my fingers. "He signed the warrant for Bow & Arrow!"

Reese freezes. "Did he? Shit. Okay."

"Is he related to—"

"Kronos? Yes, they're brothers. It's not ideal, but it makes sense why he moved into Sterling Falls. There was an obvious gap where the Titans used to be, and he would've been more aware of that than anyone."

Great.

"Okay. How's everyone else?"

Suddenly, the screen flashes.

Daniel reappears with an apologetic expression. "Sorry, Tem, we're going to have to cut this short. Any longer and it could be traced to your IP. Talk soon, okay?"

"I—"

The screen shuts down.

Not only that, but the chat, too.

After a long moment, I clear my browsing history and close out of the forum.

It was nice to see them.

I don't feel the need to mail the letters, after all.

36 ARTEMIS

Dear Saint,

There's a girl nicknamed Sleeping Beauty here. I guess she's been here a while. One of the other girls, Beckett, likes to go into her room and steal stuff. She seemed appalled that Sleeping Beauty even had stuff to begin with. But then Dr. Hawthorne mentioned that her brother still holds out hope she'll one day wake up.

Because of that hope, he spends money on giving her a private room, and he fills it with things she used to like. I guess the thought behind it is that if she does wake up, she'll feel safe and protected.

Isn't that the saddest thing you've ever heard?

A lot hinges on an if.

Beckett has been told to stop stealing from her. One of Dr. H's nurses caught Beckett in the act, and Beckett was moved to a different building.

That means a new doctor and all that.

But it's piqued my interest, Saint. I can't stop

thinking about this girl who's apparently not going to wake up, surrounded by treasure.

Whoever gave her the nickname probably nailed it on the head.

Did she prick her finger on a sewing needle, or whatever that cursed object was?

Is she surrounded by thorns, guarded by a dragon?

It's given me something to focus on, at any rate. Everyone is starting to decorate for Christmas, which will be here in two days, and everything reminds me of what I've seemed to have lost.

You. My brother and his family. Antonio.

The list would go on. It'd include Nyx, Reese, hell, even Kade can be thrown on there. Not that any of them are gone-gone *except Nyx.*

So maybe she's the one who will be with me this holiday season.

Now that I think about it, I can blame her bad influence on my need to see Sleeping Beauty. She would've been just as curious as me.

I hope you're well.

Give everyone my love.

Merry Christmas.

Artemis

MY LETTER DOES NOT ADDRESS that he told me he loves me.

It does address my burning curiosity, which I seek to

satiate immediately. As soon as I finish writing, I shrug on my zip-up sweatshirt and those stupid slip-on shoes.

Room 109. I haven't had a reason to even go down there until now.

Well, okay, I don't really have a reason.

I'm just gonna go, see what all the fuss is about, then leave.

Some part of me assumes she's going to be the boogeyman. Or perhaps she's not actually asleep?

Imagine if she was pretending?

Then letting Beckett get away with theft would be savage. Borderline criminal.

Everyone is busy with holiday preparations. They're doing a tree-decorating contest in the dining hall, and then a Christmas movie after dinner with hot chocolate and popcorn. The *residents** all seem to have accepted that they're here for the winter, if not longer.

But not me. I'm just visiting, per the asterisk.

Maybe it's an extended visit.

I reach the hallway I need. The first room is 101. Then 103. All the odds... all the way down to 109 at the end. Her door is solid wood and closed.

I knock just in case, checking over my shoulder to make sure no nurse is about to catch me. The last thing I want is to be relocated like Beckett. Not when I've been getting comfortable around the other girls.

When no one answers, I slip inside.

Soft light comes in through a large picture window. The lamp beside the sleeping girl's bed is on, too, casting a warm glow across the blankets and part of her face.

She *is* sleeping. And sure enough, the room is filled with things. The blue shoes have been returned, sitting on top of a dresser in the corner of the room. There's also a globe, a

Rubik's Cube, a puzzle box. A vase of fresh flowers is on the other nightstand, closer to the window. The blanket draped over her legs is special, and it seems extra-soft.

I drift closer.

Sleeping Beauty.

She *is* pretty. Her white-blonde hair has been well taken care of, and it lies smoothly across her small breasts. They have her in a hospital gown, maybe to better take care of her? She has a feeding tube fed through her nose, and an IV taped to the back of her hand.

My heart pulls for her.

She's really, *really* pretty. Her lips are like a bow, and the kind of natural pink lipstick companies would be envious of. Her eyelashes and eyebrows are dark blonde, and her complexion is pale.

I go to the foot of the bed to get a direct look at her.

A clipboard hangs there.

After only a moment of resistance, I pick it up and scan her chart.

Lyssa Laurent.

I drop it.

Luckily—I mean, seriously, *luckily*—it's attached. It doesn't clatter to the floor, it just swings wildly before settling against the rail.

The first thing that stands out?

Laurent. As in—Kade Laurent.

The sister with the medical bills.

Surely it can't be *her*?

And then there's another thing. Her first name... Not Alyssa. Not Liza.

Lyssa.

I've only seen that once.

My heart bangs against my ribs as I inch up to her side. I

don't really want to do this, but it's a surefire way to confirm.

I check under her gown, and the blood rushes away from my head when I spot the single pierced nipple.

"I'm going to be sick," I whisper to her.

Everything is starting to make sense.

37 GABRIEL

Two years ago

I SIT on the edge of the bed.

New bed, same situation.

Same blank expression on her beautiful face.

"I'll be here when you wake up," I whisper to her. I stroke her hair, run my hands down her body.

"Isle of Paradise will be good for her," her half-brother says at my back.

I met him three months ago, after I transferred her out of the hospital room Artemis Madden was funding. The long-term care unit, she said.

There were *vegetables* in that unit. Soulless bodies.

That's not my Lyssa.

Kade found us. The new place I picked was closer to her home, and they had her old records. They had her half-brother on file from an old emergency.

That's what he said anyway.

My mind keeps breaking. I may as well be locked in this room with her. I lose pieces of time staring out of windows.

Windows are a requirement.

This room has a big window that looks out at the water. It's pointed toward Sterling Falls, although it's too far away to see during the day. Maybe at night, the little speckles of city lights would be visible.

She's supposed to wake up, but it's been eight years.

I'm fucking spiraling.

"Come on," Kade says softly.

I wave him off and climb over her. There are nurses waiting to put a feeding tube in. She gagged when the previous hospital removed the one they had inserted. Her whole body lurched, and my heart *soared.*

But then they said it was just a reflex, like breathing.

Which she does perfectly fine on her own, they added.

They're going to give her an IV to keep her hydrated, a catheter to empty her bladder, a feeding tube for nutrients.

I hate it all.

I brace my weight on my knees, off to one side, and my forearms on either side of her head. I could stare at her for hours and never be bored.

"Shh," I whisper, pressing a kiss to her ear. "Remember what I told you, Lys? The dark can't be scary anymore. I'm here with you. We're free. Any time you're ready to wake... I'll be waiting. Just say the word, and I'll be here."

I kiss her lips, but she doesn't kiss me back.

She hasn't in eight years.

"We'll visit her soon," he promises.

I'm sick of promises.

I'm sick of keeping things together.

We're all a little mad here, aren't we?

What's the problem in showing the world?

38 SAINT

A TEXT from Kade has sat in my messages, unread, for two days.

Artemis has been gone for so much longer than that. I keep expecting new arrivals at our borrowed safe haven to be her. Instead, we've been spending our time helping people get out of Sterling Falls.

They come to Jace's home, and one of us drives the small group to the marina.

Bobby ferries them to the docks in Emerald Cove.

The first few days after Ouranos moved into Sterling Falls were utter chaos. People who tried to stand up to him were shot down. The mayor's body was carted through North Falls and left spread-eagle, naked, in the middle of Main Street.

One of Tem's old employees told us that, tears rolling down her cheeks, when she arrived to ask for help escaping. She was the first one we smuggled out, but certainly not the last.

Apollo, Jace, and Wolfe are effectively blocked from the city. Apollo tried to re-enter and was nearly shot. Having the conversation about Artemis and her addiction over the phone was not ideal.

He threatened to get her immediately, but Antonio made him see reason.

She's there to get help.

However long that takes.

But with most of our forces removed, it leaves us with both hands tied behind our back. We don't go out alone, and every run for supplies seems dangerous.

There are wanted posters around town with my face on them, along with others.

Malikai Barlow, for one. Half the Hell Hounds. Jace, Wolfe, and Apollo.

Not Artemis or Reese—although the latter says he doesn't want to risk it.

I have to agree with that. Clearly, Kade worked out some deal to protect Reese and Artemis. And when he realizes Reese *didn't* leave town like he hoped? That might backfire.

Anyway. We're not supposed to leave the property alone, and here I am, going solo. I'm on Jace's bike. It feels a bit dangerous to be out riding, but we made sure there was no sign of ownership on it. We took off the plates and replaced them with fakes from Daniel, scanned it for any sign of trackers.

I sort of relished prying Jace's anti-theft detection off it, if only to make sure it wasn't traceable back to him.

The ride to Jace's old boat house hideout is quick. I pull back the ivy-covered fence, roll the bike through, and close it behind me. Leaving the bike where it is, I stride down the sloped, curving road to the building.

It's no better than a shack.

I slow when I catch movement through the window, but then the door opens.

Malik glares at me.

He still wears his cut, and I have no doubt he's armed to the teeth. Currently, however, the only thing visible is the handle of a dagger at his hip.

"Hart," he greets me.

I incline my chin.

He steps back, allowing me inside, and closes us in. "What's the news?"

"We've been getting people out of the city," I tell him. "And your Hell Hounds?"

He grimaces. "I don't suppose you saw the smoke the other day?"

I nod slowly. We stood in the backyard and watched the brownish smoke climb into the clear sky. Vittoria was worried about Olympus, but Reese mumbled something about it being in the wrong direction.

Our only options were the Hell Hounds compound or something worth destroying in South Falls.

We didn't venture out that day. All the vehicles are out of sight from the main road, and we make sure the house looks unimposing and empty if anyone were to check it out.

"What happened?"

His expression tightens. "A group of them came in, led by the one that smiles too much."

"Gabriel," I supply.

"Right. I was in the back, but we were already aware of the wanted posters for me, my second, and the road captain. My guys got us out the back..." He quiets.

My gut twists.

"They killed everyone who tried to hold their ground. Lost a few of their own, I'm sure, but it doesn't even seem to fucking matter. They burned everything to the ground."

"Fuck."

"The Hell Hounds will rise again." He scuffs his toe on the floor. "They know where to meet me. But we're fucking laying low until we can get a better advantage."

"Understandable." *And, same.*

"Here." He holds out a piece of paper. It has a number scribbled on it. "That goes straight to my road captain. Only call it if there's no other choice."

I take it and stuff it in my pocket. "Thank you, Malik."

He hesitates. Then, "Artemis...?"

"She's out of the city," I tell him. "Safe."

My heart hurts to add that, but it's true. She's away from Sterling Falls, away from Gabriel's influence and the possibility of drugs. For now, that's safe enough.

"I trust you because of her," he says.

"I know."

He nods and glances around, then laughs a little. "I can't believe Jace slept here for six months."

It's a mess. There's a cot. A sink in the corner, a camping stove on a table with only two chairs. There's a showerhead over a drain practically in the middle of the room.

"Well, I'd rather be here than a captive of the Titans." I touch the center of my chest. I often brush over that time. I was tortured—there's no other way around it. Artemis and Elora came to my rescue. Kora, too. They risked a hell of a lot to get me out, and I still barely survived.

"Kronos was one sick fuck," Malik agrees. "Cerberus wasn't much better at the end."

I hum my agreement. Then something occurs to me—

Ouranos is keeping his identity secret.

Would blowing his cover hurt him or harm him?

"You know who Ouranos is, don't you?"

He eyes me.

"The brother of Kronos."

Malik tips his head back and laughs. It bursts out of him, a wild sound that doesn't stop until he's wiping tears from his eyes.

"Oh, that's fucking perfect." He shakes his head. "Is that why your face is posted around town?"

I don't answer.

He claps my shoulder. "Good luck, brother."

I have a feeling I'm going to need it.

39 KADE

OURANOS SITS across from me in Madness. While he appreciates the grandeur of Bow & Arrow, he doesn't quite appreciate the way Gabriel ventures closer to insanity there.

I didn't know where my sister ended up.

Terror—and the meaning behind it—was never on my radar.

When I met Gabriel, he told me a vague story of a sex trafficking ring. It didn't include most of the horrors they both went through. But then learning about it through Artemis, and seeing the shell of the place with my own eyes...

It hurts.

It's like I'm standing over her hospital bed all over again, trying not to see the white scars on her skin, or the thinness of her frame.

I didn't grow up with my father. He and my mom split, and he married her mom. They had Lyssa a few years later. My mom and I lived close to them, though. Close enough that I witnessed the aftermath of her terrible trauma. When she was six, she was attacked by a boy. Sodomized, injured, *terrified*...

My heart aches when I consider her pain. All of it, from childhood straight through to her escaping Terror with Gabriel.

I was too young to protect her, but I followed from afar. Got to know her in the quiet moments of her life. Visited her on the Isle of Paradise, where she spent years living as a teenager. She knew I was her half-brother, even though we only shared the faintest resemblance in our smiles.

Her parents gave up on her, and I took over behind the scenes. I made sure I was listed as her emergency contact with the trauma center, with the hospital and on all her medical records, even her old school.

Just in case.

And then she vanished, and no one could fucking tell me anything.

And it came in handy, because years later, I got the call that she had been checked in. It was like hearing about a ghost.

One condition of working with—*for*—Ouranos?

He holds all our secrets.

I don't know if he put together that the Lyssa I lost was the same as the one Gabriel still keeps safe at Isle of Paradise. He hopes that she will one day wake up, and it's exactly that hope that destroys him over and over.

There's no escaping his pain.

I... I've dealt with it. Sort of.

But Gabriel can't, and I think it relates back to Terror.

"Kade."

My attention snaps away from the secrets Ouranos holds, to the man himself. He has a glass of whiskey in front of him, although it doesn't look like he's touched it. In the years I've known him, one thing is for sure: those familiar vices?

He has none.

"Saint Hart," he says.

I try not to react, but I find my spine straightening, regardless.

"Tell me about him."

"I'm not sure what you mean," I reply. "What do you want to know?"

He waits.

The seconds tick past, and I dip my chin.

"He's a local. He owns a tattoo shop near the college."

"And...?"

I slowly lift one shoulder. "He makes masks for the Olympians."

"Don't make me ask again, Kade."

I meet his gaze. "I don't know what else you want me to say, sir."

He runs his finger around the rim of his glass, seeming to contemplate something. Then, "You know I don't care about your proclivities."

I stiffen.

"Men, women. It's never mattered to me who you like, or why. But I sent you here for a reason. And it wasn't to play pretend with a local." He appraises me. He's got a gaze that cuts straight through bullshit. Lesser men have cracked under such an expression. "Do you know what the worst part is?"

"I'm guessing not." My mouth is dry. Can he tell?

"You don't know what he's done. *Clearly*."

"I—"

He leans forward, his hand slamming flat to the table. This is not a man who loses control very often—and I wouldn't call this that, exactly, but he's close. A flush creeps up his neck.

It dawns on me that whatever he's about to say is personal.

Coming to Sterling Falls wasn't some whim. It wasn't an ambition on the road for more power, or a place to settle.

Stones drop into my gut.

"Tell me," I say. I need to know what Saint Hart has done to catch Ouranos' attention, yes, but I also need to know why I suddenly feel played.

"Oh, Kade," Ouranos sighs. "Of all the people you could've fallen for—"

Seems he doesn't know—or care—about my feelings for Artemis.

"—you had to pick the worst. Saint Hart killed my brother in cold blood."

I freeze.

"What?" I choke out.

He keeps staring at me, like he's more interested in my reaction than displaying any sadness about his brother.

I didn't even know he had a brother.

"Kronos ran the Titans," he says softly. "And Saint killed him. Shot him in the face. I saw my brother's body, saw the aftermath of that bloody invasion. They came into his house and attacked him and my nephew."

I ball my fists in my lap.

That can't be true.

Everything I've heard, though, indicates that the Titans' leader's sudden death unraveled the gang's organization.

"I want you to find him," Ouranos says. "Shouldn't be a problem, should it?"

I've already found him. I keep my expression neutral. No surprise, no horror, no *upset.* It wouldn't do me any good. He's always ruled with an iron fist. Debates end in death. I've seen it happen to lesser men.

But I have no doubt he wouldn't hesitate to stomp out my resistance, too.

"What do you want me to do after that?" I ask quietly.

He lifts one shoulder, then pointedly examine his nails. "Bring him here or kill him. Either option will end the same. It just depends on *you*."

Fuck.

I get up and leave Madness. My phone buzzes.

SAINT

We need to talk.

My nerves buzz, and I want to yell, *No! No, you don't want to talk. You want to stay as far away from me as possible.*

But, in the end, I'm a slave to my master's wishes.

40 ARTEMIS

Dear Saint,

I brought up Nyx in group therapy. There was a question posed about if we had lost anyone close to us, and she was the first person I thought of.

It was refreshing to talk about her. I didn't focus on her death. I told stories about how we met through Olympus, how my brother introduced me when I first got into fighting. Truthfully, that's a story for another day. I don't think I've told anyone that.

But Nyx was always a bright light. You said it, too. She was the stars, and the darkness made her shine bright. It was really true. I loved her, and talking about how she held herself, her morals, really made me miss her.

And then, in equal measure, there's you.

The thought of her will never go away, but I'm glad she's not between us anymore.

For once, I feel peace.

All my love,

Artemis

"ARTEMIS." Dr. Hawthorne approaches me at a fast clip.

Oh, shit. I got caught? I made sure to leave Lyssa's room exactly as I found it. After I registered her name, I spent the next ten minutes hunting through every item in the room. I tried to connect it back to Gabriel or Kade.

I *remember* Lyssa.

She was the dark secret we kept after I rescued them. Her and Gabriel.

They were put in the lower level of Terror, where heroin and opiates keep them complacent. It was out of Antonio's hands at that point, and I spent *months* bribing the woman who administered the drugs to help me get them out.

She gave Lyssa too much, and Lyssa never woke up. Much to Gabriel's distress. But once he moved her out of the long-term care unit Apollo was helping me pay for... well, I assumed she died.

Gabriel vanished after that anyway. It made sense to me that he would want to be far, far away from Sterling Falls.

It didn't occur to me that he would hold such a grudge against *me*.

"Dr. Hawthorne." I shift my weight and contemplate an immediate confession. It would probably be easier, right?

Do I also tell her that I know her?

Well, know *of* her?

I certainly know her brother and boyfriend. Benefactor. Whatever we want to classify Gabriel as.

"You're listed as an emergency contact for Saint Hart." She grips both my shoulders. "Did you know that?"

I pause.

Try to figure out why she's asking me that.

"Artemis?"

"Y-yes," I say.

He did it in a fit of anger a few months ago. Just one of those stupid slip-ups that required stitches, but I freaked out on him that no one had told me.

That was when I was still very much on Keep Saint Alive duty.

"Someone told them where to reach you."

"Who?"

"The hospital," she says slowly. "The hospital has been trying to reach you, through us, about Saint Hart."

My lungs stop. "Is he okay?" I force out.

"He's alive," she assures me. "But that's all they'd say. He's at the Sterling Falls hospital. If you want to go, I can travel with you."

"I—yes," I blurt out. "Of course I need to go. Right now?"

She nods.

"Okay. Okay." I slip out of her hold and rush back to my room. By the time she reaches me, I've got on my red coat and a black winter cap.

"Ready."

She nods once, all business. There's no sympathy there, and I'm okay with that. I'd crack with sympathy. She puts a hand on the small of my back, guiding me out to the waiting golf cart. The path is plowed, and wind whips at us on the way to the small dock.

A speedboat waits, one of the workers already aboard.

I scramble on and take the offered life jacket. It fits over my coat, and I stuff my hands between my legs to keep them warm. Worry bleeds through me, enough to make me forget the fact that I'm leaving the Isle of Paradise for the first time.

What the hell happened, Saint?

41 ARTEMIS

DR. HAWTHORNE STAYS WITH ME. She seems to watch me closely, although I can't tell if she's wondering about my mental status or if I'm going to immediately run away to get drugs.

I feel... stable, actually. As much as I'm worried, the thought of how heroin might help is one of the quieter voices in my head. The ride across the ocean into Sterling Falls is relatively smooth, and she ushers me into a waiting car at the marina.

Everything is arranged, I suppose.

The driver takes us to the hospital. We get out at the front entrance, and I explain to the receptionist that I'm the emergency contact for Saint.

I can barely force out the words, and my hands tremble. I ball them into fists and stick them in my jacket, needing to hide my nerves.

Dr. Hawthorne steps up and guides me down the hall, following directions I missed.

"He's okay?" I ask her.

"She didn't say. We'll talk to someone at the nurse's

station."

"Okay."

We take the elevator up to the third floor. I follow her down the hall and we stop to get an update and find out where exactly to go.

"First and foremost," the nurse says, "is that he is alive."

I blow out a breath.

"He has a concussion from the accident. Our plastic surgeon stitched up a deep gash on his head, and he has a sprained wrist that we've wrapped. He seems to be in okay spirits. We told him that we called you."

The last time I saw Saint—well, the last time I laid eyes on his face—was through the pixelated webcam. And he said he *loved* me.

I feel it.

I carry it.

And I want to say it back to his face, when I'm able to touch him. Being on Isle of Paradise... yes, it was exactly what I needed to hear to keep me going. But I'm just excited to see him, injured or not.

Especially since the nurse said he's *okay*.

"Can I see him?" I ask.

The nurse nods. "Of course. Room 305."

Dr. Hawthorne trails me down the hall, her steps slowing. "There's someone else here I should check on," she tells me. "You go on, I'll be back in a few minutes."

"Okay."

Nerves at suddenly being abandoned flitter through me, but I shake it off and enter the room.

The bed closest to the door is empty. There's a curtain pulled between it and the other one, and only the foot of Saint's bed is visible.

My heart jumps into my throat, and I hurry around it.

"Surprise!" I call, popping into his view.

He might've been dosing. His eyes snap open, and he lifts his head. It takes him a second to focus on me.

There's a bandage on his forehead, and his left forearm arm is wrapped. He has two black eyes and a scrape across his cheek. An IV in the top of his hand.

Something in me unknots.

He's *okay*.

I go to the side of his bed. "You gave me quite the scare. How are you feeling?"

His gaze goes from my head to my toes and back up again. His brows pull together.

"Artemis? What are you doing here?"

I slip my hand into his and squeeze. "They let me out so I could see you."

"Who let you out? The nurse said..." He frowns. "I'm confused."

"I..." I glance over my shoulder. "Were you expecting Reese?"

He pulls his hand out of mine.

I cross my arms, trying not to let that simple action hurt.

What is going on?

His gaze moves past me. "I wasn't expecting... that person. The nurse said family was on their way, and now you're here?"

"Yeah, well—"

"Did you drive Elora?"

I stop. "What?"

"Elora," he repeats. He cranes to the side, as if expecting someone else. "Did you drive her here? I imagine she might be a mess, hearing I was in the hospital... I didn't want her to worry. I told them to tell her I was fine."

I don't think my lungs are working properly. "You told the nurses to tell Nyx...?"

He eyes me. "Were you training at Olympus together? Is that why you came, too?"

He thinks she's alive.

He thinks she's going to walk into this hospital room.

My stomach heaves, and I swallow my nausea.

This cannot be real life.

"Saint," I say faintly. "What's the last thing you remember?"

"Why?"

"Just—"

He freezes. The blood drains from his face.

Okay. Okay, it was just a momentary thing. Confusion due to the concussion. I step forward, ready to comfort him about his lapse, but he just grips the blankets pooled at his waist. He shakes his head once, eyes wide, then grimaces.

"Please tell me she wasn't in the car with me, Artemis." His voice is hoarse. "I don't know what I'd do if I lost her. God, I don't even remember getting in the car, or the accident. Is she okay?"

Is she okay?

Well, she's not suffering. Not like me.

He's actively pulling my heart out.

He doesn't know she's dead.

His gaze slides past me again. "Did you sneak in here? Or lie about being family?"

"No. *Saint.*" My eyes burn.

"You and her just fought at Olympus the other night. She kicked your ass and made some comment about a girl in a flower mask shaking things up for the guys." He seems oblivious to my growing horror. "We went home. Fucking hell, Artemis, how much time did I lose? A day?"

"Two years," I breathe.

Give or take.

He stills.

I can't fucking move, either. We're locked in a stare, and I just wish he could read my mind and get with the program.

"Why are you looking at me like that?" he demands. "Is this some sick joke?"

How the fuck do I do this?

I bite back the words I want to say—that I love him, that I'm sorry. It wouldn't make anything easier. Not for me, and certainly not for him. If I'm in his shoes: I haven't experienced a fucking war. Torture. *Death.* I haven't grieved Nyx's terrible end for over a year.

"It's not." I close my eyes, then force myself to open them look at him. He deserves that much. "I'm so sorry, Saint. What you're about to hear... I know what happened to you the last time—the *first* time. And I guess... we're about to relive it."

"Just spit it out," he says. "You're starting to scare me."

I exhale. Tears blur my vision.

"Nyx—*Elora* died, Saint. A year ago."

He stares at me.

Stares and stares and stares.

I cannot fathom what's going through his mind.

I didn't expect this. I couldn't. I thought—well, I guess I thought I was going to be crying *happy* tears.

"Get out."

I flinch.

Is he serious?

Saint's face flushes. His chest heaves, like he had forgotten how to breathe and now can't catch his breath.

His eyes are wide open, and he slams his hand on the bed suddenly.

"I said *get out*!" he screams.

I jump out of my skin.

In all our arguments, all the long nights working through our grief—separately, together, *whatever*—he's never sounded like he does right now. On the cusp of losing his damn mind.

My heart breaks.

Two nurses rush in, and they seem to understand what's going on in an instant. One goes to the monitor beside his head, the other grabs my arm. She escorts me quickly into the hall, then down to a private room.

I sit.

"Try to breathe." She crouches in front of me. She rubs my arms. "Breathe, honey."

I can't.

I want—I need—*gah*.

The only thing that would make this better is a needle in my arm. The sweet rush of heroin taking away the pain. And that thought is the worst of them all.

My sob comes out strangled. But now, at least, I *can* cry.

The nurse gets up and the door closes behind her. I cry on my own, hiccupping and sniffling like an idiot.

When the door opens next, it isn't her.

It's Reese.

I get up and launch myself into his arms. All the misery crashes down on me.

"Don't let me use," I sob into his chest. "I don't want to start over again."

"Shh. I won't let anything happen to you, golden girl." He strokes my hair. "It's okay. Whatever it is, we'll get through it."

I focus on the rise and fall of his chest under my cheek. The steadiness of his heart.

When I finally stop hyperventilating, I rock back on my heels.

He cups my cheek and swipes away the falling tears. "What happened?"

"He—he's got amnesia, Reese. He didn't remember Nyx dying... or any of the past two years."

His Adam's apple bobs as he processes my words. Slowly, the resolve comes over him. He nods to himself like he knows exactly what to do, and I am so fucking thankful for that.

Because I am utterly lost.

42 SAINT

I'M SUPPOSED to know the man that sits beside me on the boat.

He said his name, but I wasn't focused.

All I can think is...

How could I forget her death?

They showed me the space with her name on it in the mausoleum. This guy beside me walked me up the path, head bent against the snowfall. He wore a hat and gloves, a thick jacket. Boots.

I was in hospital-issued clothes, just a t-shirt, sweatshirt, and pants. Socks and slip-on shoes. But I didn't feel the cold. The pain in my head was secondary to the stabbing in my chest. We stood in front of her so-called resting spot.

Elora Whitlock.

The darkness only makes you shine brighter.

The man next to me elbows me. "We're here."

Right.

I lift my gaze and focus first on the dock that comes closer, the boat's motor now idling as we drift in, then the golf cart waiting on the path above.

"You'll be okay," he advises me.

I sigh. "Forgive me if I don't believe you."

He shrugs.

We get off the boat, and I spot Artemis waiting for me, too.

I stiffen.

"You didn't say she would be here." My tone is accusing.

"I know." He prods me forward. "But you both need to heal, so... get going."

I don't want her familiarity.

I don't want whatever look is in her eyes.

I want *Elora*.

I want my life back.

But it turns out, the life I thought I just left, the warmth I can still imagine of Elora's body, the dazzling joy of her laughter—it's a cruel trick of my brain.

There's no coming back from that.

TO BE CONTINUED...

In Martyr (Sterling Falls Rogues, 3)

http://mybook.to/sfr3

WHERE TO FIND SARA

Thank you so much for coming along on this crazy journey with me.

If you like my stories, I'd highly encourage you to come join my Facebook group, S. Massery Squad. There's a lot of fun stuff happening in there, and they're who I go to for polls about future books, where I share teasers, etc!

My Patreon is also an awesome place to connect and get exclusive content! On release months, I do signed paperbacks. Plus, get ARCs, audiobooks, and artwork before the rest of the world. Find me here: http://patreon.com/smassery

And last but not least, here are some social media links for ya:

Facebook: Author S Massery
Instagram: @authorsmassery

WHERE TO FIND SARA

Tiktok: @smassery
Goodreads: S. Massery
Bookbub: S. Massery

ABOUT THE AUTHOR

S. Massery is a dark romance author who loves injecting a good dose of suspense into her stories. Originally from Massachusetts, she now lives in Southern California with her dog, Alice.

Before adventuring into the world of writing, she went to college in Boston and held a wide variety of jobs—including working on a dude ranch in Wyoming (a personal highlight). She has a love affair with coffee and chocolate. When S. Massery isn't writing, she can be found devouring books, playing outside with her dog, or trying to make people smile.

ALSO BY S. MASSERY

Hockey Gods

Brutal Obsession

Devious Obsession

Secret Obsession

Twisted Obsession

Fierce Obsession

Hockey Titans

Into Ruin

Ruined God

Shadow Valley U

Sticks & Stones

Heart of Thorns

SVU 3

The Christmas Playbook

Standalone Hockey

The Pucking Coach's Daughter

Fallen Royals

Wicked Dreams

Wicked Games

Wicked Promises

Cruel Abandon

Vicious Desire

Wild Fury

Sterling Falls

#0 Thrill

#1 Thief

#2 Fighter

#3 Rebel

#4 Queen

Sterling Falls Rogues

#0 Terror

#1 Nemesis

#2 Warrior

#3 Martyr

#4 Saint

DeSantis Mafia

#1 Ruthless Saint

#2 Savage Prince

#3 Stolen Crown

Broken Mercenaries

#1 Blood Sky

#2 Angel of Death

#3 Morning Star

More at http://smassery.com

www.ingramcontent.com/pod-product-compliance
Lightning Source LLC
Chambersburg PA
CBHW061636190726
48289CB00006B/1628

* 9 7 8 1 9 5 7 2 8 6 3 3 4 *